Praise for Murder 101

"Sparkling . . . romance, humor, and suspense blend perfectly in this exceptional cozy, the first of what hopefully will be a long series."
—*Publishers Weekly* (starred review)

"A romantic ending and the furthering of a girlfriend bond that we hope to enjoy in murder mysteries to come." —*More*

"An entertaining debut." —*Booklist*

"With wit and verve—a spot-on rendering of the jungles of academia." —*Richmond Times-Dispatch*

"If you love Agatha Christie, Sue Grafton, and Sara Paretsky, you'll be delighted by Maggie Barbieri."
—Sheila Curran,
author of *Diana Lively is Falling Down*

Also by Maggie Barbieri

Murder 101

Available from St. Martin's Paperbacks

Extracurricular Activities

Maggie Barbieri

St. Martin's Paperbacks

EXTRACURRICULAR ACTIVITIES

Copyright © 2007 by Maggie Barbieri.
Excerpt from *Quick Study* copyright © 2008 by Maggie Barbieri.

For information address St. Martin's Press, 175 Fifth Avenue, New York, NY 10010.

Library of Congress Catalog Card Number: 2007032329

ISBN: 0-312-94530-2
EAN: 978-0-312-94530-5

Printed in the United States of America

St. Martin's Press hardcover edition / December 2007
St. Martin's Paperbacks edition / October 2008

St. Martin's Paperbacks are published by St. Martin's Press, 175 Fifth Avenue, New York, NY 10010.

10 9 8 7 6 5 4 3 2 1

To Dea and Patrick: I love you as much as the world is big.

Acknowledgments

You've heard it before: Writing books is solitary work. But if, like me, you're fortunate enough to be surrounded by the kinds of people like the ones with whom I work, live, and call my family and friends, you never feel truly alone.

My first debt of gratitude is to perhaps the smartest, most intuitive editor in the business, Kelley Ragland. I don't say this to too many people—okay, I don't say this to *anybody*—but you are *always* right.

Thanks, too, to Matt Martz at St. Martin's Press for his support and for being so generous with his time.

Deborah Schneider, my agent, is always there to provide encouragement, feedback, and guidance. Thanks for believing in Alison and for finding the perfect home for her.

To my posse at NYU—Anna Pavlick, Kathy Madden, Juliet Escalon, Elizabeth Hardin, Norma Sparks, and Rosie Smith—thank you for everything. I'm happy we're on the bus together. I wish it made different stops, but hey, you can't have everything.

And to my dear friends and family members who have

evolved from enthusiastic cheerleaders to astute critics—and you know who you are, Lance—thank you for having the courage to tell me the truth. And the good sense to tell me over a bottle of wine.

Finally, without the love of my husband, Jim, none of this would happen. Thank you to the most patient man on earth.

Chapter 1

I have two best friends; one is a nymphomaniac and the other is a priest.

And then there's Ray.

Ray's my ex-husband and what I call a "fornicator extra-ordinaire." Not that I had any firsthand knowledge of his prowess; our sex life had consisted of a weekly roll in the hay that usually took place between the end of whatever show was on and that local news program that begins with a solemn "It's ten o'clock. Do you know where your children are?" But from the women who flocked to Ray like bees to honey, it was obvious that he held some kind of sway over the opposite sex. I had either come late to the party or didn't expect much from married sex. Either way, you could have knocked me over with a feather when I found out how many affairs he had had during our marriage.

That would be four. Two with people unknown to me, one with our neighbor, and one with one of my students. Ray has, I guess what you would call in today's psycho-babble, an issue with "boundaries."

But try as I might, I had failed to cut him out of my life. His lack of boundaries made him think it acceptable to come to my house whenever he felt like it, dropping by any time he wanted, and acting as if we were amicably divorced. He still had a key and he used it whenever he wanted. I guess I didn't send off the vibe that I wanted to cut his testicles off every time I saw him.

Ray and I both teach at the same small Catholic university; Ray is the head of the Biology Department and I'm an English professor. We see each other more than we should, which is why I can't figure out why he still drops by my house "just to see how you're doing." I'm fine! I want to scream. Leave me alone! But after having attended Catholic school myself for sixteen years, including St. Thomas, where I teach, I am unfailingly polite. I always greet him with a smile and, sometimes, a hug. And hence, because he is the least self-aware person I've ever met, and clearly doesn't know how much I detest him, he thinks we're solid. All has been forgiven.

I've spent more than one sleepless night wondering just why we married, but suffice it to say that Ray is extremely handsome and really charming. But really, my dying mother made me promise that I wouldn't become an old maid. Ladies and gentlemen: Mr. and Mrs. Raymond Stark!

It had been a long day at school. The president of the college had been demanding that a review committee be formed to reassess the English Department's curriculum; apparently, a group of students was demanding more diverse courses that took into account the changing face of the school. I had been handpicked by my boss, Sister Mary McLaughlin, to collect data from my colleagues. It was a nightmare; trying to get information from each of my colleagues, many more senior than myself at the school and many of them nuns, about what they were teaching was akin to getting the blueprints to the Pentagon. They were resentful, prickly, resistant, and clearly technophobes, because while most every other instructor at the school had a Web site with syllabi for each course they taught, the old nuns refused. Hard copy only. That complicated my task considerably. Some had been teaching close to thirty years and had been left alone during that time; asking for an accounting of their work was not something that they looked at kindly. I wasn't getting paid to do it either, which, given the St. Thomas history of low pay and long hours, wasn't surprising. So when Sister Calista, who taught American literature, practically spat at me when I asked for her syllabus, I almost gave up. Hey, Calista means "most beautiful one," I wanted to remind her as she shut her office door on my foot, not "she who can hock a loogie." And just because you're old and celibate doesn't give you the right to act however you want, lady. I'm of *un certain âge* and celibate (not by choice, of course) and still manage to get along in polite society.

It was martini time. My freezer contained two things—one, a bottle of Ketel One with a thick layer of frost on it, and two, a box of Klondike bars. Tonight's appetizer would be a big glass of Ketel One with three blue cheese–stuffed olives, followed by a dinner of two Klondike bars. I figured I had hit at least two of the major food groups with that selection; suffice it to say that I'm not making any major attempt at hanging on to my "girlish figure" as my mother used to call it.

With the vodka and prepackaged ice cream calling my name, I made my way home in record time and pulled into my driveway about fifteen minutes after I had left school. Dobbs Ferry is a pretty sleepy town but its proximity to St. Thomas makes it the perfect place for me to live. I pulled into my driveway and got out of the car, nodding to Trixie, the golden retriever who belonged to my neighbors and who stood sentry on the other side of the hedgerow that divided our property.

I guess you could call Trixie my third best friend because no matter what I do, what I say, or the kind of day I've had, she loves me unconditionally. I went over to the hedgerow and stuck my hand between the prickly branches to touch her. She responded by taking my whole hand in her mouth, licking it until it was soaked, and then giving me a nice "woof" as a send-off. She knows our time together is always brief and on the clandestine side because her owners and I don't have the best relationship. So she takes what she can get and then moves on.

Although darkness had fallen and I was sorry that I hadn't installed that motion-detecting light that Ray had been on my case about for the last year of our marriage, I did manage to make my way across the backyard without incident. I also made out a shape sitting on a lounge chair on the patio outside my back door. The moon glinted off a bald pate and I recognized my ex sprawled out on the lounge chair, his briefcase open beside him. Ray is bald by choice; he thinks it gives him "street cred" or something. I just miss seeing his head covered with a thick mop of gorgeous, wavy black hair.

"What are you doing?" I asked. "Grading papers in the dark?"

He must have been dozing because he sat up with a start, the papers on his lap spilling onto the patio. "I started grading papers when I got here. It was sunny then," he said, his voice raspy and hoarse. He stood. "How are you?" He busied himself picking up the papers and stuffing them into his leather briefcase.

I approached him tentatively. Besides his habit of dropping by unannounced, which, as I said, really annoys me, there's also the staying-way-too-long part. We didn't spend a tremendous amount of time together when we were married; I couldn't understand why we had to now. "Ray, I've got a ton of work to do tonight. I really don't have time to visit."

"I won't stay long," he promised. "Can I come in for a minute?"

I considered his request for a few minutes and stared at him. As long as a minute didn't turn into two hours, it would be fine. "Okay. Fine." I opened the back door and stood aside, letting him in. "What's the matter with your voice?" I asked.

"I've got a cold," he said. "I've had it for a few weeks. I can't seem to shake it."

I put my briefcase on the counter and offered him some tea. I immediately felt bad for being so annoyed with him; he was clearly under the weather and I wasn't so heartless as to not have some sympathy for him. We sat at the kitchen table waiting for the water to boil and tried to think of something to talk about. Even though we had a not altogether happy history, we were never at a loss for something to talk about. That had all changed, however, when I had found out that he had slept with both our neighbor and one of my students. Even though he persisted with his drop-ins, I had been extremely frosty the last few times he had come by. He didn't seem to notice.

"Max is getting married," I said finally. I figured that would either be a good conversation starter or something that would bring it to a screeching halt. Max is my best friend and Ray's archenemy. She hated him with a vengeance the likes of which I had never witnessed. His charm and good looks had no effect on her and I think that left Ray on shaky ground. Without his charm and good looks to fall back on, Ray is basically an empty husk.

He looked surprised. "That's something I never thought I'd hear." He studied the top of the table. "Is she happy?"

I laughed. "Well, sure. Most people who are about to get married are happy." Even us, I thought.

The water had begun to boil so I set about making a couple of cups of tea.

"I heard you're on the diversity council for the English Department," he said.

I took an old lemon from a basket of fruit on the

counter and examined it to find a piece that we could use in our tea. "Guilty as charged. If you find me dead in my office, Sister Calista did it."

He looked confused but he didn't ask what I meant. I could tell that he was troubled by something. I handed him his cup of tea and sat down. "What's going on, Ray?"

He shrugged. "I'm not really sure," he said, taking a tissue from his pocket and blowing his nose. "Have you ever felt like things are falling apart?"

I resisted the urge to laugh. Have I ever felt like that? Only most of the last two years that we spent together as a married couple. I kept the sarcasm in check, though; the Ray sitting in front of me was obviously in pain and I didn't want to rub salt in the wounds. I went with a vague nod.

He chuckled but he clearly wasn't amused. "I really screwed things up, Alison."

I nodded again. "Yes, you did."

"And now, in addition to dealing with that fact, I feel like I'm being followed. Or watched."

"Who would be watching you?"

He rolled his eyes; the list of suspects was lengthier than I think we both cared to admit. "Well, let's see. There's the Mob-boss father of my last girlfriend, the husband of the woman I was seeing before that . . . shall I continue?"

I shook my head. "You don't have to. I get it." I took a sip of tea. "Do you think you're in danger?"

"I don't know. But the whole thing is unsettling. I feel like someone's been in my apartment, too. Nothing's missing but I've just got this feeling . . ." He trailed off, shaking his head.

"I think we're all unsettled, Ray. Being involved in that murder investigation shook me up, too. And you were a suspect," I said. He shot me a look; obviously he didn't want to be reminded that he had been the main suspect in his girlfriend's murder. "Well, you were. I could see why you would be nervous after what you've been through."

He decided not to address that line of reasoning. He wrapped his hands around the mug. "Are you still dating that police detective?" he asked.

Well, there was a question with a complicated answer. The detective, Crawford, was a man whom I had met in the course of the murder investigation a few months earlier. And despite the fact that I thought I would never, under any circumstances, find another man attractive or worthy of my time, I had fallen for this guy so hard it had made my head spin. And although we were in the midst of a murder investigation in which I played a major role, we had commenced on a bit of a romantic journey, one that had been cut short by my discovery of the lovely Mrs. Crawford, his estranged, but very much legally married, spouse. Mrs. Crawford, who apparently was also a stickler for Church law; she refused to divorce Crawford until he agreed to an annulment, a bureaucratic "get out of jail free" card for divorcing Catholics. "No, I'm not really dating Crawford anymore," I said as cryptically as I could. I was hoping we could leave it at that.

He studied my face and I guess he saw that this was not a topic we should discuss at any length. "Do you think if I spoke to him about this he would help me? I do live in his precinct."

"If he can't help you, Ray, I'm sure he could put you in contact with the person who could." I took a sip of the tea. "Give him a call at the precinct."

"I'll do that." We sat in silence for a few minutes, drinking tea. My mind kept returning to the contents of my freezer and I sneaked a glance at my watch to see what time it was. It really didn't matter what the hour was, but it was time for Ray to leave.

Dejection was etched on his gorgeous face. "Do you think that things will ever be the same between us?" he asked.

I laughed out loud. "God, I hope not!" I blurted out. I immediately regretted being so caustic. To lessen the blow, I leaned across the table and gave him a quick hug. "Ray, the fact that we can be in the same room and I don't feel like killing you is a huge step for us."

He looked at me, not knowing whether to laugh or get mad. That was familiar territory for both of us; he never quite got me or my humor.

"I guess I have to take your word for it." He moved back. "Besides everything," he started, "we had some good times, right?"

"If by 'everything' you mean your four affairs, I guess we had a good day or two in between," I said truthfully and without a trace of sarcasm.

He pursed his lips and thought for a moment. "I think it was more than a day or two, but we don't have to argue about that."

I focused on a red wine stain on the tabletop so that I didn't have to look at him. "Tell me something, Ray."

He raised an eyebrow. "What's that?"

"Why did you marry me?" I asked, finally prepared to hear the answer that I hadn't wanted to hear until now. "And don't give me your 'I'm in love with love' bullshit or anything like that. I want the truth." I looked up from the counter and held his gaze.

"You'll never believe me," he said, looking down.

"Try me."

When he looked back up, he was smiling sadly. "Okay. The reason I married you is because I loved you. Part of me still does. I may not have shown it, but I was in love with you."

I let out a sound that was somewhere between a laugh and a sob. "Oh, Ray. You can do much better than that."

He drank the rest of his tea and got up from the table, turning to leave. "I told you that you'd never believe me." He put his hand on the doorknob and, seeing that I had nothing else to say, quietly let himself out.

Chapter 2

Father Kevin McManus called me later that week to invite me to dinner and I jumped at the invitation. My social life had come to an abrupt halt after my divorce from Ray and then the hiatus of my more recent romance with the sexy, yet married, cop named Crawford. A night out with a friend was just what I needed, even if he was celibate and really into God. School was well under way and I was happy to be back into my old routine.

I hadn't seen too much of my nymphomaniac best friend, Max; she was involved in her relationship with a police detective that took up most of her time and made good use of her nympho skills. And Kevin, well, I guess he was busy saving souls or turning water into wine, but I hadn't seen him in weeks, either.

So I had thrown myself into preparing for a new year of school. I had minds to shape, theory to espouse, syllabi to collect from mummified nuns . . . heck, a paycheck to cash. Let's face it, the minds I was shaping weren't all that interested in theory I was espousing, but I always faced a new semester with high hopes.

I straightened up my office, waiting for Kevin to arrive. A knock at the door interrupted my weak attempt at filing, which consisted of a file that was called "miscellaneous" and housed everything from syllabi to standardized tests. I reached over from my position in front of the filing cabinet and opened the door.

Ray stuck his head in. "Hi. Can I come in?"

If you must, I thought. I looked at my watch and saw that I had fifteen minutes until Kevin arrived, plenty of time for Ray to ruin my good mood. I hoped we weren't going to walk down memory lane again. "Sure."

Ray took a seat across from my desk, folding his hands in his lap. "I called your friend Detective Crawford."

"Good. Did he help you?"

"He asked me to come down to the station to make a formal statement but I haven't had a chance."

Ray had been in the precinct for questioning earlier in the year and I was sure he was in no rush to go back.

"I need to talk to you about a student, Alison."

I sat down at my desk. "Who and what is the problem?" I knew if Ray was coming by, there was a problem and that the student must be his advisee. Great. A biology student with an English literature problem. Professors usually don't get involved in each other's business unless some student has come whining to us about unfair treatment, what they perceive as too-tight deadlines, or a grade about which they disagree.

"Julie Anne Podowsky." He looked out the window of my office, a floor-to-ceiling affair that afforded a great view of the cemetery at the top of the stairs that led to the building. He looked back at me. "She's my advisee and she told me that she's having trouble in your Modern Lit class."

She was right about that. "She's handed in one paper late and gotten a D on the latest quiz."

He squirmed in his chair. What was that about? I wondered. "See, here's the thing. She's taking the MCAT soon and she's trying to get into a good medical school, so she needs her grades to be tops," he said. "Preferably As."

"Well, then she should study harder and get her work in on time," I said. What the hell was he thinking? I didn't want to presume that he was asking me to give her a pass, but it seemed like he was heading in that direction. Given what I knew about Ray the philanderer, it made sense, but given what I knew about Ray the professor, it didn't jibe.

Unless . . . so there it was. Yep, I'm a little slow on the uptake sometimes. But the thought entered my mind and stayed there. I had hoped that Ray had enough sense not to get involved with a student again, but apparently I was wrong. I looked at him. "You should leave. Now."

People who have been married have a sort of telepathy and now we were communicating without saying too much. "She's twenty-one," he said.

I shook my head. "Doesn't matter." I stood. "Let's forget that we had this conversation, Ray. And tell Ms. Podowsky that I wouldn't want a doctor practicing medicine on me who thinks that Robert Frost was the author of *Chicken Little*."

He decided that that didn't need or deserve a response and he huffed out of my office. Talk about a man who let his johnson do his thinking for him. I shook my head in silent wonder at his lack of judgment.

Kevin showed up at my office a few minutes later and looking at his outfit alone lifted my mood. He was in his "casual" outfit—shorts, a LIFE IS GOOD T-shirt, and sandals. Kevin liked being a priest but hated the uniform; if he didn't have to wear his Roman collar, he didn't. Most of the time, he coordinated a pair of jeans to the black shirt/white collar ensemble; other times, he wore black pants and a regular shirt. Tonight, he had gone completely over the top and looked like a middle-aged surfer as opposed to a man of the cloth.

Whenever Kevin and I ate out, we either went to Maloney's for wings—a local campus hang-out—or to the River Edge Steak House when we needed more sustenance. We headed out the back door of the Administration Building and up the concrete steps to the parking lot. After deciding that walking would be in both of our best interests given the amount of time we spend behind our desks and what we planned to consume, we headed down the avenue and arrived at the Steak House about ten minutes later.

We sat down in the cool comfort of the dark-paneled room, and ordered drinks; me, my usual Ketel One martini (with extra olives . . . it's a drink, and an hors d'oeuvre, my favorite kind of beverage), and Kevin, a glass of chardonnay.

After taking a sip of my drink and feeling white heat travel down my esophagus and into my stomach, I started to relax. Just being away from school and out for the evening, even if my date was a priest, was a vast improvement over what I had originally planned, which was laundry followed by more laundry.

The waitress appeared at the table and took our order. Kevin and I both ordered the Steak House's famous giant sirloins with baked potatoes and asparagus on the side. I held up my almost empty martini glass and waved it toward the waitress. "And I'll take another one of these, if you wouldn't mind."

Kevin asked me how things had been going.

"Eh. Boring."

He gave me a pitying look.

I laughed and polished off my drink. "That about sums it up."

"No word from Crawford?"

"Not a one."

Kevin gazed out the window. "Why do you think that is?"

I laughed ruefully. "I asked for time. He's pretty literal."

"That doesn't remind me of anybody I know," Kevin said, rolling his eyes. He ran a hand through his shaggy blond mop of hair, a blatant time killer.

"Cut to the chase, Kevin."

He waited another beat or two. "Do you think it's time to move on?" he asked quietly.

The waitress put salads in front of us, delaying my answer. I dove into the pile of iceberg lettuce and Russian dressing with more enthusiasm and fervor than the wilted plate of greens deserved. I pointed to my full mouth with my fork.

"I'll wait for your answer," he said. "I've sat in darkened confessionals in silence for hours. Your iceberg-filled mouth isn't very daunting. Trust me."

I chewed and thought about his question. Was it time to move on? I didn't know. I did know that I missed Crawford terribly and hoped I would hear from him. I wished I was more twenty-first century and could pick up the phone and call him myself, but I always hesitated; I don't know why. "I don't know, Kevin. Do you think I should move on?"

He turned pensive. "I do. And I want to bring something up about that and now is as good a time as ever."

I waited.

"I have a brother . . ."

I put my hand up. "No!"

". . . and he's single."

I shook my head.

"He's not married. Or separated and married. Or not separated. He's completely available. His name is Jack and he works for the Rangers. You know, the hockey team?" he asked, knowing full well that I knew who the Rangers were. I was intimately acquainted with many of the New York Rangers, if only in my sweat-soaked sexual fantasies. Besides that, I liked hockey. A lot. Kevin took a sip of his drink and waited for my response.

I had nothing to say. I would rather have a root canal without anesthesia than go on a blind date, but I kept that tidbit to myself.

"You haven't really done a lot of dating since your divorce."

Fortunately for me, his cell phone trilled, preventing me from having to strangle him on the spot. He pulled the phone from his cargo shorts, peering at the caller ID. "The convent," he said. He clicked the phone on. "Hello?"

I continued eating my salad, listening to his end of the conversation. He hung up a few seconds later. "Sister Bertrand needs last rites," he said.

I knew Sister Bertrand from my days as a student at St. Thomas; she was the Latin professor and a formidable conjugation adversary. The only thing that saved me was the fact that I was bilingual, having been raised in a French-speaking household, and I could sometimes figure things out without killing too many brain cells. Of course that was before I had discovered the joys of ice-cold vodka and olives. "Oh, Kevin. I'm sorry."

"Leukemia," he said. "Hospice brought her back to the convent to die, and it looks like it will be tonight. I'm sorry," he said, getting up. "If it's not too much trouble, would you mind having them wrap my dinner? You can leave it at the desk in my building." Kevin lived on the top floor of the men's dormitory on campus; my car was parked in front of the building, as always, so he knew that I would be returning to that area within the evening.

"Of course." I stood and embraced him. "I'll say a prayer for Sister." I watched him leave before sitting back down and returning to my salad. The waitress delivered my second martini. I looked out the window at the traffic outside, people walking past the restaurant looking as wilted as my salad, baking in the unseasonably warm weather as they made their way home from the express buses stopping at the corner. I raised my drink to my lips and focused on the opening to the main dining room. I froze.

Crawford, his wife, and his two daughters entered,

smiling and chatting with each other, joking with the hostess as they made their way to a table that was thankfully as far away from mine as you could get. A waitress glided past me, a stack of menus in her arm.

I grabbed her. "Hey, could I have one of those?" I asked.

She stopped at my table. "Do you want to change your order?"

No, I want to crawl in a hole and die, I thought, but a menu in front of my face is the next best thing. "Um, I just want to look at the dessert menu." She handed me a menu. "And my friend had to leave. Emergency. Could you wrap up our dinners to go?"

She looked at me as if my medication had worn off and I wasn't making any sense. "Sure."

I held the menu up in front of my face and pretended to read it, peeking out over the top every now and again to make sure that the Crawford family was ensconced at their table and not making any sudden moves. Thankfully, Crawford's back was to me, as was his wife's; his daughters faced me, but I felt like I was far enough away that they wouldn't recognize me if I had to suddenly give up the menu. They had only seen me once during what was now known in my mind as the "great hospital debacle," an event that occurred when I had stopped in to visit Crawford while he was recuperating from a stabbing incident. While there, I introduced myself to his wife—a wife I didn't know he had. I hoped neither one had inherited their father's gift for observation.

I continued reading the menu and arrived at "chicken breast marinated in our own combination of ginger, soy sauce, and garlic" when I felt a tap on my shoulder. I looked up and focused on the crotch of a very tall man. Crawford.

"I can see you," he said.

"This is an extremely interesting menu," I said. When

he didn't respond, I offered a stupid-sounding chuckle. I looked over at his table, where his family was all turned in their chairs, staring at me. His wife gave me a tentative wave, which I returned. "Who saw me first?"

"Meaghan," he said. "She spotted you, even behind the menu. She recognized you as the woman she saw at the hospital."

So one of them had gotten the observation gene. I threw my head in the direction of their table. "You don't seem too separated," I said, alluding to his wife. I regretted it the moment it came out of my mouth.

He closed his eyes for a moment and sighed. "Christine is going away tomorrow morning on an overnight and asked me if I would take the girls for the whole weekend. She offered to drop them off and I offered to take everyone to dinner. Nothing has changed."

I snorted. "Great." If nothing had changed, it meant that they were still separated. However, it also meant that they were probably still legally married, which, for me, was the deal breaker.

He shifted uncomfortably from one giant foot to the other. "I've been meaning to give you a call. I wanted to see you."

"Well, here I am!" I said and threw my hands up, knocking my drink over. Icy vodka flew up in the air, almost in slow motion, and settled right into Crawford's crotch. With his entire family watching this scenario, I resisted the urge to press my napkin into his zipper and, instead, watched as his face went from almost contrite to a mask of consternation.

He looked down at his pants, the moisture spreading into the shape of Italy. He gave me a slight smile. "Maybe we could try this again at a later date?"

"Yeah. I could do without the Greek chorus," I said, shooting a glance at the three women at the front of the restaurant who were fixated on our conversation. "Please tell them that my usual greeting doesn't consist of flying martinis."

He smirked. "Well, the first time we met, you vomited on me, so this is a vast improvement."

That didn't deserve a response so I was grateful when my cell phone rang. "I have to take this," I said, before looking down and seeing that I really didn't have to take it: it was my ex-husband. No phone call from him could result in anything good. Crawford stood over me for a few more seconds, and when it was clear that we had nothing else to say to each other, he drifted off, looking over his shoulder with a doleful expression on his face.

I flipped open my phone. "Hi, Ray."

"Alison . . ." He trailed off.

"Ray?" I said.

"Alison. I really want to talk to you about the situation with Julie Anne again." The connection clicked in and out as if he were in a bad cell area. I heard him say my name and then what sounded like "can you hell" but the line was dead. I scrolled through the contacts menu on the phone and hit send when I came to Ray's name.

The waitress came by again. "We have a no-cell-phone policy," she said.

Of course you do, I thought. You should also have a no-home-perm policy, too, but of course then you wouldn't be able to work here. I got up and went outside through the back entrance so I wouldn't have to see *la famille* Crawford again. The phone rang in my ear and, after five or six rings, went to Ray's voice mail. "Ray, call me back." I walked to the front of the restaurant and caught a glimpse of Crawford and his family inside.

I stood for a moment on the street corner watching the bustling activity on the avenue. After a few moments of thought, I made another call. The message was short and to the point, and the decision, I hoped, not one that I would live to regret.

"Hi, Kevin? Yes, tell your brother I'd love to meet him."

I dropped Kevin's dinner off at the dorm where he lived. On my short drive home, I thought about running into Crawford, a situation that could not have been more awkward. I wish I had been able to keep my cool, but something about seeing him with his daughters and his wife made me lose whatever modicum of composure I actually had. And from what I had heard about his wife from the little he told me and from the details that his detective partner, Fred—who as luck would have it was also engaged to Max—had filled in, she was a veritable Mother Teresa, lovely and kind and devoted to her daughters. Crawford had said that they would be getting divorced, but when? It was not something that I felt we could delve into at the Steak House in any meaningful way.

I thought about my impulsive decision to green-light a date with Kevin's brother. A minor twinge of guilt gnawed at my insides; I was really crazy about Crawford, probably more than I ever had been about my ex-husband, but what was I supposed to do? How long was I supposed to wait while he figured out his personal life? Denial is a powerful thing, however; by the time I had reached my exit off the Saw Mill River Parkway, I had completely justified going out with Jack McManus and felt much better about things. I hadn't paid too much attention to what Kevin had told me about his four brothers, but I seemed to remember that one brother was a little too into Madonna and liked to "vogue" at family parties. He also had another brother who was really into *Star Wars,* and had an adult-sized Chewbacca costume that he donned every Halloween. I prayed that neither of them were named Jack.

I pulled into my driveway and gave a nod to Trixie, who looked at me as she always did, tongue hanging out to one side, her black lips pulled back into what seemed like a huge smile. It was nice, after having adjusted to living alone, to have someone or something greet me every evening.

Darkness had settled over everything in the backyard and I carefully picked my way around lawn furniture and trash cans to get to the back door. Damn that nonexistent motion-detecting light. At least there was no ex-husband lounging on my patio furniture. I managed to insert my key into the back door and get into the kitchen without much of a problem and my eyes began to adjust to the blackness of the house. I flicked on the kitchen light and dropped my bag onto the table. It was in that instant of doing the familiar, the normal, the rote, that I noticed that I wasn't alone.

Sitting at the kitchen table, the ends of his wrists bloody nubs, was Ray, my ex-husband, a tortured look forever etched on his handsome, lifeless face.

Crawford walked into the precinct that evening; he was pulling a double shift so that he could have all of Saturday night and all day Sunday with his girls. He had left the girls with his aunt Bea; although they were old enough at sixteen to stay in his apartment by themselves, he preferred them to be there when his aunt was in the apartment downstairs. She rarely left after six in the evening unless there was bingo at the church or some devotional hour. Tonight was her television night so she was in, they were upstairs, and he could work without letting his mind wander as to what they might be doing. He had a ton of paperwork to do, never mind if he caught any new cases that night. He opened the door to the main area and the stench of the building—a cross between old gym socks and decaying leaves—hit him and ruined his joie de vivre immediately. He walked behind a gray-carpeted partition and toward his desk.

"Hey, Mr. Best Man!"

Crawford looked at him, confused.

"Fred tells me you're the best man for the big day," Champy said, pulling at the waistband of his pants. "Nice going. Lots of responsibility with that role. You know, taking care of the bridesmaids and everything." He wiggled his substantial brows lasciviously.

"Hey, Champy." He pulled out his desk chair and sat down, clearing a space on his desk for the cup of coffee that he had bought at the deli. "What's going on?"

Champy, about the same age as Crawford, but red faced and old looking after a lifetime of bad food and excessive drinking, stood up behind his desk. His given name was Arthur Moran, but he had gotten the nickname of "Champy" some years before. As a uniformed rookie, he and his partner had been sent on a call to a Lower East Side gay strip club—"Champy's"—to break up a fight between a dozen or more drag queens; when everything was sorted out, he ended up with the unfortunate responsibility of escorting one Dusty Rhodes out of the bar in handcuffs. Dusty was a six-foot-seven drag queen with a blond beehive of hair and a thing for cops. As they exited the bar, a photographer for the *Daily News* snapped their picture, Dusty's lips plastered to Champy's baby face. His reputation, and nickname, was solidified on that day. Forevermore, he was "Champy"—a name he wore a little too proudly. He smoothed down his blue and yellow tie, about three inches shorter than it should have been, given his height. "We're catching together today."

Crawford looked around and saw that they were the only two detectives in the squad and groaned internally; Fred never worked nights and that meant a new partner for the shift. He was hoping that at least one other detective was in the rotation but Champy was alone in the squad room. A day with Champy was not on his list of "things I really love," but more akin to a colonoscopy, an IRS audit, or having his fingernails ripped off one by one. Although he was one of the best detectives in the squad when it came to clearing cases—perps usually gave it up as quickly as possible in order to get away from him as quickly as possible—his style was different from Crawford's. Whereas Crawford liked to follow the rules as closely as he could (within reason), Champy worked a fringe detail where nothing really mattered besides solving the case. Civil liberties? Never heard of them. Innocent? Champy would make you believe you were guilty if it meant getting out of work earlier. And he never met a perp he didn't like for a crime. Crawford steeled himself for a very long day.

"Don't look so happy, Bobby," Champy said, a bit dejected as he sat back down at his desk.

Crawford felt instantly guilty. "I'm thrilled, Champy. You and I don't get to spend enough quality time together." He went through the stack of folders on his desk. "Anything happening?"

"Not too much. Casey and Mariano are working the double from Kingsbridge."

Two people had been killed in an apartment in the Kingsbridge section of the Bronx the week before and Casey and Mariano were still working the canvass of the neighborhood and following a couple of leads. The original theory was that it was drug-related, but they weren't sure. "Anything from Alex?" Crawford asked.

Champy shook his head, annoyed. "That guy is less of an informant than a fucking pain in the ass. I told him to keep his ear to the ground, gave him another twenty, but he hasn't given me shit."

If it had to do with drugs, Alex would know. Crawford had had more meals with Alex than he cared to admit, but every once in a while, he got something valuable. "Maybe he'll come through."

Champy snorted. "Yeah, and maybe my wife will give me a blow job."

Crawford looked up from the file he was reading.

"In other words, my friend, it'll never happen."

"Keep the faith, Champy. Anything's possible." Crawford smiled. The world of Champy. Not one he'd want to spend too much time in, but an amusing stop every once in a while. He went back to the file on his desk.

"Oh, and I took a call from a guy named Stark," he said, crossing the room and handing Crawford a pink slip of paper with a name and number written on it. "Dr. Ray Stark, he said. Wants to set up a date to talk about that statement you asked for. Sounded dramatic," Champy said, rolling his eyes.

Crawford took the slip from Champy and shoved it into his pants pocket. Dealing with Ray Stark's "dramatic" situation, as Champy had dubbed it, was not high on his priority list.

He turned when he heard Danny Concannon, the Homicide Division's lieutenant, open his office door and emerge.

Concannon was fifteen years past retirement—he had put in his requisite twenty years, but was a "lifer." Mandatory retirement at sixty-two was what he was striving for, and at age fifty-eight, what he would eventually attain. He was a big and blustery man and Crawford loved working with him. He was the kind of guy who started every fourth or so sentence with "If they can put a man on the moon, then . . ." but he was honest and forthright and treated all of his cops with respect. Crawford knew that it could be very different from his own experience on the

PD. Danny scanned the detectives' bullpen and saw that only Champy and Crawford were at their desks.

"Moran! Crawford! Body parts in Van Cortlandt Park. Right by the stables. Patrol's got hands and feet. Nothing else. Get over there."

Champy pushed his chair back from his desk. "How do we know it's a homicide?" He stood. "Maybe we've got some John Doe running around . . . excuse me . . . hobbling around with no hands and feet."

Concannon stood in front of Champy's desk, staring at him in disbelief. "Moran, get your ass out of here and go look at the hands and feet." He started back to his office, muttering, "If they can put a man on the moon, they can give me a cop who can figure out that a vic without hands and feet IS DEAD." He slammed the door to his office.

Crawford stood. "Let's go." His night with Champy had begun. They would work through the night in a desolate park. They didn't call it the graveyard shift for nothing.

Chapter 3

As I've learned from the other murder investigation I was involved in, nothing screws up your weekend like finding a dead body.

"Ray?" I managed to squeak out, knowing instinctively that he was not going to answer me. I edged closer to the table and tentatively touched his shoulder, succeeding in making him list to the side. Fortunately, the wall prevented him from sliding off his chair.

His eyes were open and he stared at me, unseeing. I, however, stared at him for far longer than I should have. I don't know how much time passed but I felt as if I were glued to the floor. Finally, my flight instinct took over and I backed out of the kitchen, first slowly, and then gaining speed as I crossed over the threshold of the back door.

I stumbled backwards out of the house, going ass over tea kettle when I hit the wrought-iron table on the patio. The racket brought my neighbor to the left, Florence, out of her house in record time. I have to carry her recyclables out every week because of her sciatica or lumbago or whatever her disease of the week is, but once I hit that table, she flew out of the house like an Olympic sprinter. From now on, she was carrying out her own goddamned recyclables. Florence loves a good drama; she had watched, with rapturous glee, my marriage unravel from between the vertical blinds in her kitchen. Trixie set up a howl that was ear piercing. It crossed my mind that a man had been murdered inside my house and nobody raised an eyebrow; I, however, fall over a picnic table and the National Guard practically appears.

Florence got a look at the body, and pronounced Ray officially "dead." She was then so kind as to call 911. I sat on the grass with my head between my knees rocking back and forth and hoping that I would wake up and realize that it had all been just a horrible dream. And that my ass wouldn't hurt like a mother once the shock of finding a dead body passed. Florence stood sentry at the bottom of the driveway so that she could show the cops where the body was. I guess "it's in the kitchen" would have been too much of a stretch for them, in her opinion. She was a major player in this drama and she would not be denied.

The police came quickly. After all, we live in a sleepy suburban town. Unless someone forgets to pay for their Dunkaccino at the local doughnut shop, there's not a lot going on. A dead body? Well, that was big doings. They really didn't know what to do with me; I guess they kind of considered me a suspect, but not really. It was clear that I had been shocked and awed by the discovery and that counted for something. I also didn't look like someone who could wield a chain saw with ease, and the person who had hacked Ray up seemed to have been a professional, given the "signature" of the missing body parts. Nevertheless, the detective assigned to the case—one Joe Hardin—asked that I go down to headquarters with one of the uniformed cops and make a statement. I was more than happy to oblige. Anything that got me out of the house and away from the scene of gore was more than welcome.

Oh, and there was one more disturbing fact: not only were Ray's hands missing, so were his feet. And they were nowhere to be found. My entire house had been searched and nothing had turned up.

Before I left, I asked Detective Hardin if I could make a quick phone call. Despite the way things had been left with Crawford, I knew that he was the only person I could count on to truly help me in a situation like this. Hardin, a hound-dog-faced fellow who looked perpetually sad, cast a glance in my direction and asked me who I wanted to call. I tried to look as convincing as possible and said, "My priest." I figured it was better than "my lawyer" or "my married boyfriend, the cop."

He gave me a dubious look and a nod. Even though I didn't think I was the most viable suspect, Hardin seemed liked the type who wouldn't rule anything out before making a decision. Or maybe he thought I was Jewish and was wondering why I had a priest. He weighed my request. "I'm not going to ask why you need to call your priest, but call him if you need to," he said after a few seconds of thought.

One of the cops had brought me my bag and I punched the numbers into my cell phone; Hardin walked a discreet distance away, convincing me of my notion that they really didn't think I was a maniac with a chain saw. When the call connected to Crawford's cell, it went directly to his voice mail. I left a calm and casual message that gave him the details: Ray was in my kitchen, he was dead, and he had been dismembered. Hey, could you give me a call when you get a chance? Thanks. Buh-bye.

I didn't want to push it with Hardin, so I didn't ask for another phone call. I wanted to get down to the station as quickly as possible, get my statement recorded, and then get out of there. It didn't occur to me until I was in the cop's cruiser that I would probably have to stay in a hotel that night because my kitchen was blood soaked. I didn't think Magda, my cleaning lady, was up to that challenge. She could barely wield the attachments on my Electrolux. But she was a whiz with grout.

The police station wasn't far from my house. I had led a pretty law-abiding life up until this point, so I had never been inside its charming Tudor-style walls. I was not shocked to find it clean, well lit, and stocked with Starbucks coffee. I had once been in a precinct in New York City and can testify that it was not clean and that the lighting made everyone look deathly ill. And no Starbucks coffee. The uniformed officer asked me if I'd like a cup of that delicious coffee, but I was so jittery from my discovery that I passed.

"We have decaf, too," he said, anticipating the fact that my shaking hands might preclude my having some caffeine.

I accepted the decaf; I didn't want to disappoint him. He seemed hell-bent on making a cup of coffee. After he handed it to me, complete with the little guard that surrounds a very hot paper cup, he led me into a brightly lit room with a long mahogany table and close to a dozen comfortable chairs around it. I wasn't sure if I was going to get questioned or make a presentation on the fourth-quarter sales goals of Wal-Mart. I took a seat at the end of the table and waited to make my statement.

I thought about Ray while I sipped my French roast and tried to sort out my feelings. I was still stunned by seeing him in the kitchen but I didn't feel like crying. And I cry when I see the hurt look on that caveman's face on the insurance company commercial when he realizes everyone is making fun of him. But my hands danced to a rhythm all their own, and I sat on them to keep them subdued. I kept seeing Ray's face, in death, and while I felt profoundly sad, I wasn't at the point of true grief yet. I wasn't sure if I ever would be. How are you supposed to feel when something this horrible happens to someone about whom you have such conflicted feelings?

The uniformed cop interrupted my reverie and poked

his head into the room. "Do you have a boyfriend who's a cop?"

I chewed on that question for a moment. That would be harder to answer than "who would want to kill your ex-husband?" "Uh, he's not my boyfriend, really, because we're kind of broken up right now, but . . ." I stopped when I saw the cop looking at me with a mixture of confusion and boredom. "I guess so," I said, as definitively as possible.

"He's on his way over," he said and pulled his head out of the room again, leaving me alone.

So I guess Crawford had gotten my message and, in true Crawford style, wanted to lend a hand. Why was I attracted to fabulous, but unavailable, men? And why, with my ex-husband dead in my kitchen, was I obsessed with understanding why this was so?

I picked my coffee up with my shaking hands, and took a careful sip. The hot liquid stuck in my throat as I thought about Ray, the way he looked, his missing digits. The contents of my stomach started wending their way up my digestive tract and I took a deep breath, holding it until my nausea subsided. I have a hair-trigger nervous system and have been known to unleash its power at the most inopportune times. I focused on a picture of the mayor of Dobbs Ferry which hung over the door and waited for a feeling of calm to overtake me again.

Fortunately, I was able to hold it together until another detective, this one a woman named Catherine Madden, entered the room to talk to me about my gruesome discovery. I put her age at around fifty or so and she reminded me of someone who had spent many years in the convent before finding that her true passion was police work—short, unstylish hair, sensible shoes, navy blue suit with white shirt. A gold cross dangled from a short chain around her crepey neck. She offered nothing in the way of pleasantries, just a curt "Start at the beginning. What happened?" She jotted down what I thought were the most salient points of my accounting, putting her pen down when I was finished.

"So, who do you think did this?" she asked, pursing her lips together in a very unattractive frown. Didn't she know that if you made unattractive faces, your face could freeze that way? Geez.

"I don't have the slightest idea," I said. And that was true. If I just thought about cuckolded spouses or pissed-off parents, the list of suspects was long: Peter Miceli, Mob boss and father of Ray's last girlfriend, a nineteen-year-old college student who was now dead; my neighbor Jackson, husband of Terri, Ray's paramour before the Mob princess; presumably the parents of Julie Anne Podowsky, the worst modern literature student ever to grace my classroom; and probably dozens of other spouses, boyfriends, fathers, and brothers of the women that Ray had slept with over the years and had dumped when he was done. Not to mention the actual women. I didn't have any family to blame, fortunately; I'm an only child, and my father—the most gentle of French-Canadian men—had been dead for nearly twenty years. Unless Uncle Claude in Baie-St.-Paul in Quebec had heard of Ray's philandering ways and had decided to kill him on my behalf, I had no viable suspects on my side of the family.

"And you?" she asked. "Where were you between the hours of two and six?"

"I was teaching and then I went to dinner with a friend. Who's a priest," I added helpfully. Who wouldn't believe a priest?

She stared at me for a few minutes. "I can check that alibi, you know."

"Please do," I said, holding her gaze. I prayed that my

students had been awake and would know that it was I who had taught their classes that day. There was a good percentage of them who didn't even know what class they were taking, never mind the name of their instructor.

She continued to stare at me. I spied Crawford's face in the glass pane of the door. Yep, still gorgeous. Madden turned around when she saw my attention on the door and beckoned him to come in. "Can I help you?" she asked.

"Detective Crawford, NYPD," he said, flashing his gold shield and shaking her hand. "I'm a friend of Dr. Bergeron's." He put his shield away. "I have some information about this case, too. Can we step outside?"

I tried to eavesdrop on what they were talking about but I couldn't hear anything. I watched them through the window in the door. Madden got a concerned look on her face and scurried off down the hall. Crawford watched her move away and came into the room.

"I'm sorry," he said.

I nodded. "I know."

He stood by the table and shoved his hands into his pockets. "Listen, I have something to tell you."

He imparted some truly sobering news: Ray's hands and feet had been found next to a horse stable in Van Cortlandt Park. It was the one detail that completed the story of Ray's demise and moved me from a state of shock to one of pronounced grief. I'm not sure why, but it was in that moment that I realized just how much Ray had suffered, and any feelings of ill will that I may have had toward him melted away in a flood of hot tears.

Chapter 4

My other best friend—the one who isn't the priest—defies description but I'll give it a shot.

Her name is Max, she's all of five feet two and a hundred pounds, but gorgeous and sexy in a way that many women attempt but few succeed at. She comes off as a total dumbbell, but in reality, she has an IQ of one hundred and sixty, runs a cable television station, and can add, subtract, multiply, and divide numbers in her head with a speed that is frightening. Especially if they pertain to the ratings of one of her shows, like the illustrious twenty-part reality series *Housewives: The True, Untold Story of Their Lives, Loves, and Passions*.

I spent a few nights billeted at her Tribeca apartment in the guest room, which reminded me why I never wanted to live with Max ever again. She keeps weird hours, has strange dietary habits, and engages in loud phone sex. But she's also loving, kind, and was willing to put me up and take me out to dinner until my house was restored to a blood-free state, a time period of about a week.

We didn't really talk about Ray that much; Max hated Ray and I'm sure that his death, while gruesome, wasn't a tragedy to her. For me, there was no handbook on dealing with your ex's death, so I tried to sort out my feelings in private, without her help. I was a bit more upset by Ray's death than I ever could have imagined. I had thought about killing Ray a hundred times, but never did I think he would meet such an untimely and gruesome demise. I found myself welling up at odd moments and realized that if I was going to move past everything—the marriage, our divorce, and his murder—I was going to have to deal with this. It occurred to me that I may not be equipped to deal with it on my own, but the thought of visiting the campus psychologist, Nancy Martin, was not an option. She wore too much patchouli and that made me suspect anything she had to say. I think if I dug deeply enough in her overflowing desk drawers, I would be sure to come up with a picture of her mud covered and half naked at Woodstock. And that was just not something I was prepared to see.

Dealing with the state of my house was much easier than dealing with the state of my emotions: Crawford had called some company that, interestingly enough, specialized in cleaning up crime scenes. I wondered what you had to have on your résumé in order to get a job there ("1989–1991: Responsible for all cleaning and disinfecting of Jeffrey Dahmer's apartment"). Their specialty was getting blood out of carpeting, and although I didn't have any carpeting in my kitchen, Crawford assured me that they would be equally effective on ceramic tile. As a fallback, I always had Magda's grout-cleaning wizardry. I took his word for it. I didn't know if I would ever go back into the kitchen, which wasn't a terrible loss; I don't cook and I mainly use it as a cut-through to the backyard and driveway.

The days after Ray's death were a blur. The murder spun the campus into turmoil again, just like Kathy Miceli's murder had a few short months before. And I was in the eye of the storm, the murder victim being my ex-husband and all. I tried to keep a low profile, going to school, teaching my classes, and returning home at the end of the day. Kevin's and my usual socializing was canceled for the time being. I felt like I was becoming a pariah, having been peripherally involved in two heinous crimes, and really didn't want to spend too much time in public. I knew that public stonings had been outlawed, but didn't want to take any chances.

I took in the tabloid headlines every time I passed the faculty receptionist, Dottie's, desk; they screamed of the blood and gore of Ray's murder. "Out of a Limb!" "Dismember of the Faculty!" And a picture of me, snapped when I had gone out to get my mail: "Dr. Doom!" Seems I was getting a bad reputation what with my close proximity to dead bodies becoming common.

My phone rang as I was finishing up at school. I had just returned to the safety of my office fresh from syllabi reconnaissance. Sister Calista and her wicked coven of English instructors were freezing me out now; when I knocked on their office doors, they pretended that they weren't at their desks, even though I could see the outline of their bonnet-shaped wimples through the glass. Neither Sister Mary nor President Etheridge was any help on that front, either.

When I picked up the phone, it was Max. As usual, she was mid-conversation with me even though I had just joined in. "You have to get a dress." We had talked about this topic ad nauseam while I had been living with her, yet she was smart enough to sense that I wasn't really going to take an active role in dress shopping unless she held a proverbial gun to my head. I hate shopping.

"Okay." I picked my briefcase up and put it on top of my desk, balancing the phone in the crook of my neck. "When?"

"When's the first day you can go?" she asked, screaming to someone to get her a latte. "No sugar!"

I reached into my briefcase and pulled out my planner. Every day was blank, with the exception of the notation regarding a meeting with the department heads a week in the future. "Anytime." Loser.

"Go to Nordstrom *as soon as possible,*" she said, "and pick something out. No black."

Black was my fallback color. "Black is the new . . . black," I said, striving for a little humor.

"Black is *blech,*" she said. "I like black just as much as the next washed-out New York beatnik, but not for my wedding. Find something sexy. Fun."

Sexy. Fun. Who did she think was buying this dress? Certainly not me. Right now I was dour and morose, but I didn't think Nordstrom had a section devoted to those adjectives. I could see the tagline now: "Dour. Morose. The latest in wedding glamour." "I'll give it my best shot, Max," I said, but she had hung up.

I took my car keys from my pocketbook and started to walk to my car, parked in the lot right behind my office. I heard my name being called and I stopped, turning to look around the dark lot. The person in the shadows was a few feet away and small, thin, and dressed in black. I squinted in the hazy charcoal of dusk, trying to discern who it was and my breath caught in my throat when I made out the outline of Gianna Miceli.

"Gianna?"

She approached me tentatively, one hand outstretched. "Alison."

Gianna Miceli and I had a complicated history. We had attended St. Thomas at the same time, and although she was two years older than I was and we shouldn't have had anything to do with each other, we found ourselves linked together by tragedy. Gianna's daughter, Kathy, had been murdered earlier this year, an event that had rocked the campus and my own world. A couple of sordid things come to mind when I think of her death: one, that she had been found in the trunk of my car, and two, that she had had a relationship with my ex-husband. I hesitate to call it an "affair" because what nineteen-year-old girl sets out to have an affair, a word that has serious and somewhat tawdry connotations? I preferred to think of it as a relationship because I was sure that Kathy thought that's what it was.

I walked toward her and embraced her, at the time the obvious thing to do. The dark circles under her eyes highlighted the grief etched on her face and it was apparent to me that she was still in the depths of a fathomless despair. I held her at arm's length. "What are you doing here?"

She motioned to a dorm across campus. "I came to clean out Kathy's room. This is the first day I've been able to face it."

Students had been in the dorms for a couple of weeks already, so Gianna was a little late to the task. I guessed that the Housing Office had decided against opening the room to new students and would leave it unoccupied for at least the year, if not longer. I looked down at her, her face illuminated by a spotlight hanging off the dorm behind us.

"How is the rest of your family?"

She shrugged. "Fine."

"Max is getting married," I said, for want of something else to say.

"Who's Max?" she asked.

I started to explain that she had known Max at St. Thomas but gave up. It didn't seem to matter if she remembered Max or not. I decided to shut up.

Clearly, we had nothing to say to each other. Despite the history we had we were nothing more than acquaintances bonded in death and tragedy. I thought back on our shared time at St. Thomas—she was the rich golden girl whose father had a dubious occupation; on the surface, he owned a restaurant but talk ran to his now-confirmed Mob connections. When she took up with Peter Miceli in her junior year, a fat, prematurely balding guy with absolutely no game or brains to speak of, we were all very surprised. What I remember about Peter was that he was always trying to get me to ride in his Trans Am and that I always declined. Even then, when I should have been throwing caution to the wind and living the life of a carefree coed, my common sense ruled. I had been right about him all along but it still didn't explain to me why this seemingly bright, attractive woman had ended up with him. It only explained why I hadn't.

I remember Gianna pouring her heart out to me and Max one night at Maloney's, our favorite bar back in the day. Sal Paccione was her boyfriend and the bartender at Maloney's. His reputation was one of a nice guy who was basically a gigolo; although Gianna seemed to overlook his wandering ways, they were obvious to any girl who had ever bought a beer from him at the bar. Except for me, of course; I thought he was just an inordinately friendly guy. A lingering glance, an extra hand squeeze when change was returned, a wink in your direction—I always thought it was his way of drumming up more tips, but Max assured me that he was a cad, plain and simple. The night that Max and Gianna and I had spent at the bar, it was clear to us that she had had enough but she wasn't prepared to do anything about it. Until she caught him kissing one of the other bartenders in the alley behind the bar.

Then, all hell broke loose.

Gianna, unbeknownst to me and Max, was a woman with a temper. A tiny, hundred-and-ten-pound spitfire, who turned that bar into the eye of a hurricane in about ten seconds flat. Rumor had it that her father had paid for all of the damage and then some so that Billy Maloney wouldn't press charges, something that I'm sure wasn't really on his mind, given her father's *alleged* occupation of whacking people.

Sal didn't fare as well as Billy Maloney. He was gone the next week and never seen again.

I hugged her again. "I have to go," I said, knowing that this was probably the last time I would ever see her. I turned to walk away.

"Peter sends his regards," she called after me, something in her tone causing me to stop.

I turned slowly. "What?" A chill crawled slowly from the base of my spine to my neck.

"Peter sends his regards," she repeated, a small, cruel smile playing on her lips.

Her husband was a gangster, a murderer, and involved in more illicit activities than I could keep track of. I had more than a sneaking suspicion that he was responsible for Ray's death, too. He had kidnapped me a few months earlier, threatening to kill Max and Ray if I didn't provide him the details of Kathy's murder investigation. He had lost interest in me once the murder had been solved but had professed to "owe" me for treating Kathy with kindness when she was alive. I hated and feared him and to hear Gianna speak of him in relation to me was frightening and a little nauseating. I continued looking at her, unable to fashion a reply.

"Just wanted to let you know," she said coldly. She started to walk away and I resisted the urge to scream at her to tell Peter to leave me alone but I stood in the growing darkness in silence.

Fred Wyatt was the perfect partner in every way. He was the first guy in and the last guy out. He was the one Crawford wanted beside him when shots were fired. But his singing drove Crawford to the edge of insanity. He sang love songs, Motown songs, heavy metal songs, show tunes . . . anything to hear the sound of his own voice. And, Crawford expected, to drive him completely insane.

Fred's MO was simple: if he sang to Crawford, he wouldn't have to talk to him about anything more complicated or intense than what they were having for lunch. At that moment, he was in the middle of his homage to Def Leppard with a rendition of "Pour Some Sugar on Me."

Crawford and Wyatt had been pulled out of Homicide temporarily and put in the Robbery Division to track a mugger who was preying on wealthy women in the Riverdale section of the Bronx. The deputy mayor's great-aunt had been mugged and taken for a thousand dollars, and therefore, every available cop in the Fiftieth Precinct was now looking for this asshole. Champy, because of his high clearing rates for homicides, had been left on the case of the hands and feet, as Crawford had dubbed it in an effort to distance himself from the troubling detail that the victim was Alison's ex, something that put him in a foul mood.

Despite the fact that Crawford and Champy were only in possession of Ray's hands and feet and Dobbs Ferry had most of the body, NYPD had taken on the case. It could have been a jurisdictional thing, but Dobbs Ferry had been more than gracious about giving up control.

"That's because it's a bag of shit," Fred had said in his usual delicate manner. A "bag of shit" was a case nobody wanted, and Crawford supposed that Hardin and Madden had their own, Westchester version of the phrase to describe the Ray Stark case. Probably had something to do with old foie gras or something equally highfalutin.

For the past six hours, Fred and Crawford had been watching a female police officer in a borrowed diamond necklace walk up and down the avenue, checking her police-issue Rolex now and again and flashing wads of cash as she purchased items of a variety of name brands from the vendors on the avenue of a variety. They were across the street, idly examining newspapers, walking up and down the avenue, trying to remain as inconspicuous as two men over six feet three can remain on a fairly crowded street. Crawford and Wyatt were the "catch team"—the cops that watched decoys as they put themselves in harm's way to catch the people who preyed upon the innocent.

Crawford was in a particularly bad mood because he hated a disruption in his routine and he hated being pulled away from the job he was good at—investigating murders. He missed another Saturday-night dinner with his daughters. And that was a disappointment he couldn't handle; he saw them once a week and valued his time with them. Missing out on seeing them for work was unacceptable.

Fred moved on to the *Saturday Night Fever* collection.

> *If I can't have you*
> *I don't want nobody, baby*
> *If I can't have you—*

"Shut the FUCK up, Fred." Crawford took a few steps away from Fred; with Fred singing to him, they looked less like cops than a gay couple in the middle of an argument.

He had been holding the same cup of coffee for the last hour; he took a swig of lukewarm sludge and grimaced.

Fred turned and looked at him. "And what is your problem?"

Crawford folded his arms across his chest. "I'm sorry," he said, none too convincingly. "Just stop singing." He watched the woman across the street play with the diamond necklace on her neck as she shot them an impatient look. She was as tired as they were, and she got to parade up and down the avenue in a four-thousand-dollar necklace and Manolo Blahnik shoes instead of standing in the hot sun with a partner who wasn't as funny as he thought he was. Crawford avoided her gaze and focused on his shoes.

"We've got to get back on the Stark homicide," Crawford said.

Fred grunted.

"What?"

Fred kept his eye on Carmen but addressed Crawford. "You're a little too interested in the case, don't you think?" Fred took a sip of cold coffee. "Do you want to solve it to close the case or do you want to get back into someone's good graces?"

Crawford tensed. He and Fred never disagreed about anything; they knew each other too well. But Fred was treading on rocky territory, and if Crawford were really honest with himself and his partner, Fred had a point. He was more than a little ticked that they had been pulled off the case; any breaks in the case would give him an excuse to talk to Alison and, hopefully, see her.

"That case is a bag of shit," Fred repeated.

"Why do you say that?"

"It's a Miceli hit, Bobby. Plain and simple. And we know that with Miceli hits, whoever did it is in the wind."

Crawford shook his head. "I'm not so sure. I think we can find who did it."

The conversation ended when Fred tensed. "What's that?" he asked and pointed across the street.

A scraggly-looking man came out of the alley between a shoe store and an Italian deli and approached the female police officer. He reached for her throat and attempted to pull the necklace from it, only to find himself in a half nelson.

Fred was into the middle of the street before Crawford had a chance to react. When it finally registered what was happening, he leapt over a parked car and darted into traffic, doing a forward roll over a taxi and landing on the double yellow line flat on his feet. Cars screeched to a halt and horns blared as the two ran across the avenue. Crawford grabbed the gun on his hip and pulled his shield from beneath his shirt as he bounded up to the female cop and her quarry.

"You okay, Carmen?" he asked. Carmen Montoya was small but strong, and had the perp on the ground, a stiletto heel straddling his neck. He flailed beneath her as she checked her manicure. Carmen had been a classmate of Crawford's in the academy, and while she had a little "junk in the trunk"—the term Fred liked to use to refer to her sizable backside—she was as tough and smart as they came. She smiled at him as she adjusted the strap on her five-hundred-dollar shoes. Fred took over for her and pinned the perp to the sidewalk, reading him his Miranda rights as he huffed and puffed from his sprint across Riverdale Avenue.

"Way to stick your landing," she remarked, having witnessed his gymnastics across the cab. "Do I have to give back the shoes?"

Crawford let out a laugh. "I think so."

She reached up and pinched Crawford's cheek, leaving her hand there. "You so cute, Crawford," she said in a Puerto Rican accent that she affected for his benefit. She had a master's degree from John Jay and was on the sergeant's list. "When we gonna hook up, papi?"

"When your four kids go to college and your deputy inspector husband is on a respirator," he said, pulling the perp up from the sidewalk by his handcuffs.

She walked off, her backside packed into a black skirt, tottering on her high heels. "I'll see you later," she said.

Crawford dragged the perp across the street to the

Crown Victoria, parked in front of the Avenue Steak House.

"Don't tell me you never thought about it," Fred said, thrusting his head in Carmen's direction while opening the back door of the Vic.

Crawford shook his head. If only it were that easy.

Chapter 5

Another weekend came and I was still rattled by Ray's death, and, truth be told, by my encounter with Gianna. Nothing says creepy like being in the sights of a Mob wife. Even though she was a seemingly innocuous Staten Island housewife there had been something cold and somewhat calculating about her and in the way she conveyed Peter's message to me. Was that a hint of jealousy that I had discerned or nothing at all? Whatever it was, I was unnerved, and being as I'm slightly nervous about everything to begin with, this new state wasn't a welcome addition to my psyche.

I awoke, at seven-thirty, to the sound of a chain saw, in clear violation of the town's noise ordinance. No chainsawing, no lawn mowing, no noisemaking until eight o'clock. I looked out my bedroom window and saw my neighbor, Jackson, sawing a stump on his front lawn. Given the recent developments and my thought that a person with a chain saw had killed my ex-husband, I decided to forgo giving Jackson a hard time about it and let him saw away.

The phone began to ring. The last person I expected to hear from was Max. But indeed, she was up and at it, probably still awake from the night before.

"I've got two tickets to some Shakespeare shit up by you for tonight," she said, yawning while talking. "My mother gave them to me in the hope of culture-fying me. You want to go with?"

I took a breath and tried to compose myself. "Shakespeare shit," I said. "Sounds lovely." I pushed my hair off my forehead. "Do you think you could be more specific?"

"Hold on," she said. "I have to find the tickets." I could hear her rooting around near the phone. "It's at Boscobel," she said, referencing an estate near Cold Spring that overlooked the Hudson River and West Point, "and they're performing *The Merry Wives of Windsor.* I don't know what the hell that is. Is that even Shakespeare? It sounds like porn."

"Yes, it's Shakespeare." I really didn't feel like seeing this particular Shakespeare play, but since I didn't have anything to do, I was inclined to accept. "Where's Fred?"

"Working." She waited a second for my reaction to her invitation. "Do you want to go? I figured you could tell me what's going on during the play. It's supposed to rain, but not until after dark."

"Sure," I said, and lay back on the bed. I loved Boscobel and hadn't been there in a few years; Ray and I had gone every year to the summer Shakespeare performances, but since our divorce, I hadn't renewed my subscription. "We can bring a picnic and have dinner there. How does that sound?"

"Good. What time do you want me to pick you up? The show starts at seven."

It would take about forty-five minutes to get to Boscobel, and factoring in picnic time, I figured we should leave my house a little before five. I told her that I would buy dinner and prepare it.

"Of course you will. If you leave it up to me, we'll be eating stale Wheat Thins and drinking flat Diet Coke." She hung up without saying good-bye; that's her trademark. No beginnings and no endings.

I took a shower and got dressed. There was a gourmet shop in Tarrytown that would provide all of the food we would need to enjoy our evening. I went into the kitchen and grabbed my car keys from the counter. I peered out of the window over the kitchen sink and looked into the back of Terri and Jackson's yard; the coast seemed to be clear. I had been trying to avoid the two of them ever since I had found out the little tidbit about Terri sleeping with my ex-husband. To me, Terri's one-dimensional; she's a slut and nothing else. I had no use for Terri, and while I felt a little sympathy for her husband, Jackson, he was a pompous jerk who was constantly looking at me with pity. I wanted to remind him that he had been cuckolded, too; we were kind of even on that score. I headed to the back door.

With my hand on the knob, I was almost free and clear, until I heard a persistent knocking at the front door. I threw the keys back on the counter and headed down the front hall. I opened the door to find the last person who should have been at the door: Terri.

I tried to remain impassive, but the sight of her made my blood boil; I felt my cheeks go hot. I didn't give her the satisfaction of any courtesy; I stood in silence, slouched against the door but with my hand gripping the knob, staring at her.

She gave me an awkward smile and straightened to her full five feet two inches. "Alison. Hello."

I stared back at her.

"Can I come in?" she asked, opening the screen door and not waiting for my consent.

I stepped back and let her pass. She walked down the hallway to the kitchen and took a seat at the table. She looked back at me expectantly, her blue eyes pooling with tears. I reluctantly started back to the kitchen and stood at the counter, my arms crossed.

She started talking as if we were in the midst of the conversation already. "I feel terrible about Ray."

As would anyone with a modicum of human feeling, I thought. I continued to stare at her. Although I'm not scary in any way, shape, or form, the fact that I towered over her by a good eight inches obviously intimidated her somewhat. I stared down at her and she averted her eyes.

She started crying, a hiccuping serenade complete with runny nose and leaky eyes. "I'm actually devastated by his death," she said. She got up and leaned into me, expecting a hug, I presumed, but my arms hung at my sides. "You found him, right?"

"Yes, Terri. I found him."

"Oh, my God! That must have been awful!" she cried.

More than you'll ever know, I thought. I stood there while she wept into my shirt, waiting for her to stop and tell me her reason for coming by. I didn't think she had come by to wail about Ray, but I had been wrong before. Maybe she had.

After a few minutes, she composed herself and pulled back. She saw that I wasn't going to engage in a conversation about Ray, so she took another tack. "It wasn't always like this, you know."

"Like what, Terri?" I was beyond exasperation and waited for her to get to the point.

"Like it is now." She didn't do anything to stop the tears and they fell freely onto the front of her T-shirt and my kitchen table. "We used to be happy. I thought we had a good marriage."

"Well, I guess your cheating put an end to that." We had moved very quickly from her devastation over Ray's death to a conversation about her marriage; I shouldn't have been surprised, but I was.

She looked at me, resigned. "You've got every right to be angry. You must hate me."

"First of all, I don't need your permission to be angry,

and second, hate doesn't even begin to describe how I feel about you."

She pursed her lips. "Ray loved you. He just didn't know how to be in a committed relationship."

My anger boiled to the surface and I used every ounce of self-control that I had not to throttle her. I kept my voice even and measured. "I'm going to have to ask you to leave, Terri, and ask that you never come back here or speak to me again." After a second, I added, "Please."

She gave a rueful laugh. She wiped her hands across her eyes, smearing her mascara across her forehead. "I had this realization this morning," she started. "Besides you, and of course, Ray, may God rest his soul," she said dramatically, "I really don't know anyone in this neighborhood." She paused. "And I need a friend, Alison." She let out a choked sob.

We were only a few feet apart and her fear was palpable.

"What would you say if I told you that you didn't really know Jackson?"

I sighed. "I would have to agree, Terri."

She pushed her hair back with both of her hands. "I'm in a bit of a bind, Alison."

My head was spinning. I didn't know why she was here, I didn't want to know, and I wanted her to leave. Immediately. I didn't want to hear this story and I didn't want to be involved in her life in any way. She wasn't responsible for my divorce in any direct way or in Ray's death, I assumed, so we really didn't have anything to talk about. Ray had cheated on me before and after her, but I was suspicious of women who had affairs with men who were clearly attached, never mind married. I could never hurt another woman in that way and tried to stay clear of women who could. Even Max, for all of her liberal views on sexual recreation, drew the line at married men.

I finally pulled a chair out and sat down. I don't know

if it was compassion or stupidity, but I felt sorry for her. I looked at her. My expression said "tell me your story." And she did.

Crawford did the paperwork on the hump who had attacked Carmen and got him through the system before logging out. It was close to six at night and he had been at work since a little before six in the morning. He was bone tired and more than a little cranky. He wanted a shower, a beer, and his bed. Nothing more.

He lived on the top floor of a brownstone on West Ninety-seventh Street, with his mother's sister-in-law, Bea McDonald, below him in the small, one-bedroom unit. Bea and her husband, Bobby, had owned the house since the late '50s and had raised their six kids in the upstairs unit where he now lived. When Bobby died after a long battle with lung cancer some twenty years earlier, Bea had offered Crawford ("little Bobby" to her despite the fact that he was almost a foot and a half taller than the five-foot-tall Bea) the apartment for him and his growing family. He moved in and never left. Which is more than he could say for the rest of his family.

He tried to let himself into the ground floor of the house as quietly as possible. Bea was a great housemate, but sometimes, especially late on a Saturday night, she liked to visit with him. He had barely planted his size-fourteen feet on the long staircase up to his apartment when he heard stirring in the first-floor apartment. The door opened and Bea's round face peered out. "Bobby?" she called.

He stopped, midstep. "Hiya, Bea."

"How was work?" she asked, opening the door all the way. She got up on her tiptoes and tried to kiss him; he bent at the waist and met her halfway.

There was no polite answer to that question, so he went with a grunt and a shoulder shrug.

"That good, huh?" she responded. "I've got some left-over pot roast in the kitchen. Some dinner?"

He thought back to his last meal: some peanuts and a cold cup of coffee in the Crown Vic. He could muster up a little conversation for Bea; her pot roast was the best. He didn't know too many people who prepared pot roast on a hot September night, but he was glad she had. He nodded and told her he would be back after "washing up," which euphemistically meant "putting my guns where nobody will find them." He didn't enjoy eating with a Glock on his hip or the smaller gun on his ankle.

"I've got a few bottles of that Canadian beer that you like, too," she said.

"I'll be right back," he said, returning to her apartment within five minutes of her invitation. He walked through her living room and into her kitchen, where she had set a place for him. The apartment was cool, thanks to a large wall unit in the living room that cooled the living room and kitchen. An ice-cold bottle of Labatt's sat on a place mat alongside a fork, knife, spoon, and napkin. He took a seat at the table and a long drink from the Labatt's bottle, finishing half of it. "Thanks, Bea. This is nice."

She stood at the stove piling oven-browned potatoes, carrots, peas, and pot roast onto his plate. "You look tired. I heard you leave a little after five this morning."

He stretched his long legs out under the maple table. "Fred and I had to ghost a decoy on Riverdale Avenue. Mugger. Beats and robs wealthy women in the neighborhood." Bobby McDonald had been a beat cop in the Four-six Precinct, so Bea was well acquainted with all of the cop lingo.

She set the plate down in front of him. The pot roast smelled so good that he almost started crying. "Did you get the bastard?" she asked, her language at odds with her sweet, round face. She took a seat across from him.

"Got him," he said, and forked a piece of meat into his mouth.

"Good job!" she said, and offered the palm of her hand for a high five.

He reciprocated with a hand slap. "Got the whole sob story," he said, taking another swig of beer, almost finishing it. Bea got up and took another bottle from the refrigerator; Crawford spied a freshly baked apple pie on the counter next to the refrigerator. "But he's a junkie. And he left a seventy-year-old woman with a black eye and a broken nose. I don't want to hear the backstory."

She smiled. "My Bobby used to say the same thing."

Crawford chuckled. "That's probably where I got the expression."

Bea jumped up suddenly. "Oh, I have rolls, too." She opened the toaster oven and pulled out a couple of hot rolls. She didn't ask if he'd like one; she was sure that he would. She put them on a plate and brought them to the table.

Crawford tore one open and slathered butter on it from the butter dish that was perpetually on the table, regardless of the season. He didn't want to think about the bacteria that resided in a butter dish that sat out in the heat and ate his half of the roll, parasites be damned. "Thanks, Bea. This is great."

She folded her hands on the table. "I'll feed you any night of the week, Bobby. You just have to show up."

He finished his first beer and opened the second.

"I'm a little worried about you," she said, after a few minutes of watching him eat in silence.

He looked up from his potatoes. "I'm okay."

She leaned in. "Are you sure?"

He nodded and studied the remaining food on his plate.

"What's going on with that woman you met?" Bea searched her memory. "Alison?" Crawford's personal life was of great interest to his mother—a woman in whom he confided nothing lest the entire Eastern seaboard get an update—so Bea was their go-between. Marie (née McDonald) Crawford wanted nothing more than for her son, estranged from his wife for six years, to get on with his life, and have it move beyond the police department.

CIA interrogators had nothing on Bea. A little pot roast, a couple of beers, an apple pie—he'd give it all up for those few comforts. But he tried to keep his mouth shut. There was nothing—and everything—to tell.

Crawford tensed. "Nothing's going on. We're trying to work things out."

"Is she nice?"

His nerves were frayed and he was exhausted, so his overreaction was understandable, if not justified. Crawford dropped his fork onto his plate, making a racket. "Of course she's nice," he barked. "Would I be going ahead with my divorce and that goddamned annulment unless she was nice?" It was out of his mouth before he could think and he looked at Bea. He pointed a finger in her direction. "That is between you and me."

Bea smiled; her job here was done. "Of course it is."

Chapter 6

I had finally managed to get rid of Terri an hour and a box of tissues after she had arrived, hearing all of the sordid details of her five-year marriage to Jackson, recovering drug addict and alcoholic. To me, he seemed like an affable, rather innocuous, suburban guy, albeit with the pompous-jerk side. To hear Terri tell it, I was living next door to Sid Vicious.

When she finally blurted out everything, it became clear to me that she had one thing on her mind and one thing only: she thought that Jackson was responsible for Ray's death. She told me that they were in counseling and that Jackson had been diagnosed with "anger management" issues. Who doesn't have anger management issues? I certainly did, but I attributed them to my husband and his roving penis.

I wasn't sure how seriously to take her concerns—she was a bit of a drama queen—but I counseled her to go to the Dobbs Ferry police, who would know what to do with this information. She claimed that on the night Ray had been murdered, Jackson hadn't been home. And that when he came home, he was in a bad mood. Those two things together didn't a murderer make, but Terri didn't appear to be the sharpest knife in the drawer, so I went along with her line of reasoning, just for argument's sake. I often came home late and in a bad mood, and I didn't murder anyone. I didn't think her theory would hold up in a court of law if it didn't hold up in my kitchen.

Jackson didn't strike me as a murderer at all, but who knows? Maybe he had gotten sick and tired of being cheated on and wanted to do something about it. Could he have been that angry about Terri's cheating that he could murder Ray in cold blood? Why hadn't he just murdered Terri, my preferred victim? I didn't have the energy to murder Ray; I was hoping for a more supernatural solution to the problem and had hoped that he would just disappear into thin air.

I didn't know what she was going to do, but it seemed like the shit was going to hit the fan next door and I didn't want any part of it.

After Terri left, instead of crawling into bed and staying there for the remainder of the day (my first inclination), I got into the car and headed to my favorite Italian deli in town. There's nothing like a good Italian sub to take my mind off my troubles. My plan to head to Tarrytown was scrapped by the hour that Terri had eaten up with her tale of woe. I was forced to stay local if I wanted to squeeze in the much-needed nap that I had promised myself.

Tony's Delicatessen was only about a quarter mile from my house but I decided to drive anyway. I needed a lot of food and even more wine to erase this day from my mind, so I didn't want to make the trek on foot. I set out in my car, thinking about Terri and how she could possibly imagine that I would lend a sympathetic ear. I guess I come across as as much of a patsy as I thought, having lent her that sympathetic ear for far too long.

I love to eat but I hate to cook and Tony's had become my go-to place for all things deli. As luck would have it, I had married a man who lived on protein shakes and power bars, so cooking was a nonissue. Also, I'm spec-

tacular in bed and that made up for any culinary deficien-
cies. At least that's what I tell myself. My ex apparently
didn't share the same regard for my sexual prowess.

After stopping by the liquor store and buying several
bottles of wine, I arrived at Tony's. His face lit up when I
entered the deli and he looked genuinely happy to see me.
Two things about Tony: (a) he seems to carry a torch for me
and (b) he knows the kind of sandwich I like and calls it
my "usual." For some reason, that sends me over the edge.
I don't want to be the paramour of a little, fat Italian deli
owner widower and I definitely don't want to be the kind
of woman for whom chicken salad on rye is the "usual."
I'd like to think of myself as more exotic—the kind of
woman about whom people say "and she just loves foie
gras"—as misguided a notion as that is. I had avoided going to Tony's very much and the joy on his face when I
walked in reminded me why. Your deli man shouldn't be
that happy to see you.

"The usual?" he asked, reaching across the counter
and grabbing my hand. Tony is sixty-five if he's a day,
widowed, and the father of eight children, two of whom
are older than me by at least six or seven years. If I ever
did decide to marry Tony, I wondered how those middle-
aged children would feel about his young wife cutting in
on their deli inheritance.

I took a step back, ostensibly to visit the beverage case
but more to avoid the make-out session that Tony seemed
to have in mind. "No, thank you, Tony. I have a list," I said,
dropping the list on the counter and backing away. I made
my way to the refrigerator and picked out a couple of bottles of water and that disgusting, high-caffeine drink that
Max consumed by the case. I set them down on the
counter and waited while Tony assembled the sandwiches
I had ordered.

"How is everything, *mi amore*?" he asked, turning

slightly from the meat slicer to get a look at me. Judging from his expression, I must have looked pretty hot.

"Everything is great, Tony," I lied, putting a plastic smile on my face. I made a great show of looking at the food in the glass-fronted case and tried to avoid making eye contact with him. "How's the family, Tony?"

He turned back and focused on the meat slicer. "They're good," he said, pulling off some roast beef and throwing it onto a roll. "I didn't see you at all this summer. Vacationing?" he asked.

"A little vacationing, some work. I tried to get some rest before school started," I said, plucking a couple of bags of chips from the display behind me. He kept looking back at me and I desperately hoped that he would turn his attention back to the slicer; a day at Phelps Memorial Hospital for microsurgery to attach his missing digits did not fit into my plans.

He cut to the chase. "Are you still dating the detective?" he asked, unable to meet my eye.

Damn that Magda. As cleaning ladies go, she's the best. However, her great big mouth was starting to mitigate her ability to get mold off the grout in my shower. I only laid eyes on her occasionally because she came while I was at work, but she seemed to know every intimate detail of my life, as did every Hungarian in Dobbs Ferry and, apparently, Tony.

"Not really, Tony," I said.

He smiled. "So, I still have a chance!"

I smiled back. "I guess so!" I said, with as much enthusiasm I could muster for my new life with a widowed senior citizen. Getting into the movies with his AARP card would be a nice by-product of our relationship, but that was about it.

He leaned over and kissed me on the cheek, the smell

of freshly sliced roast beef rising from his hands and apron. "You . . . I've always loved you. You're a nice girl. Those men were no good for you," he said, shaking his head sadly.

I didn't want to get into the "Crawford isn't as bad as Ray" conversation, so I just let it go.

Tony looked at me, his expression so sad that I knew where he was going next. "And your poor husband. Ray."

Not my husband, not poor in any way, shape, or form. But I played along. "Yes. Terrible."

His eyes narrowed. "And you found him? No hands and feet?"

I nodded.

He whistled through his teeth. "Must have been some sight."

Yes, indeedy. Can I have my food, please? "I don't really want to talk about it, Tony."

He stared at me for a few more seconds before getting the rest of my food. I think he wanted the gory details but I wasn't about to provide any. He put it into a big bag and rang up its contents on the cash register. I handed him a couple of twenties and waited for my change.

"Don't be a stranger," he said in his lilting Italian accent, using the return of my change as another opportunity to hold my hand.

"I promise, Tony." I picked up the bag.

"One more kiss," he said, putting his stubby fingers to my cheeks and pulling me close.

I gave him the quickest peck I could and extricated myself from his grasp. "Okay! That's it! No more kisses," I said as pleasantly as I could, grabbing the bag and backing up toward the door.

He called out his usual parting greeting, "Anytime you're ready, I'm yours!" as the screen door slammed.

I ran down the street with the bag half obscuring my face, my pocketbook hitting the outside of my thigh with every step. I had a five-pound bag of deli food for two people and I had to make it last for a while; I was never setting foot in Tony's delicatessen again. At least not while I remained single. Part of me was starting to get the impression that Tony wasn't kidding; I was his new "amore" and nothing was going to get in the way of our love. I shuddered at the thought—although being with a man who had unlimited access to Boar's Head products was somewhat appealing—while I rooted around with my free hand for my car keys, mentally constructing a "Dear Tony" letter in my head that began with "Although we'll never be together in *that way* . . ."

I finally reached the car; I put the bag of food on the front hood. I heard my name, but unfortunately, the caller was too close for me to pretend to be deaf. I looked up and spied Jackson ambling up the street with Trixie, who was on a leash. I thought we had some unspoken agreement whereby we didn't speak to each other. At all. But apparently, he hadn't gotten the memo. Or decided that the statute of limitations had run out on our silence. Trixie bounded up to me and planted her nose between my butt cheeks, her usual greeting.

He gave the leash a little tug but didn't make mention of Trixie's seeming love of my ass. Trixie's ass love was the most lovin' I'd had in two years. "Hey, Alison!" he said, a big smile on his face. "Boy, I haven't seen you in a dog's age," he said, laughing. "No pun intended."

None taken. "Hi, Jackson."

"Where the heck have you been?" he asked, pushing back a lock of his light brown hair. I could see that he had recently stocked up on whatever superhold hair gel he liked to use; individual strands of hair were artfully arranged atop his hair in a messy, Abercrombie & Fitch model kind of do. He realized that his question was probably self-explanatory. Where had I been? Living somewhere else while my house was being cleaned, fumigated, and repainted. He looked down at the ground.

"Oh, here and there," I said, bending down to pet Trixie. I stole a look at him from my crouch; he didn't seem like a drug- and alcohol-addled, anger-obsessed murderer. But, hey, you never know. I wondered if I should be a little more concerned about him, but the look on his face was pure fecklessness and the vibe he gave off was not threatening in any way.

"I'm really sorry about Ray," he said in that condescending way that made my skin crawl.

I nodded a thank-you at him.

"What a mess, huh?" He toed the ground with his fancy nonathletic sneaker. I didn't think any serious athlete would be caught dead in an orange sneaker with pink trim, but that's just one woman's opinion.

"Yes, it was a mess," I concurred.

That out of the way, he decided to commence with the small-talk portion of our conversation. "Did you take a summer vacation?" he asked. Holy subject change, Batman.

Jesus, we're going to have a whole conversation, I thought. Did I take a summer vacation? "Yes. I went to Quebec."

"Très bien!" he said. "Parlez-vous français?"

My last name is Bergeron and my parents were French Canadian. What do you think? I tried to be nice. I didn't want him murdering me in a drug-induced rage. "Yes, I do."

"Moi, aussi!"

"Great!" Or more appropriately: *fantastique!* I plastered

a big grin on my face. "I'm kind of in a hurry, Jackson. I've got to run," I said, opening my car door. Trixie sat beside me, looking up at me with her sad/happy dog face.

He put his hand on my arm. "Listen, I know we had a rather unpleasant spring."

I'll say.

"Things are better, though. Terri and I are in counseling and I think we're going to be able to work through everything."

What planet did this guy live on? First of all, why did either of them think I gave a rat's ass about their marriage? I lived through a marriage that couldn't qualify as remotely happy and yet I only confided that in my best friend. Okay, and my priest. Secondly, his wife was painting him as a crazed substance abuser and murderer and he's living on Sunnybrook Farm. "That's great, Jackson. I wish you the best of luck," I said. I looked at him closely; nope, not scary at all.

"You know how this is, Alison. Either you throw it away," he said, looking at me pointedly, "or you try to work things through. We're going to make it," he said with a confidence that really wasn't warranted, given what I knew.

I was one of the "throw it away" people he was referring to, so I didn't have a reply. When your husband's penis has as many stops as the local Metro North train line, I think you have the right to "throw it away." I smiled again.

"Terri's been taking night classes at your school, too. She wants to finish her degree," he said.

"Great." My guess was that she had declared a biology major what with Ray having been head of the department.

We stood, looking at each other for a few seconds. He reached out awkwardly and gave me a hug. I let my arms hang at my sides and waited for him to release me.

"I've really got to go," I reminded him.

He let me go. "Oh, and Terri has hired Magda to do our house cleaning!" he said. "I forgot to tell you."

"She's a great cleaning lady," I said. Magda could really spread her gossip wings cleaning that house. I got into the car and gunned it out of the spot, leaving the happily married Jackson and beautiful Trixie standing on the sidewalk.

There was something up with that guy, but I wasn't sure what it was. Again, he didn't strike me as a murderer. But what does a murderer look like? I decided that Max and I would have a lot to talk about on our drive to the play.

I managed to get home without running into any of the other undesirable people in my life. I walked through the back door, closed it, locked it, and rested my head against the cool granite counter. I was starting to think that perhaps I should join an online grocery service and teach my courses strictly on the Web. Leaving the house was presenting a whole new set of challenges.

I filled Max in on Terri's story on our way to Boscobel. I finished with my account of running into Jackson on the street.

"The dog is the only one who doesn't turn my stomach right now," I said.

Max responded with just the right amount of indignation and disgust the story deserved. "She needs to stay away from you," she said, making a right onto Route 9D in Garrison. We were about ten minutes from Boscobel and it had taken me nearly the entire ride to tell her my tale of woe. "But let's think about this. I like Jackson as a suspect."

It certainly made sense.

"Do you think he has the cojones to have killed Ray?" she asked, chewing the inside of her mouth.

"They're in counseling, Max. He seems like the 'let's talk about this' kind of guy, not the 'I'll cut you to bits with a chain saw' kind of guy." I looked out the window and studied the scenery for a few minutes. "Maybe she did it," I said.

"Now that's an interesting theory," Max said. "She's potentially setting him up for the fall by using you. Framing the husband. Interesting. Let's ponder that." She pursed her lips. "You know, we really need to Google this whole hands and feet thing. See where it comes from. It's clearly not an accident that Ray lost a few appendages. Maybe we've got a dormant serial killer on the loose again."

The thought of that made me queasy. I was more comfortable with a crime of passion committed by my graphic-designer neighbor than with a roving serial killer.

I turned and looked out the window, hoping to see the yellow sign indicating that Boscobel was approaching. I remembered that I hadn't told her about seeing Gianna; her jaw fell open at that revelation. "And then she said this really weird thing, like 'Peter says hello,' but in a very creepy way."

"Ewww," Max said. "He kind of sniffed around you in college, though. Remember?"

I grimaced at the thought of it. "No," I said emphatically. "We took a class together, but that was it."

She shook her head. "Whatever. I've been thinking about this ever since he reappeared. I definitely remember him being just the wee bit interested in you," she said. "Remember how he was always offering you rides in his Trans Am?"

"I guess," I said. "So you think Gianna has been carrying some kind of grudge for all these years, Max? Hardly," I said. "Plus, she's gorgeous and he's a troll. That guy should thank his lucky stars every day."

The yellow sign appeared and Max maneuvered into the parking lot, putting the conversation to an end. She was directed to a spot close to the great lawn of Boscobel by a green-shirted employee of the estate. Max had sold her Jaguar and bought herself a very un-Max-like car: a silver Volkswagen Beetle. It was quirky and sporty, and unlike anything she had ever owned. She explained it away by saying the Jag was too "conspicuous." I actually thought that was why she liked it. Whatever her excuse, I hadn't seen her drive anything so small since the late eighties when we were both starting out in our careers and really couldn't afford anything bigger or better than a tuna can with wheels.

We got out of the car and opened her trunk to remove the picnic basket that I had packed. In it was all of the food I had gotten from Tony and a delicious German Riesling that I had found in the wine shop in my neighborhood. I had also thrown in some grapes and a couple of apples that I had bought earlier in the week at the A&P. Max had an old comforter in the trunk and she removed that for us to sit on while we dined. We made our way across the lawn and found a perfect spot near the estate, yet with a panoramic view of the Hudson River and West Point on its western shore. Max spread the blanket and I began taking the food from the basket.

"Any chocolate in there?" she asked, peering into the wicker basket.

"Yes, but not until you eat all of the other food that I brought." If it were up to Max we would eat the chocolate, drink the bottle of wine, and skip everything else. I took out everything that I had bought and arranged it on the blanket. People were scattered all around the grounds of the estate, doing exactly as we were: drinking wine and eating dinner. There was a festive feel to the gorgeous evening and I rejoiced in being out of my house, with my best friend, and preparing to enjoy the performance.

Max pulled a white paper bag out of the basket and opened it. "Oh! Cookies!" she exclaimed, pulling them out.

I hadn't bought any cookies. Max held them up: two heart-shaped cookies with the word "amore" written across them. Tony.

She looked at me and gave me a sweet smile. "I love you, too," she said, kissing my cheek.

"I didn't buy those for us, Max. I think maybe Tony, my deli boyfriend, put them in there."

She dropped them back into the bag as if they had burst into flames. "Ewww."

I opened the bag further but only the two cookies resided at the bottom. Thank God . . . I was hoping not to find an engagement ring embedded in a salami.

"Crawford could take a page from this guy's book. He's very romantic," she said. Max stretched out on the blanket, her shirt riding up to just beneath her black bra, exposing her flat stomach. Max doesn't engage in any kind of physical activity besides yoga and sex, and both were keeping her in very good shape; you could bounce a quarter off her abdominal muscles. I pointed to her six-pack of muscle. "Sex or yoga?"

She picked her head up and looked at her stomach. "A little bit of both. You should try at least one of them." She rolled over on her stomach and surveyed the crowd. She let out a disgusted groan as I saw her eyes fall on a couple a few blankets away who were rolling around in the throes of passion. "Get a room, for God's sake," she said, and turned back to me. She popped a grape in her mouth and held out a wineglass for me to fill. "If *The Merry Wives of Windsor* isn't porn, then I don't want to be watching that," she said, throwing her head in the direction of the amorous couple.

I stayed focused on the couple in question and almost

threw up when the man rolled onto his back and off the woman; I got a look at his face and gasped out loud. The woman sat up and put her hand to his cheek. Her breathy giggle wafted over to our blanket on the fragrant breeze.

Terri. And Jackson.

Chapter 7

It took me a minute to really understand what I was seeing. Fortunately for me, Terri never saw me, jumping on top of Jackson soon after I spotted them to resume their juvenile public make-out session.

"Look who that is," I whispered. She turned her head to look and I hissed, "Don't look!" Max isn't really very good at the art of surveillance. But she did catch a look at my supposedly murderous neighbor and his supposedly terrified wife. I don't know—if you really think your husband is a cold-blooded killer, do you make out with him in public? I think not.

"It's Jackson," she said. "I'd know that weak chin anywhere."

"Does that look like a woman who's afraid of her own husband?" I continued to keep them in my peripheral vision; although they were far enough away that I could spy unobserved, I turned to the side in the hopes that they wouldn't see me.

Max eased up onto her elbows, looking like she was setting up her position in a foxhole. She studied them for a few minutes and then looked at me. "Do you really want to see this play?"

"Let's go," I said, throwing all of the food back into the paper bag and rolling up the picnic blanket. I handed her the paper bag and threw the blanket over my shoulder.

"But we're not breaking into their house," I said, knowing that that was exactly what she had planned.

"Whatever," Max said, walking toward the parking lot. I grabbed her arm. "Promise me."

"You don't have to break in anywhere. I'll do it."

"Max, I'm serious."

" 'I'm serious,' " she mimicked. "Well, I am, too. How do you expect to find Ray's killer if we don't do a little sleuthing?"

"Breaking in is not sleuthing," I said. "It's a felony."

She continued to walk toward the car with purpose. I ran to keep up with her, turning around every few seconds to see if Terri or Jackson had spotted us. They continued to roll around on their own blanket, seemingly oblivious to everything and everyone around them, so I figured we were safe.

We reached the car and put everything into the Beetle's miniscule trunk and started for home. She drove along Route 9D and came to the turnoff that would take us across Garrison and back toward the road that would take us to my house. "So, the Terri thing this morning was a giant setup."

I was looking out the window and didn't really hear her. "What?"

"Terri. It was a setup. She's got something to hide."

Of course, she was right. I had been had. And now, we had to figure out why.

Even though a steady rain had begun to fall, and lightning crossed the dusky sky, we made it home in record time. Max pulled into my driveway and turned off the car. She turned to look at me, her mouth set in a thin line of determination. "Are you in or out?"

I got that queasy feeling in my stomach that signals the onset of intestinal distress. "What do you think you're going to find? A bloody chain saw? A diary entry with 'Dear Diary, today I killed Ray . . . get saw blade re-sharpened'?" I sighed. "Remember the last time we broke in somewhere? We almost got arrested!"

"Well, I guess I've got your answer," she said, and got out of the car. She shimmied between the hedgerow and strode across their backyard with purpose. I didn't know whether to be in awe of or terrified by her force of will and lack of judgment.

It was in that instant that I remembered to tell her about Trixie, the massive golden retriever who, at ninety pounds, weighed nearly as much as Max. It was too late. By the time I reached the hedge, she was already on the ground, Trixie on top of her covering her with wet, sloppy kisses. As watchdogs go, Trixie sucks. But as a lovable family pet, she's clearly the tops. Max struggled beneath the weight of the dog, her white T-shirt covered with muddy paw prints, the back of her pants wet and soggy.

"A little help here?!" she gasped, her hands on the dog's belly in an attempt to liberate herself from Trixie's underside.

I plowed through the hedge. "Trixie! Here, girl!" I called and Trixie bounded toward me, freeing Max from her canine clutches. She tackled me, which left Max free to find access to the house. I wondered if Terri and Jackson ever let this poor animal in the house; every time I came home, she was outside and tonight was no different.

It was not unusual to find doors unlocked, even open, in our town. Nobody is too cautious about locking things up, especially when they've gone out for a short period of time. I, myself, had been guilty of this lax attitude toward security, so I wasn't surprised when Max opened up the sliding glass door on the patio and slithered inside the house. I guess it wasn't breaking in, technically, if the door is unlocked. I suspected, however, that Crawford might beg to disagree.

I sat with Trixie in the backyard, in the rain, and waited for what seemed like an eternity for Max to emerge from the house. As we sat and watched the back door for activity, my ears perked up to the sound of a car driving slowly up the driveway. The intestinal distress kicked up a notch as it dawned on me that the car belonged to Terri and Jackson. With the rain now coming down in a steady downpour, it was obvious that they had fled Boscobel rather than sit under the leaky tent where the play would be performed.

"Come up with a story," I muttered to myself, stroking the dog. I looked deep into Trixie's eyes, hoping to figure out what to say when they got out of the car. I didn't know how I was going to keep them out of the house long enough for Max to leave but my mind was working overtime as I watched them make their way from the driveway to my side.

They were damp and looked a little bewildered as to why I was sitting in their backyard. "Hi," Jackson said, a question in his voice. His hair gel had made his hair harden into a weird helmet that made him look like an extra in a Pompeii reenactment.

"Hey," I said, drawing out the syllable for as long as possible. "Hey."

Terri looked at me and furrowed her brow. Jackson produced an umbrella and gallantly put it over her head, leaving me to get soaked. "What are you doing, Alison?"

I got up from my crouch next to Trixie. "It started to rain and I saw the dog and she was wet and then I thought 'gosh, the dog is wet,' and so I felt bad and then I thought I would come out here and get her and then I saw you drive up," I babbled. I cast a nervous glance at the house but couldn't tell if Max was in or out. "Wow!" I screamed as loud as I could, hoping that she could hear me. "It's really raining!"

Jackson stared at me as if I had gone insane. "Well, we're back now so we'll take Trixie inside." He took the dog by the collar and pushed her in the direction of the house. Trixie stayed firmly planted by my side.

"And I need sugar!" I cried. I pushed a wet lock of hair off my forehead.

"Okay," Terri said. "Come inside and I'll give you some sugar."

I followed them inside and stood at the edge of their kitchen, next to the sliding door, trying not to get their gleaming wood floors wet or muddy. Terri went into the kitchen and rooted around in the maple cabinets for sugar. She produced an entire five-pound bag and pushed it at me. "Here. Take the whole thing."

"Oh, I couldn't!" I hollered, hoping that my voice was carrying throughout the entire house.

"Yes, you can!" she hollered back, convinced of my sudden onset of deafness.

I stalled for another minute, looking around the kitchen, which was attached to a large family room with a stone fireplace. Their wedding portrait, re-created in oil paints, had a prominent place over the mantel. It appeared that the antebellum South had been their theme. Terri was seated on what looked like a toadstool with a parasol at her feet; Jackson stood over her with one hand on her shoulder, the other in the pocket of his suit vest. He was sporting a Vandyke goatee/soul patch sort of thing on his chin which he had since had the good sense to shave off. Yuck.

I put my hand on the door handle and pushed the slider aside. "I'll be going now. Thanks for the sugar." I stepped through the door and back out in the rain, offering a prayer that Max was out of the house and safe somewhere.

She was sitting at my kitchen table, in exactly the same place in which I had found Ray, waiting for me to return. She looked disappointed. "No bloody chain saws," she said. "But did you get a load of the toadstool and the parasol?"

Crawford met his daughters at Grand Central Station early Sunday morning. The girls, twins, were going to be seventeen in a few months and their mother had finally relented to letting them take the train from Greenwich to Grand Central with the caveat that their father meet them at the train doors and make sure they were seated on the right train when it was time to go home. Crawford waited on the track, right where the third car would open its doors; it was their plan and it was foolproof. The doors would open and they would race out, as always.

Meaghan and Erin Crawford had been born three minutes apart in the midst of a December snowstorm; their mother had been escorted to the hospital by two police cars, her husband walking a beat somewhere in the Bronx and unable to get back to the Upper West Side to get her there himself. He arrived just in time to see Erin, then Meaghan, be born, the first blond, the other dark.

The train doors opened and Meaghan, a full six feet, preceded her smaller sister. She jumped into his arms and kissed him, forgetting that she was almost as tall as he and not a little kid anymore. He stumbled backward at the force of her embrace. Meaghan was the more gregarious of the two, an athlete and honor student. Erin was small, like her mother, and more reticent. Crawford didn't get a lot from her in terms of affection and had given up trying to figure her out. She was who she was and probably more like him than he cared to admit. Erin waited for her sister to finish before standing on her toes to kiss him on the cheek. They hadn't brought any bags since this was only a day visit; he had missed his Saturday-night visit with them but had made sure he could spend the entire Sunday with them.

Meaghan grabbed his hand. "Did you catch the skel?" she asked. Their mother had explained to them why their father had had to cancel his usual Saturday visit.

He turned to her, surprised. "Skel? Where did you hear that word?"

"I saw a documentary about the NYPD on television and they used that word a lot."

He shook his head. "Okay, that's not a word we're going to use in normal conversation. Got it?"

She nodded. "Got it," she said, flashing a grin that was identical to his.

Erin slipped her hand into his free one, smaller and more fine-boned than that of her younger sister. "What do you want to do today?"

He gave her hand a squeeze. "Well, Bea suggested we attend the Divine Mercy Hour at Trinity Church, but I told her we had a full day of Stations of the Cross on the agenda." The girls chuckled; Aunt Bea was an old-time Catholic and hated the fact that Crawford didn't enforce a weekly mass ritual on Sundays. His time with them was precious; he didn't want an hour eaten up going to church. "What do you want to do?"

They walked across the wide-open space of Grand Central, the girls looking up every now and again to get a look at the beautiful planetarium scene on the domed ceiling; they never tired of it. Crawford ushered them up the great staircase that led to Michael Jordan's The Steak House on the right and the Campbell Apartment on the left, an intimate bar and bistro that he had never been to but had passed a hundred times. The girls told him that they were starving and wanted brunch. They exited at Vanderbilt Avenue and walked a block and a half to an Irish pub.

They took a booth away from the bar and toward the back of the restaurant. Crawford let them choose where they wanted to sit; they chose to sit together, across from him, where they could both see him.

The waiter appeared and asked them if they'd like a drink. Crawford looked at his watch and saw that it was just after ten. He ordered the girls their usual glasses of water and a coffee for himself.

Erin cut to the chase. "Mom said you're going ahead with the divorce."

Meaghan shot her a look. "Nice going. Can we have a drink before we get into all of that?"

Crawford sighed. He and Christine had a relatively good relationship, amicable mostly, but sometimes, she let the girls in on things that he would just as soon keep between them. She was very open and, admittedly, he was a little closed. It had been one of the things that she had grown to dislike in him, but it was who he was and he was not great at change. He spread his hands out on the table, looking down at his fingers instead of into their eyes. "We're moving forward with the divorce," he confirmed. Technically, that was true. But they still had the lengthy annulment process in front of them before everything was finalized. He didn't think Christine was signing the divorce papers until the process had at least commenced.

Erin's eyes filled with tears, something that he didn't expect.

"Hey," he said, grabbing her hand. "Don't cry. Everything's fine." He touched her cheek with his other hand. "Nothing's going to change. Everything is going to be exactly the same except that we won't be legally married anymore."

Meaghan put her arm around her sister. "We've talked about this a lot, but she still thinks there's a chance."

Crawford was puzzled. A chance?

Meaghan explained. "That you'd get back together."

He hadn't considered that either of them would ever think that was a possibility.

Erin wiped her eyes with her napkin. "I'm sorry, Dad. It just makes things so final." She let out a quiet sob.

He nodded. He understood. The holding pattern that he and Christine had been in for six years was hardly fair to anyone, least of all their daughters.

"Does it have something to do with the woman we saw at the restaurant that night?" Erin asked, keeping the napkin pressed to her eyes. "The woman from the hospital?"

Crawford pulled a folded handkerchief from his pocket and handed it to her. He took the balled-up napkin from her and pushed it to the side of the table. "It does."

Meaghan, remarkably composed, started the interrogation regarding Alison. "How did you meet?"

Crawford explained that they had met when he was investigating a murder.

Erin kept his handkerchief over her face, not wanting to look at him. "Do you love her? Are you going to marry her?"

He didn't know and he told them as much. "She's a little mad at me right now."

Meaghan laughed. "What did you do?"

He was in awe of her maturity. She didn't seem the least bit fazed by the conversation and had obviously come to terms with her family situation. He found himself looking at a very confident young woman and couldn't remember when the transition from childhood had taken place. "Well, I didn't explain our situation all that well. She met Mom at the hospital and . . ."

Meaghan winced. "I get it." She looked down at the table. "You really blew that one."

He had to agree. He asked Meaghan to change seats with him and he slid into the booth next to Erin. He pulled her close and she sobbed on his shirt. He stroked her hair and waited until she didn't have any more tears left.

She pulled back. Her face was red and tearstained. "I'm sorry, Dad."

"It's okay," he said. The waiter came and delivered their drinks, assessed the situation and said that he would be back in a few minutes to take their order. "I'm sorry, too." He looked at Meaghan. "Are you all right with everything?"

She nodded and took a long sip from her water glass. "I'm all right with everything." She smiled, a little sad, but resigned to the truth: her parents were better off apart. And as divorced, or almost-divorced, families went, theirs was pretty functional. Neither parent used Meaghan or her sister to their own gain, they saw their father as much as they possibly could given his crazy work schedule, and their parents seemed to genuinely like each other, even if they didn't love each other anymore. There were no financial issues to speak of; their father took very good care of them and made sure they wanted for nothing. There was no ill will or resentment in the air when their parents spoke. As she tried to tell Erin, it could be much, much worse. She gave her father a punch in the arm. "And frankly, Dad, you need a woman. You're getting awfully cranky."

Chapter 8

I woke up the next morning after a fitful night's sleep. I dreamed that I was making mad, passionate love to Crawford, only to find that it was really Ray when all was said and done. And next to us in bed was Terri.

You didn't have to be a psych major to figure that one out. Calling Dr. Freud . . .

Max and I had spent a couple of hours on the computer Googling all sorts of things related to murder. It became apparent to us that a corpse missing its hands and feet had been killed by a Miceli foot soldier before; that seemed to be their trademark in murder. Something about identification being harder without fingerprints and all. I guess the Micelis had never heard of facial identification, dental identification, or DNA. What a bunch of morons. I made a mental note to tell Crawford, even though I assumed he was smart enough to have already researched this signature and was all over it.

But if we could Google and get this information so easily, so could anyone with a computer and Internet connection. It didn't really prove anything beyond the fact that someone knew how the Micelis signed off on their executions. And that still left Jackson and Terri on my short list of suspects.

I got up and stumbled around the bedroom. I had on the oversized navy blue NYPD T-shirt that Crawford had given me in the spring and a pair of underpants. I padded out to the hallway and down the stairs, hoping that I had enough coffee beans in the cupboard to make a big, strong pot of the stuff. I was half asleep and only slightly cogent, but I could make out the outline of a bowling-ball-shaped person standing in my kitchen. When my eyes adjusted and I made out who it was, I nearly fell to my knees.

Peter Miceli.

He turned from his task—arranging biscotti on a tray—and greeted me with a huge grin and a wave. Having a Mob boss in my kitchen was not a normal occurrence, but Peter had this habit of acting like we were old friends (we weren't) and that I was always happy to see him (I wasn't).

"Alison, hi!" he called.

I stood still, rooted to my spot in the hallway.

He held a large paper cup aloft and waved it back and forth. "I've got coffee," he said in a singsong voice. "And biscotti. The best on Staten Island. Gianna made them."

I couldn't find my voice or the will to move, so I stayed where I was.

He waved me into the kitchen. "Come on in. I want to have a chat."

I remembered the last time we had a chat; he had thrown me out of his car and I ended up with a cut on my leg from which I still had a scar. I shook my head at him.

He took a few steps toward me. "You might feel better if you get some clothes on." He gave my bare legs the once-over. "Go get dressed," he said softly.

I headed back up the stairs and closed my bedroom door. I looked around wildly for some kind of escape hatch, but since my room was on the second floor at the front of the house, there was nowhere to go. I ran to the window and pulled the shade up only to see Peter's black Mercedes in front of my house, a beefy, black-clad goon standing beside the car with his hands folded in front of him.

I decided to take Peter's advice and found a pair of jeans. Maybe if I was dressed, I would be able to formulate a plan. After standing in the middle of my room in my jeans for a full five minutes, I was no closer to any kind of action.

I picked up the phone and held it to my ear. There was no dial tone. And my cell phone was in its usual place in my pocketbook.

I had no choice but to go back downstairs and face Peter. I left the bedroom and returned to the hallway, going down the stairs slowly, my heart pounding so hard that I could almost hear it. I went to the kitchen doorway and stood. Peter was at my kitchen table, dunking biscotti into his coffee cup.

I've seen Peter three times since his daughter, Kathy's, murder: once at her funeral; once when he broke into my house previously "for a little chat"; and the final time, when he kidnapped me. Two of those three times, he had been wearing golf attire; today was no exception.

He saw me looking at his golf shirt, a bright salmon color. "I'm headed up to Hudson National to hit the links," he said.

I continued to stand in the doorway. "What do you want, Peter?"

He nodded, his bald head gleaming. "Well, first of all, Alison, I owe you an apology."

I'll say.

"I was out of my mind with grief when we took that drive together." He threw his hands up. "Out of my mind! Didn't know what the fuck I was doing!" He grimaced. "Pardon my French." Dunk, sip. "But things are better now. Gianna is better. We're getting better. It was an awfully hard summer, but I see a light at the end of the tunnel." He took a huge bite from the biscotti and continued talking, coffee and biscotti spraying onto my kitchen table. "Counseling is a fantastic thing, I tell you. Fantastic! That head shrinker has given us hope, Alison."

I leaned against the doorjamb and crossed my arms.

"And she's taught me to make amends. I need to make amends, Alison. With you, in particular." He jabbed a fat, sausagelike finger in my direction. "Remember," he said gravely, "I owe you."

Peter had left a note on my car last spring to that effect. I didn't know why he felt like he owed me and I didn't need any favors.

"Peter," I said slowly, finding my voice, "the only thing I need from you is for you to leave me alone."

He nodded. "I can understand why you would feel that way. I think that's called 'empathy.' Or is it 'sympathy'?" He shook his head, confused. "I can never remember. But here's the thing, Alison: I owe you way more than you could ever know."

I shook my head. "You don't."

He insisted. "I do! You were so kind to Kathy, you did everything you could to help find her killer . . . hell, you found her killer! You solved the case! The fucking NYPD couldn't even do that with all of those fucking detectives working overtime!" He grimaced again. "Sorry. I have to stop cursing. Old habits die hard."

My stomach was sick and I was getting light-headed.

"Here's the thing, Alison," he said, his voice changing slightly. "I need to tell you how sorry I am about Ray."

I waited.

"I didn't have any fond feelings for the man, obviously," he said, tears filling his eyes. "I actually wished he would die. But you married the man, you had a life together. I'm sure you're very sad about his passing." He shoved half a piece of biscotti into his mouth. "Does your boyfriend have any idea who did this?"

"He's not my boyfriend," I clarified, as if it mattered.

"And Crawford doesn't tell me anything about any of his cases." I was babbling, but it was the truth.

Peter stared at me, looking for some kind of sign that I was telling the truth. He chewed on his pinkie nail and considered what I said. I wondered if he was trying to find out if Crawford was linking him to the murder. It made sense, after all. A grieving father, who was also a Mob boss . . . Peter clearly had motive and opportunity. After a few minutes of tense silence, he got up.

I decided to go for broke even though I knew I wouldn't get the truth. "Did you kill Ray, Peter?"

He looked stunned but I assumed that acting was part of the criminal repertoire of false reactions. "No!"

I sighed. "Okay, let me rephrase that. Did you have someone kill Ray?"

He shook his head sadly. "Now why would you think that, Alison?"

"Oh, I don't know, Peter. Maybe you thought that killing Ray would be one way to repay me for my kindness? Or maybe to avenge your daughter's death?"

He smiled slyly. "Now, there was a good idea. Too bad I didn't come up with that on my own." He looked up at the ceiling. "You'll let me know if they find out anything, won't you, Alison?"

I wasn't sure why he would want to know who did it or who the police suspected. I took a step back. No, I wouldn't let him know anything that I found out, but I stayed silent.

He approached me and put his hand to my cheek, leaving it there for a few long seconds. He rubbed his hand against it.

"I'd really like you to leave," I whispered. My face was hot beneath his clammy hand.

He dropped his hand to my shoulder. "I always liked you."

And I never liked you, I wanted to say, but didn't. Unable to meet his eyes, I focused on the collar of his shirt.

"Remember when we were in school together?" he asked.

I nodded. Peter went to Joliet, a mile or so away from St. Thomas and the original "brother" school to my formerly all-girls college. His proximity, coupled with the flashy Trans Am that he drove, made him tough to miss.

"You were very cute. Nice girl. Quiet. Not like some of those other slutty girls at St. Thomas."

"Thank you, Peter," I said. "What you think means so much to me." I didn't know if sarcasm violated some kind of cosa nostra code of ethics, but I was beyond caring.

He gave my shoulder a little squeeze. "I know," he said, and gave me a patronizing smile.

God, this guy really believes his own hype, I thought. I could only imagine what his Joliet transcript looked like. Whacking: A+. Subtlety in Language: F.

"I'll reconnect your phone now." He chuckled. "Bet you didn't know I used to work for AT&T?"

I didn't know if he was kidding or not, but it really didn't matter. I'm sure he had a little familiarity with wiretaps and such, but I didn't see him as a lineman for the county. And I'm sure he knew that the first thing I would have done when I went to put my clothes on was call someone to tell them that Peter was in my house.

He held out his arms. "Come here," he said. When I hesitated, he repeated, "Come here."

I walked toward him because it didn't seem like I had a choice and held my breath while he grabbed me in a massive bear hug and put his lips to my cheek. He smelled like he had bathed in cologne. The stench, combined with the fact that his arms encircled me, made it so I could barely breathe. He finally let go and stepped back. "Enjoy the biscotti," he said. "The best on Staten Island. Gianna made them."

"I know, Peter," I said, nodding. I didn't know what else to say, so I said, "Thank her for me."

He threw his arms out wide. "And now, off to the links! What a glorious day." He exited through the back door.

I stood in the kitchen until I heard the Mercedes pull away from the curb five minutes later, hearing the gravel spray onto my front lawn. I picked up the phone on the counter and listened for the dial tone.

It was back. I dialed a number I knew by heart.

Crawford put the girls on the train, walking them all the way down the platform and making sure they were in their seats and on their way to Greenwich before leaving. He watched their faces as the train pulled away and took some solace in the fact that Erin actually smiled at him and blew him a kiss. Meaghan was too busy fooling around with her iPod to notice that he was still there.

He stood on the platform until the train lights were out of sight. Every time they left was hard; it never got any easier. He had gotten used to the fact that they didn't live together, but he wished there was more time to be together. Work had taken hold of his life and wouldn't let go. He'd be interested to see how Fred would make it work once he was married. Crawford certainly hadn't figured out how to balance on the high-wire act of life versus the "Job."

He had just passed his sixteenth anniversary on the police department. Graduating from the academy just five months before his daughters were born, he felt like he had everything: the job he always wanted, a wife, and soon, a family. It all came very quickly, shortly after he had left college, but it was what he wanted. Nothing more. His father had fought him on joining the police department; Frank Crawford had spent twenty unhappy, tedious years as a beat cop, hating every minute, counting down the days until he retired. But Bobby saw it as his calling; his time on the Job would be different from Frank's. He promised Frank that he would finish college at night, as soon as the twins were born and things settled down. Frank wasn't stupid; he knew that that would never happen and it never did. Bobby had managed to eke out two full years of school, but never got his bachelor's degree. A couple of courses at a community college got him his associate's, but he had never found the time to make good on his promise to Frank.

Christine had been with him since high school. They had met in the neighborhood; her father owned a local bar and she worked there. She was inclined to agree with Frank—she saw Bobby in a different job but she accepted that police work appeared to be his calling. But she had supported them while he attended NYU, slaving away in her father's bar, and she was tired. She wanted to go to college, too, but had sacrificed in order to make sure he got out of school first. The police department, to her, was her ticket out of drudgery. From what Crawford could tell, she never anticipated the strain it would put on their marriage.

He took the crosstown shuttle to Times Square and then the subway home to Ninety-seventh Street. He knew that Sunday night was Bea's bingo night at the church, so he was safe. He walked in, no tiptoeing, and made his way up to his apartment at the top of the stairs.

Upon entering, he threw his keys onto the dining room table and checked his phone messages, his nightly ritual. The machine sat on the counter that separated the galley kitchen from the dining area. He went into the kitchen while the tape rewound and took a beer from the refrigerator.

"You have two new messages," the disembodied voice announced. The first message clicked on, but nobody spoke. He could hear breathing on the other line and then silence as the line disconnected. The second message came on immediately. "Bobby, it's me." Fred. Crawford listened to the message, detailing Peter Miceli's visit to Alison, and then hit the button that told the day and time of the call—it had come in right after he had left for Grand Central that morning. Fred said that he and Max were on their way to Alison's to check on things.

He grabbed his keys and left the apartment.

He found himself speeding through the Brooklyn Battery Tunnel, not sure how he had gotten there but completely aware of where he was going. Everyone knew where Peter Miceli lived; his house had been used during a movie shoot and its location had been both published in every New York paper and broadcast over every major news station in the area. Crawford knew exactly where he was headed, even if he wasn't really sure why he was going.

Staten Island is really part of New Jersey, Crawford thought, and flashed back to the secession movement that had gripped the borough in the late eighties. It borders the really ugly part of New Jersey and is virtually impossible to get to from the five boroughs. It's an island only in the most literal sense without all of the attendant lushness and beauty that usually accompanies the word. Crawford had found out—after they had gotten married—that Christine's late mother's family lived way out on Staten Island. Somewhere in the back of his mind, he remembered Christine casually mentioning her family out there, but when push came to shove, he would swear under oath that he never remembered her saying that they visited said family twice a month. He, Christine, and the twins had spent many a Saturday afternoon sitting in traffic on the Gowanus Expressway, inching their way closer to hell: Christine's Polish grandmother, her spectacularly bad

Polish food, and her small, overheated, figurine-filled Cape Cod house. Trying to keep toddling twins away from a display of Precious Moments figurines almost became Crawford's full-time job during those days; an ill-timed trip to the bathroom to relieve himself of the cheap, domestic beer he consumed while there could spell disaster. And a Polish curse on his house from his suspicious grandmother-in-law.

He wondered, just for the sake of argument, if failure to disclose Staten Island relatives was a reason for annulment.

He exited the Staten Island Expressway and made his way onto Richmond Road, where small, attached homes eventually gave way to old, big, expensive estates. Peter Miceli's Italianate stucco monstrosity was somewhere off Richmond Road and Crawford knew that he would find it easily. When he got a sense of the house numbers—evens on the left, odds on the right—and saw that they were getting larger as he drove, he knew he was getting closer.

Miceli's house was about a quarter mile down the road on the left. Surprisingly, there was no gate in front of the house and Crawford was able to pull right up to the front door at the center of the circular drive and adjacent to the fountain in the center of everything. Peter's Mercedes, as well as other cars, were in the driveway—all late model and all American made—making Crawford think that perhaps the Micelis were entertaining. He pulled the Passat up as close as he could and turned it off, taking a few deep breaths as he sat in the car.

He had no second thoughts as he walked up the wide stone steps to the front of the house. He pushed the doorbell and waited, hearing footsteps falling on marble inside the foyer. When the door opened, he was surprised to find himself face-to-face with Peter Miceli.

Miceli, on the other hand, didn't appear surprised at

all. Recognition flashed in his porcine eyes and he smiled broadly. "Detective!" he bellowed, as if he had been waiting for Crawford all night.

Crawford shoved his hands deep in the pockets of his jacket, fingering the gun under his right hand. "Mr. Miceli."

Peter held out his hand, forcing Crawford to remove his from his pocket to shake. "What brings you here on this balmy evening?" Peter asked, sniffing the breeze. "Smells like rain."

"Can I have a word with you, Mr. Miceli?" Crawford asked, his voice barely above a whisper.

Miceli stepped out of the house and onto the grand front porch. Once off the inner step of the foyer, he lost several inches and stood at his full five and a half feet, looking up at Crawford. If Crawford had to guess, he would say that they probably weighed the same, however. "What can I do for you, Detective?" he asked, an innocent gleam in his eye.

Crawford got right to the point. "I'm going to have to ask that you leave Alison alone, Mr. Miceli. She doesn't know anything and can't help you with whatever it is that you want." He tried to remain fairly convivial; he was already in violation of about half a dozen department rules and he didn't want Miceli to feel threatened in any way.

Peter considered what he said, staring up at Crawford's face. He pursed his lips and narrowed his eyes. "She's an old friend, Detective. She was very kind to my daughter. Occasionally, I like to drop by and remind her of how grateful we are." His face turned hard. "I don't see what business it is of yours."

Crawford took a step back. "It's entirely my business, Mr. Miceli."

Peter paused another moment. "Stay out of it, Detective. It doesn't concern you anymore. From what I hear, Alison doesn't want to spend a lot of time with you right now." He smiled. "You've got a wife. I'm sure that didn't sit well with Professor Bergeron."

Crawford swallowed. "Please. Stay away from her."

Peter laughed. "Or what? Are you gonna have me arrested, Detective? For what? Visiting an old college friend?" He gave Crawford a look. "You're out of your league here, Detective. Let it go."

Crawford looked down at him. "Don't go there again. That's all I have to say." He turned to leave, making his way down the first two steps of the porch.

"Let it go, Detective!" Peter called after him. "After all, it's not like I visited your wife and daughters on Donald Street in Greenwich or anything like that. You know, beautiful Meaghan and Erin? And Christine?"

Crawford was back up the stairs before he had a chance to think. He grabbed Peter by the throat and squeezed; when Peter's face began to turn red, he let go. He got a small satisfaction out of the fact that the smug look that had been on Peter's face had been replaced by raw fear. "Don't ever, ever, say anything even remotely threatening about my family again. I will—"

"What? You'll what, Detective? Kill me?" Peter said, rubbing the red mark on his throat. "Think about your alternatives, Detective. When you do, you'll realize you don't have any." Peter turned and went back in the house, calling out to his guests that he would be returning to the dining room shortly.

Crawford stood on the porch, shaking with rage. His hands were trembling and his face was hot. He went back to his car and got in, his hands gripping the steering wheel. This may not have been the stupidest thing he had ever done, but it was close.

Chapter 9

Fred and Max had stopped by later in the afternoon, after Peter's visit. I had called Max at her downtown apartment after Peter left the house and she could tell immediately that I was shaken. Fred had worked a double shift the day before and she didn't want to wake him to fill him in, so she waited until he awoke on his own, which wasn't long after I called. I'm convinced that cops have a sixth sense about these things. As soon as he heard what she had to say, they took the forty-minute ride up to Dobbs Ferry to get a handle on what had happened.

I was calmer than I had been in the morning, but still unnerved at the ease with which Peter was able to get into my house. He was all about intimidation, and intellectually, I knew that. But I also knew about his history and his business. He had people killed just for saying the wrong thing. What was to stop him from killing me if I didn't entertain his flights of fancy and his wish to "make amends" with me?

I hadn't called Crawford this time. I had a couple of reasons for this: one, he was my go-to guy every time something happened and I didn't want him to lose patience, and two, the next night was my blind date with Jack McManus. I didn't want him to become embroiled in my life on the one day when I was poised to betray him. I know, it sounds dramatic to say it like that, but that's how I felt.

Fred listened to the story and agreed with me that

pressing charges really wouldn't be wise or necessary. I couldn't think of a surer way to end up in a garbage bag at the bottom of the Hudson River than crossing Peter Miceli and told Fred so.

Max and I tried to bandy around a few theories about Ray's murder; she had already filled Fred in on the Terri and Jackson scenario but now we had Peter to truly add to the list of viable suspects. Fred wasn't having any of it. He remained quiet while we talked, not interested in sharing what he knew about the case. We tossed out our theory about Ray having been killed by a Miceli associate but Fred is the master of the poker face; we couldn't tell whether or not he thought this was the case, too, or that he thought we were out of our minds. In our discussion, however, we conveniently left out the part where Max went into Terri and Jackson's house; she hadn't found anything anyway, so what was the point in sharing that with him?

So we focused on Peter and the whole biscotti thing. Max was barely able to keep a straight face every time I said the word. I was becoming convinced that Peter was truly out of his mind. And what could be more dangerous than being in the sights of a crazy wise guy who could have people killed at will? Or force-feed them biscotti?

We shared a pizza and a bottle of wine and they left around five. I sat at the kitchen table deciding what to do next—bath, martini, or television, my three go-to activities—when my eyes landed on the keys sitting on the place mat across from me. And then it dawned on me.

I had a key to Ray's apartment.

In his quest for us to be completely open, amicable, and friendly, he had given me a key to his new place on Kappock Street. I didn't want it, had almost thrown it out even, but I had to put it on my key ring because, at the time, he had refused to leave until I had done so. In time, I had forgotten about it. But now it seemed like a message from beyond the grave, so I grabbed the keys and ran out the back door.

I navigated the labyrinthine streets of Riverdale trying to discern which building could be Ray's. I finally found it, and one of those ever-elusive city parking spots, after driving around the block five times. As I started to get out of the car, it occurred to me that I didn't know which apartment Ray lived in, but I assumed that there was a mailbox with clearly delineated floor and apartment numbers.

Wrong. There was a surly doorman, though.

The doorman opened the door for me, taking in my disheveled appearance; in my eagerness to get over to Ray's apartment, I hadn't taken the time to brush my hair or put on an ensemble that even approached acceptability. My baggy jeans, T-shirt, and high-top sneakers did nothing to inspire confidence.

"Leave the menus with me," he instructed, holding out his hand.

"What?"

"The menus. Leave them with me." He lost patience with me when I didn't proffer the requested menus. "Aren't you from Shanghai City?"

"No." Do I look Chinese?

The doorman gave me another look and then returned to his post at a circular desk. "Then what can I help you with?"

"Can you tell me which apartment Ray Stark lived in?" I asked, wiping a hand across my brow; my nervousness over pulling this off had produced a thin sheen of sweat on my forehead.

"Not unless you can tell me that you're a member of the PD," he said, quite impressed with his authority.

Give a guy a uniform and he automatically thinks he's in charge, I thought. I knew better than to try to impersonate a member of the police department so I went with the truth. Wow, that was a refreshing change. I took another couple of breaths and held the keys before him. "I'm his ex-wife. I have a key." I tried to think about something sad, willing tears to my eyes. The best I could conjure up was the feeling I get when I watch the first *Rocky*. Between his love for mousy Adrian and his inability to form a complete, cohesive thought, I was a sucker for his plight. I thought about Rocky in his boxing shorts and my eyes welled up. Thinking about Sylvester Stallone's post-Rocky career probably would have produced more genuine sadness and tears, but that didn't occur to me at the time. It wasn't exactly an award-winning performance but the doorman looked at me with something approaching sympathy. "It's just been so hard," I gasped. "I still loved him!" I wailed.

He waited a moment, obviously considering his response. He gave a look that I interpreted to mean "you look pitiful and I think I'll help you out." His voice was so soft that I missed what he said the first time. "Four D." He stopped me before I took off for the elevator. "Listen, if anyone finds out . . ."

My tears abated as quickly as they started. "I won't tell a soul."

He nodded again and held his hands out in a conciliatory gesture. "We have rules here."

Obviously none that protect against the wearing of mullets, I thought, but I kept my lip zipped. Business in the front, party in the back . . . and not the hairdo for a man living in the new millennium. I dug into my bag and pulled out a five.

"I won't forget this," I said. But I realized that *he* had to. Before I left for the elevator, I went back into my bag and came out with a twenty; hopefully, it would be used at a hair salon. "This is between us, okay?" I made a sound like a sob, but it was a little over the top. He nodded nonetheless, so I ran for the elevator in the hopes that this guy couldn't tell what a giant faker I was.

Ray's apartment was a short walk from the elevator, and despite my nervousness about getting into the apartment, the key didn't require any extra jiggling or special insertion to open the door. The yellow NYPD tape hanging across the door should have been a deterrent to me, but it wasn't. I'm an old hand at yellow crime-scene tape by now. I opened the door and scooted under the tape to find a small living room with a nice balcony off it, a galley kitchen to my right, and a hallway off the living room leading to a large bedroom. The bathroom was across from the bedroom. It was decorated in early dorm room, with some Ikea furniture that was propped up by milk crates. Apparently, the money I had given Ray to buy him out of the house had gone entirely toward his new car. Figures.

Since Ray had been killed elsewhere, the apartment was not technically part of the crime scene, but obviously the police had been through here pretty thoroughly. Ray wasn't the neatest guy in town, but the place had been tossed but good. I didn't know what I expected to find, and particularly, what I would find that the police hadn't, but I thought it was worth a little look-see.

But first, there was the more pressing matter of my bladder. I had had to go to the bathroom since leaving Dobbs Ferry, and while I had been able to keep the discomfort at bay, now that I was in the presence of a toilet, the situation had gotten critical. I went in and used the toilet, reaching behind me for the roll of toilet paper that sat on the back of the tank. It skittered out of my hand and rolled behind the toilet, just out of my reach.

"Dang it," I whispered. I got off the toilet and onto my knees. "This is classy," I commented to myself. I stuck my head between the toilet and the vanity next to it, praying that I didn't get wedged in. My cell phone was in my pocket, so I knew that if I got stuck, I could call for help. Crawford would love to find me, with my pants around my ankles, stuck between two fixtures in Ray's bathroom. My guess is that would put an end to any romance we might have had.

My fingertips grazed the toilet paper and I finally managed to get a good hold on it, dragging it toward me. But before I backed out of the space between the toilet and the vanity, something shiny, affixed to the back of the toilet tank, caught my eye. I reached up and yanked it off.

It was a plastic jewel case and inside was a DVD.

I guess the police hadn't been over this place as thoroughly as I had thought.

I finished up in the bathroom and went into the living room. Damn that Ray. In addition to having the nicest car I had ever seen, he also had a giant flat-screen television. I took the disk and inserted it into the DVD player, finally figuring out how to sync the player with the television. As big as life, the surround sound of his voice making it seem like he was in the room with me, was Ray. Well, actually, it was just Ray's crotch, but being as I had some familiarity with that crotch, I recognized it immediately. Yep, there was his appendectomy scar and the mole on his left hip.

"Oh, no," I said out loud. I sat on the couch and watched the scene.

Ray was sitting on his bed. I could tell it was him even though his head was cut off in the shot.

"Say hi to the camera, baby," he said to a blurry woman.

"Hi, there," she said and gave a little wave.

The woman was standing close to the camera. All the camera took in was a shot of her torso; Ray was apparently quite the amateur sex-videographer because all we had here was a sex tape with a blurry torso, indescribable penis, and no heads. Eventually, she walked away from the camera and I could make out a large heart tattoo on her lower back.

Well, that's not very helpful, I thought. I watched more of the tape but it became clear that I would never find out who she was. I didn't recognize her voice because she mostly spoke in whispers and moans, so unless I had a tryst with this woman and got her to moan like that, I wasn't going to find out her identity anytime soon. I took the DVD out of the player and popped it back into the case.

Okay, so that gave me another suspect: Miss Blurry Tattoo Ass. Had she had second thoughts about the sex tape and had she tried to get it back from Ray? Had he denied her possession and had that made her mad? Was that why it was so well hidden behind the toilet? It was hard to tell but it gave me a lot to think about. Although I couldn't see her face, she had appeared pretty tall in the video. Her head came up to the top of the bookcase in Ray's room, so I went in and measured myself against it. Yep, she was about two inches taller than me, putting her at a good six feet. Wow. That was one tall woman. With the most toned thighs I had ever seen.

But any titillation I might have gotten from the sex tape was mitigated by the fact that everything was blurry and I couldn't tell what the heck was going on beyond some murmurings of "you're the best, Ray" and "oh, yeah, that's how I like it." Blurry and unoriginal. I felt sorry for Ray. His lasting legacy as a champion cocksman would now be sullied by a sex tape in which everything was out of focus and in which he clearly hadn't satisfied his partner.

That poor guy just couldn't catch a break.

Chapter 10

The next day, I taught my classes, ran interference with Sister Calista—who was still holding out on me—and visited with Kevin for a few brief minutes before heading home. I got home with an hour to kill before I had to take the train into the city. On top of everything that had been going on, tonight was my blind date with Jack McManus.

On the drive home from Ray's, I had made a decision: the sex tape was mine. If Crawford or his colleagues ever found out that I had been in Ray's apartment, I was toast. And what did a barely viewable sex tape have to do with anything anyhow? Maybe Miss Blurry Tattoo Ass was a suspect and maybe not. That was for me to find out.

So, I focused on the event at hand: I had a date. With a single man. Is there any law on the books—either legal or moral—that says you can't go on a date shortly after your ex-husband has been murdered? As I brushed my teeth for what seemed like the seventeenth time in the past hour—it was the oral version of the clean underwear edict uttered by every mother in America—I justified my decision to go out with Jack. At first, all I had to feel guilty about was cheating on my married boyfriend; now, I had the added pressure of thinking about a handless and footless Ray (an image that was seared in my brain). I finally came to the conclusion that a diversion with a man, even one who potentially loved Madonna and loved to vogue, would be an acceptable way to spend my time. I hadn't been on a date since Ray first asked me out nearly ten years earlier; Crawford didn't count. We had never been on an official "date" and he still had that . . . well, wife.

Jack and I had spoken on the phone not too long after my dinner with Kevin, but we all know what happened in the interim, and that made my life extremely complicated. Jack had been so kind and understanding that I thought perhaps he was the vogueing brother, sensitive enough to "strike a pose" and caring enough to respect my feelings after losing my ex-husband to a crazed, knife-wielding maniac. He had called back earlier in the week, equally kind and persistent, and had asked if I could meet him at Madison Square Garden, home of the New York Rangers, that evening. He sounded like a very nice guy indeed and that gave me hope. Kevin told me he was very attractive, but being as Kevin has been celibate for at least the last fifteen years and maybe more, I didn't put too much stock in his assessment. And what was he supposed to say? "My brother is a troll. Have fun!" I assumed that he looked like Kevin—myopic, about my height, blond, and rumpled. Imagine my surprise when a man an inch or two over six feet with jet-black hair peppered with a little bit of gray and the most gorgeous blue eyes approached me at the ticket window at Madison Square Garden, our appointed meeting place. The Rangers were playing a preseason game and Jack had invited me to go. I had met Kevin's parents—also blond and myopic—and could only conclude that there were some most excellent recessive genes in this clan.

See, here's the thing with blind dates, in my experience: they never involve anyone remotely handsome. The handsome guys are usually married or gay and not interested in a blind date with me. The blind-date guys are usually guys you wouldn't consider spending the rest of your life with, never mind the two hours it takes to eat dinner. Or, the fifteen minutes it takes to drink the cup of coffee that you agreed to because you overheard your date taking a puff off his inhaler while you were scheduling said date. Rather, you are usually subjected to the guy wearing the "Bikini Inspector!" hat who lives with his mom, is lactose intolerant, or has some other not immediately obvious medical condition that would, under normal circumstances, make him ineligible for you to accept a date from. Jack McManus was not wearing the "Bikini Inspector!" hat and, while not drinking from a huge glass of milk or eating a hunk of cheese and simultaneously having an allergic reaction, did not look lactose intolerant. Or deathly allergic to bees. Or suffering from Dutch elm disease. In other words, he looked like a winner.

I looked at his shoes to see if he was trailing toilet paper from his heel, another dead giveaway. Nope. And when he smiled, all I could see were two rows of the straightest, whitest teeth ever to reside in one man's mouth. This guy was a veritable poor woman's George Clooney. If you find that kind of thing attractive. Which I don't, I reminded myself. I like Crawford. Crawford is the guy I like. I repeated that mantra over and over while I stared at this gorgeous man in front of me, steeling myself for "the catch" that I hoped would reveal itself early in the evening so that I wouldn't get my hopes up.

He approached me tentatively and held out his hand. "Alison?"

"That's me!" I said cheerfully. Mentally, I took a deep breath and tried to reorient myself. Okay, I told myself, pretend you're a fairly attractive, grown woman, with lots of confidence and more than your fair share of mojo. Or at least someone who can follow up a hearty "that's me!" with some intelligent conversation.

"Jack McManus," he said. We shook. Nice hands. Not

smooth like Kevin's, which were unused to manual labor, but definitely the hands of someone who knew how to hold both a hammer and a woman's hand, although preferably not at the same time.

The Garden was abuzz with people arriving for the hockey game, and Jack took me by the elbow, steering me through the throngs. In the past when I had gone to Ranger games, I had taken the escalators that wended their way at an alarming speed up through the Garden. More than once I had felt nauseous riding those escalators. I had never had great seats, so my escalator rides had always ended in the nosebleed section. But tonight would be different, from what Jack told me, because he worked in the public relations office for the team and had access to second-row, center-ice seats, right behind the home team's bench. For a French Canadian like me, it was about as close to heaven as you could get.

We arrived at our seats just as the pregame practice was ending. We really hadn't spoken on our way to the seats, so when Jack sat down next to me, I realized that it was "showtime." He asked me if I wanted anything to eat.

"No, thanks," I said. I had never met this man before. I wasn't going to display my chowing prowess in the first half hour of our time together. Nobody likes a woman who can inhale a foot-long hot dog in three bites. Except maybe Crawford. The guy I like, I thought, as I admired Jack's chiseled jaw.

"A glass of wine? A beer? Soda?" he asked.

I gazed into his blue eyes for probably longer than was socially acceptable. "Wine would be nice," I said.

Jack told me that he would be back in a few minutes, so I settled into my seat. When I was sure that he was out of sight, I dug my cell phone out of my pocket and dialed Max. I wanted her to watch the game to see if she could get a peek at me; with seats right behind the bench, I was confident that I would be on television at least once or twice. I needed input on my hair. I had been going for a Barbra Streisand in *Funny Girl* look and wanted confirmation that I had succeeded. She answered on the first ring, as she normally does.

"Max here."

"Hi, it's me," I shouted over the crowd noise. "Listen, are you watching anything on television tonight?"

"No," she said, chewing loudly in my ear. She mentioned that her favorite reality show wasn't on so she wasn't watching anything. Max loves reality television more than life itself and watches every single reality show with a devotion and solemnity normally reserved for religious ceremonies.

"Great." I smoothed my hair down. "Put on the Rangers. I'm out with Jack McManus and I want you to see how I've done my hair."

She gasped. "Cheating on your married boyfriend already?" she cried, with mock alarm. She knew about this date but wouldn't miss an opportunity to rib me about it. "Well, I never!"

"Max, seriously. I need help. I haven't been on a date in this millennium. Help me."

She turned on the television and we chitchatted while she waited to get a shot of me. She continued eating what sounded like an entire bag of tortilla chips.

"Wait," she said, "there's the bench . . . and there you are." She paused for longer than I would have liked. I started to get nervous. "You look like Barbra Streisand in *Funny Girl*."

"Great! That's what I was going for!" I said.

"But not in a good way," she added. "Take that piece that you've artfully arranged behind your ear and pull it forward."

"Like this?" I pushed some hair around.

"Got it."

"Oh, and Max, I went to Ray's apartment yesterday and guess what I found?"

I took the massive crunching in my ear for her response.

"A sex tape."

"Is it good?"

I rolled my eyes. "That's not the point, Max. There's a woman on there. Do you think she might be a suspect? She's awfully big. I could see her being able to overpower someone."

"Bigger than you?"

"What's that supposed to mean?"

A hand on my shoulder interrupted our conversation; Jack was back. I pretended to be on an important phone call. "I appreciate your concern about your grade, Anne Marie, and will reassess the points you made tomorrow. Have a good night." I snapped my phone shut.

Jack sat down next to me and handed me a crystal goblet filled with red wine. "Here you go."

We had already covered all of the basics of our lives on our "predate interview" as I liked to call it, over the phone: we were both single, professionals, but whereas I lived in Westchester County, Jack had stayed close to his and Kevin's Queens roots and had a condo in Long Island City, which was fast becoming the hot new area in New York. I attempted to make conversation, pretending to myself that I was out with someone in whom I had no interest, didn't find the least bit attractive, and with whom I had spent many an evening.

"So, Kevin tells me you're a Joyce scholar," he said, and took a sip of the beer that he had brought back for himself.

"Guilty." Nothing says sexy like someone who reads obtuse Irish writers.

" 'Love loves to love love. And this person loves that other person because everybody loves somebody but God loves everybody,' " he said, a faint blush appearing on his cheeks as it may have occurred to him that quoting Joyce was either a show-offy move or one that would give me the wrong impression of our first date.

Neither possibility crossed my mind. "I'm impressed," I said, and it was the truth. Not only did he quote correctly, but it was a quote from well into the text. That was a quote correctly rendered from someone who had read the book from start to . . . well, at least the middle.

He focused his attention on the game. "I've always loved Joyce. His writing has such a musical quality, it's hard not to love it."

We cheered as the Rangers scored a goal. I was careful not to jump up and down, spilling what tasted like a fine merlot all over my date. "So, what else did Kevin tell you about me?"

The look that passed over his face told me that Father Blabbermouth—my rather improper nickname for gossip-loving Kevin—had given Jack chapter and verse on the many sordid aspects of my life. How I had married a scoundrel but stayed married to him for seven years. And how the dead body of one of my students had been found in the trunk of my car. And how I had fallen in love with a very attractive, yet very married, detective. And how aforementioned scoundrel was found dead in my kitchen. It was all there, written on his kind face.

"He told me that you love hockey," he offered weakly. "I hope that's true."

Nice save. "Yes, it's true," I said, and exhaled. "My mother and father were from Quebec and while my father was a dedicated Nordiques fan, once he moved to New York, he changed teams. I grew up a Ranger fan."

"College professor, Joyce scholar, Ranger fan," he said,

smiling. "You don't find too many people in this arena with that pedigree." The buzzer sounded, ending the first period. "How about another glass of wine?" he asked.

I looked into my glass and saw that it was nearly empty. "Why not?" I said, and handed it to him. The moment he left his seat, my cell phone chirped. Max.

"You're showing quite a lot of boob tonight," she observed. "Unless that's the glare from the ice bouncing off your cleavage."

I peered down into my chest area; my cardigan sweater was unbuttoned just enough to say "yes, I'm a college professor but, boy, have I got game." "Am not."

"You're doing quite well," she said. "I've been watching your entire date on television."

"He's cute, right?"

"He's very cute, I think. The guy sitting in front of the two of you has a huge head. It's enormous. He should get that looked at." And with that, she ended the conversation.

Jack returned with wine and some hot dogs, one of which I devoured as daintily as I could. I stretched out my consumption to five bites this time but he didn't seem to notice. After the second glass of wine, the conversation flowed a little more easily and I found myself really enjoying his company. The game ended with the Rangers winning, leaving both of us in a great mood.

We left the seating area and returned to the lobby, where we had begun our date. "Did you drive in tonight?" he asked as we went with the crowd toward the front door. The night air was chilly even though, technically, summer had just ended.

"I'm taking the train home," I said, and pulled my jacket tight around my body.

"I've arranged a car service to take you home. Let's walk outside; the driver should be waiting out here on Thirty-fourth Street." He took my hand and led me out to the street. Just as he predicted, a driver was parked along the street, holding a sign bearing the name "Bergerson." Close enough.

I turned to face him. "Jack, thank you. This was a really lovely evening."

He leaned in and I girded myself for a kiss. But instead, he took a piece of my hair and put it behind my ear, reestablishing the look that I had so carefully constructed before I had left the house. He rested his hand on my left cheek, rubbing it slightly with his thumb, and leaned in and kissed the other one. "Good night. Maybe we can do this again?" he asked.

I nodded. "That would be great." I got into the car and gave him a little wave as we drove off. I pulled my phone out of my pocket and saw that I had a text message from Max. It read: "You have mustard on your left cheek. It's been there since the second period. xoxo"

Chapter 11

I went to school the next day with a spring in my step. For one night, at least, I was able to forget about Ray's death and focus on something fun and pleasurable.

Every time I thought of Crawford's face, I tried to put it out of my mind. Why the hell did I feel so guilty? After all, I had a lot of lingering hurt and ire left over from the Crawford "I'm married but not really" debacle of the spring. I had very strong feelings for him—of both the love and lust variety—but the sting of not knowing about his estranged wife, who was adorable and seemingly lovely, was still painful.

I bounced into the office area, nodded a quick hello to Dottie, our crazy "never met an eyeshadow she didn't like" faculty receptionist, and went to my office. She was also dating one of Crawford's colleagues, a fireplug of a man named Charlie Moriarty, with whom she had fallen deeply and madly in love during the Miceli case. I was surrounded by women dating cops. I wondered what would have happened had I set a small fire in the office area instead of ending up with a dead girl in the trunk of my car; would everybody be dating firefighters? Or if I had caused some kind of international mail incident by sending a toxic package to my cousin Giselle in Quebec? Would letter carriers be part of all of our love lives? I went in and fell into the chair behind the desk, musing on the attraction of civil servants to single women and closed my eyes.

A soft knock at the door interrupted my thoughts. "Come in," I said, running my hands through my hair and standing. Frank, the mailman for our division, opened the door and tossed in a packet of mail, rubber-banded and thick; it hit me mid–solar plexus and I let out a little grunt in surprise. Frank is middle-aged, suffers from obsessive-compulsive disorder, and lives with his mother, who also works in the mailroom. He's been on campus for as long as I remember, going back to my undergraduate days. "Thanks, Frank," I said, surprised to see him. He usually puts the mail in the boxes behind Dottie's desk.

"Dottie said that you looked like you had a late night," he said, "so I thought I'd bring you your mail this morning." Frank is nothing if not painfully honest, something that on most days, I appreciate. Today was not one of those days. "Do you dye your hair?" Frank is also king of the non sequitur.

I dropped the mail on my desk and put my hands back up to my head. "No."

"You should." He started to pull the door closed. "And don't wear red. It makes you look green."

I looked down at my red blouse. "It's garnet!" I called to the closed door. I hastily pulled a hand mirror out of my drawer and examined my face; it didn't look green to me but maybe I wasn't getting the whole picture. My phone rang as I looked for a larger reflective surface around my office. "Dr. Bergeron."

It was Sister Mary, my boss. She wasn't my biggest fan but she wasn't my biggest detractor, either; she was somewhere in the middle on me. I attributed this to my geeky undergraduate years at St. Thomas. "Alison."

I suppose I had to guess why she was calling. I stalled. "Sister."

"Alison. We are sitting in Dr. Etheridge's office awaiting your arrival."

Awaiting my arrival. I gave up the hunt for a larger mirror and immediately went to my day planner, still turned to two days prior. I turned the page to the current day and saw in giant red letters "Staff meeting. Don't be late." And in smaller letters "You were late to the last one." I resisted the urge to curse and went for the always-courteous abrupt hang-up. I smoothed down my sleeveless *garnet* blouse and ran out of the office, skidding down two flights of stairs until I reached of the office Dr. Etheridge—"little Napoleon" as I liked to refer to him—where my illustrious humanities and social sciences colleagues were gathered. I ran past Fran, Etheridge's secretary, who shot me a death look, and ran into the room. With the plethora of pocket protectors jammed into short-sleeved dress shirts and knee-hi panty hose peeking out from beneath peasant skirts, it resembled a meeting of the local chapter of *Star Trek* conventioneers. In my garnet blouse, black printed skirt, and high-heeled pumps, I looked, frankly, like a hooker compared to this crew.

"Sorry I'm late," I mumbled and slid into the only empty chair in the room, the one right beside Little Napoleon at the conference table. Sister Mary glared at me from across the table and I looked down at my hands.

"Thank you for joining us, Dr. Bergeron," Etheridge said. "Now that you're here, perhaps we should have a moment of silence for our departed colleague, Dr. Stark. And perhaps a word from Dr. Bergeron?"

I looked around the room and all eyes were on me. Why me? I had only been married to the guy for seven years; some of these clowns had worked with him for far longer. Silence, the man said. Surely I couldn't be expected to say something about Ray?

"Alison? Would you like to say something?" Etheridge asked.

Oh, I've got a lot to say, I thought, but I shook my head instead.

"It really would be nice if you could share something about Ray," he persisted.

Share something? How about how he made me pay off the credit cards after we divorced, and then bought a fifty-thousand-dollar car? Or how I'd learned he was catting around mere hours after we returned from our honeymoon? Or how he had managed to produce the most boring sex tape known to the world of amateur porn? I clasped my hands together and cast my eyes downward. "Dear Lord, watch over Ray as he makes his way from purgatory to heaven." That was the best I could do.

I looked up and all eyes were still on me, except this time, instead of pity, the eyes were filled with wonder. At my prayer. Sister Mary put her hand over mine and patted it gently. "Do you really think that Ray is in purgatory, Alison?"

No, I think he's in hell. My marriage was purgatory. "I don't know, Sister. But let's hope he makes it upstairs to the big guy as soon as possible."

If I had any doubts that Etheridge thought I was a giant buffoon, I was fairly confident at that moment that that was the case. He stared at me from behind his glasses and considered what I had said. Finally, he broke the silence and returned to the matter at hand: why we were all in the conference room together. "We were just discussing the potentially changing demographic landscape for . . ."

Blah, blah, blah, I thought, as I chewed on "potentially

changing demographic landscape." There was so much wrong with that phrase that I couldn't even begin to focus on what he was saying. I watched his mouth move and thought about my raging headache when in my half slumber I heard him ask, "And what do you think?"

I sat up a little straighter. "Sounds good."

David Morlock, the history chair, caught my eye and gave his head a little shake to warn me.

"Sounds good?" Etheridge asked. "So, you're proposing that we reverse our policy?"

Whoops. The blood in my veins turned to ice as I considered my options. I had a fifty-fifty chance of getting the answer right—or wrong for that matter—so I stalled by putting my finger to my nose in a gesture of contemplation. "Hmmm . . ." I said. "Interesting dilemma." I looked around the table and saw that all of my colleagues were staring at me. After a few seconds of silence, David spoke up.

"I think what Alison means is that there are two schools of thought on the issue of gay rights and that allowing a queer studies program into a Catholic school has both pros and cons," he said. He continued talking, and after a few tense seconds, all eyes were off me and onto him, an eloquent orator and all-around good guy.

I almost fell in love with him at that moment, but being as he is sixty-seven, has terrible halitosis, and lives with four cats, I was able to keep my emotions in check. I shot him a grateful look and returned to studying my cuticles. I also said a silent Act of Contrition to make up for all of those "Morlock the Warlock" jokes that I found so hilarious during my sophomore year.

Etheridge asked me if I had collected all of the syllabi that he had requested. I felt the blood drain from my face as I realized that I hadn't. I didn't even have one.

He stared at me from behind his frameless lenses.

"And when do you think you'll be getting them, Dr. Bergeron?"

"Any day now," I proclaimed unconvincingly. Damn that Sister Calista and her cabal of ornery sisters. Now I knew why they were so resistant to giving me the information I needed; the school was thinking about offering some courses in gay and lesbian studies and they weren't having any part of that. I could save Etheridge a lot of time and tell him exactly how many gay and lesbian literary figures were included on those syllabi: none. And I could also tell him who'd be happily teaching a queer studies course if it were offered in the future: me. So, he could have saved me a heck of a lot of time and energy by just being honest with me from the get-go. Those nuns had turned on me and I would never be able to turn them back.

After an arduous forty-five minutes of debate, during which I was able to keep my mouth shut, the meeting adjourned and I slunk back to my office, no closer to understanding what decision had been made or why.

I was hungry. The hot dog from the night before was a distant memory and I needed more processed nitrates if I was going to make it through the morning. I looked at my watch and determined that I had one entire class period to spend in the cafeteria eating breakfast. I grabbed my wallet and headed out of the office area.

I stopped in at the campus bookstore to get a *New York Times* to read while I had my breakfast. It was between classes and there were more students than usual browsing the stacks of books and magazines in that section of the store.

A student in a blue and gold St. Thomas sweatshirt was bent over at the waist examining the newspaper choices on the bottom shelf of the rack. As is the case with many of my female students, this one was wearing the ubiquitous thong underwear that they found so attractive; it peeked from the waistband of her low-rider jeans. I tried not to stare but her butt crack was inches from my face, as was a huge, red heart tattoo.

Miss Blurry Tattoo Ass.

She stood and turned and I was only mildly surprised to find myself looking at Julie Anne Podowsky.

"Oh, excuse me, Dr. Bergeron. Am I in your way?"

I tried not to do a double take, instead opting for the old clear-your-throat time killer. "Oh, no. I just want to get a *Times*."

She bent over and picked one up, handing it to me. I had on heels so I couldn't tell what the height differential was between us, but since we were eye to eye, I guessed that she had about two inches on me. A picture of her blurry, naked breasts popped into my mind and I looked away.

"I really need to talk to you," she said.

"About your grade?" I asked, picking up a copy of *Marie Claire* and thumbing through it. I couldn't look at her; I had seen her naked. Kind of. It was uncomfortable.

She bit her lower lip. "Well, that, and maybe something else."

I am so not going there with you, I thought. "My office hours are posted online." She seemed like a very sweet girl, but she had forearms that would rival a lumberjack's. And having seen her thighs, I knew they were mighty powerful, too. Her demeanor didn't say "killer" to me but what did I know, really?

She nodded. "I'll find a time that works for both of us."

I nodded. "Good enough." I made my way to the front of the store and threw some coins on the counter to cover the cost of my paper. I walked across the bottom floor of the building without incident, crossed through the student center, and progressed down the long hallway to the commuter cafeteria. I had just reached the doors of the cafeteria, the smell from it not entirely appetizing, when I spied Crawford ambling down the hall toward me, coming from the direction of the convent. Weird, I thought; maybe he's hooked up with a nun? Based on our lack of physical contact, I guessed anything was an improvement. He looked a little shocked when he saw me and more than a little surprised; there was a slight hitch in his step like he was reconsidering his straight path toward me. Kevin was close on his heels, not exactly with Crawford, but not exactly not with him, either.

I stopped, my hand on the handle of the cafeteria door. "Well, well, well. If it isn't Detective Crawford and his ward, Father McManus. You gentlemen out fighting crime together? Where's the Batmobile?" When they didn't laugh, I explained why I was there. However, it didn't explain why Crawford was there. "I was just going in for breakfast. Care to join me?"

Kevin made a great show of looking at his watch. "I have an appointment," he said and scurried off down the hall, his black jacket billowing out behind him, the sound of his loafers click-clacking on the tile floor like he was warming up for *Riverdance*.

I looked at Crawford. "I guess that leaves you. Coffee?" I asked, and held the door open for him. He appeared to be considering his options, finally deciding to follow me in. I approached the counter and put him in charge of getting coffee. "Can you handle that?" I asked.

"I think so," he said, and wandered off to the coffee bar. I watched him stand before the large coffee dispenser, trying to figure out what I would like and what I would take in my coffee.

"Large! Milk!" I called after him and turned my attention to Marcus, my favorite cafeteria cook, who was making omelets behind the counter. "Hi, Marcus," I said.

"Could I have two scrambled egg and bacon sandwiches on rolls, please?" I asked. I looked around. The cafeteria was sparsely populated since the second class of the day was in session, and only a few students, all plugged in to something or other—headphones, MP3 players, or cell phones—hung around the outskirts of the room. Marcus whipped up my sandwiches which I paid for and brought over to a table by the window.

Crawford joined me with two large cups of coffee and sat down across from me. I handed him a plate with a sandwich on it.

"So, what's going on, Crawford? Anything to report on Ray's murder?" I asked, digging into my sandwich with gusto. I had thrown up on this guy's shoes; I didn't need to pretend I was a dainty, delicate flower when it came to eating.

He shook his head. "Not a thing. We're working a couple of angles . . ."—he paused when he saw my eyebrows shoot upwards—"the details of which I will *not* share with you."

Party pooper.

"Did you talk to my neighbors? Jackson and Terri?" I asked.

He knitted his brows together. "Yes. Why?"

"Right after Ray was murdered, Terri came over and basically accused Jackson of the murder." I went on to re-count my visit with Max to Boscobel, but left out the part where Max rummaged through their underwear drawers. "Does he seem like a suspect to you?"

Crawford thought for a moment. "I'll go back through my notes, but my initial reaction was that he seemed pretty innocuous." He took a bite of sandwich and gazed out at the river, glistening like a jewel beyond the great lawn of the building in which we sat. "Why would his wife accuse him and then carry on with him like that, though? I think I'll talk to her again, too."

"Good idea," I said. "And I guess you're looking at the Miceli family, too?"

He remained quiet on that subject. I took that as an affirmative.

I decided to change the subject; as much of an amateur sleuth as I'd become, talking about Ray's murder took its toll on me emotionally. "What are you doing here, Crawford?" I asked. I tried for that nonchalant insouciance that I always attempt, but am never successful at pulling off. Because, good Lord, he was handsome and I was a sucker for tall guys with chiseled good looks; call me crazy.

"I came to see you," he said, unconvincingly.

"Liar." I'm not all that observant, but I had this sneaking suspicion that he had been with Kevin prior to seeing me. That could mean one of two things: he was getting spiritual direction or help with his annulment. I didn't let my mind wander too long as to the purpose of their visit. The look on my face must have conveyed other emotions or feelings because Crawford went into full mea culpa mode.

"Listen, I don't know how many times I have to tell you this, but I'm sorry." He tried to look at me, but couldn't.

I didn't respond. What was there to say? I knew that he was sorry, but it didn't mitigate my feelings of humiliation of having met the wife I didn't know he had.

"I don't know what I have to do to make this up to you." He rubbed his eyes, either just plain tired, or tired of this conversation.

I spoke quietly but made my point. "You just have to get divorced, or annulled, or whatever it is that will make you available."

He nodded, almost imperceptibly. He had mentioned

to me that he had finally signed his divorce papers but, in doing so, had promised his wife that he would go through the annulment process, her main stipulation in dissolving their marriage, but a process in which he did not believe. It was the proverbial catch-22: he would be free of his marriage, but have to compromise his ethics in the process. And I knew Crawford well enough to know that that caused him more than a few sleepless nights.

So while the papers were signed on his end, I didn't know if Christine had signed them as well and I certainly wasn't going to ask. Crawford was nothing if not intensely private and while I was dying to know how long this would take, I resisted the urge to probe him further on the subject. Kevin had hinted that an annulment could take upward of two years and that left me in a bit of a moral quandary: would I hold out that long or compromise my own ethics by dating a technically still-married man?

"What's the matter?"

I realized that I had been staring at him the whole time that I had been working all of these details out in my brain. And I also realized that while staring at him and working out those details, I had inadvertently thought about my date with Jack. Damn that brother McManus and his straight white teeth. They had left quite an impression on me. "Nothing," I said, and took a bite from my sandwich. I looked out the window.

"You seem, I don't know, nervous," he said, and leaned in a bit. "Are you blushing?"

"No," I protested, my mouth full.

"You are," he said, a bit amazed. "Now, why would you be blushing?"

I shrugged and smiled nervously.

"Does it have anything to do with the . . ."—he paused dramatically—"*date* you went on last night?" The look on my face must have been priceless, because he burst out laughing. "Alison, if you're going to go out on a date and you want to keep it a secret, make sure you're not on television."

I swallowed my food and gulped slightly. "Sorry?" I said.

He looked at me and it appeared that he was deciding whether or not to be angry. The tables had turned and now we were off his divorce and onto my dating life. I looked down at my sandwich, crumbled egg falling out of the side of the roll. That coupled with the acids in my stomach churning took away any feelings of hunger that I had.

"How was the hockey game?" he asked, smiling.

"It was great. Bouchard had a hat trick," I said casually.

"I know. I watched it on TV," he reminded me.

"Right," I said, nodding.

"Are you going to go out with him again?" he asked. He finished the sandwich, and pulled a few napkins out of the holder, wiping his fingers.

No, I thought. "I don't know," I said out loud. Big mistake.

"Oh." He shoved his napkin and paper plate into his coffee cup; the look on his face told me that that hadn't been the right answer. God, it was getting so I could almost teach a class in sticking one's foot in one's mouth. "Are you bringing him to the wedding?"

"God, no," I said. I thought that was obvious; I was the matron of honor and Crawford was the best man, so *he* was my date. But he really had gotten the wrong idea watching me on my televised date.

"Well, how would I know that, based on your last answer?" He stood. "I've got to go. I have to go to work."

I stood and pulled at his sleeve. "Wait."

He looked down at me, his face sad. "I really have to go," he said quietly.

I nodded. I had blown this one but good. And no amount of bacon and eggs was going to make it better.

But a lesson had been learned: cheating on your sort-of-married boyfriend with your priest's brother can only come to no good.

Chapter 12

With just two days to go before the wedding, I finally found a dress and shoes and got Max off my back. I did as she instructed and went to Nordstrom, returning with a sophisticated black dress that defied Max's edict of "no black" and that had cost me a fortune. The outfit was stylish, not too bridesmaidy looking, and suited my slightly gone-to-pot beach-volleyball-player build. The day of the wedding, I went to the beauty salon in Manhattan that Max patronized. Although I had what amounted to a giant bouffant the likes of which hadn't been seen since Angie Dickinson played Pepper Anderson on *Police Woman*, I drew the line at wearing the diamond tiara that Max had bought for me and just went with big-ass, hooker hair. When I was fully dressed, however, I had to admit that the hooker hair looked better than I would have thought and I made my peace with it.

The day of the wedding dawned bright and beautiful, a vintage New York September day. I hadn't seen Crawford since *le désastre cafétéria* and until the rehearsal dinner the night before. There was so much happening at that event we didn't have a lot of opportunity to chat; I had to reminisce with Max's entire family, the Rayfields, and Crawford apparently had promised never to leave Fred's side because the two remained side by side for the entire evening. I loaded up on vodka martinis and pigs in a blanket and let Max's uncle Richard grab my ass during "The

Girl from Ipanema," so I had been a little preoccupied during the proceedings.

I don't know why I had blurted out that I didn't know whether or not I would go out with Jack McManus again; based on Crawford's revelation that things were moving forward on the divorce, I should have leapt into his arms and professed my undying love for him. But I hadn't done that. I had gone on a date and been vague about my intentions toward my date.

I would like to be able to say that I left my marriage to Ray unscathed, but based on my behavior the last few months, it would be hard to say it with any conviction.

Max and Fred got married at the chapel at St. Thomas, which was the same location as my wedding to Ray, but the similarity between the two unions stopped there. My wedding had been a small affair with only forty or so people; Max and her parents had invited just shy of two hundred and fifty people, while the Wyatts had more like sixty on their side. The Wyatts, come to think of it, looked a bit overwhelmed by the loud and boisterous Rayfields and stayed on their side of the church, staring solemnly at the altar.

The chapel is spectacular, with a long marble aisle and burnished oak pews. Max floated down on the arm of her father, smiling and crying. Fred, standing on the altar with me, Crawford, and Kevin, wept openly as he watched her approach.

Fred, despite his earlier assertion to me that he belonged to some kind of ancient Samoan religious sect, had actually been baptized Catholic, even though he had received no other sacraments. Kevin fudged some of the paperwork so that it looked like he had made his first Holy Communion and Confirmation, but he never really admitted to me just how much he had lied in order to make this church ceremony take place. I didn't want to know; the Vatican police are rough on heretics and liars. Despite a history of social justice, the Catholic church has been known to set a few people on fire or feed them to lions. So, Max, despite not having set foot in a church since 1987, in an effort to please her parents, was permitted to marry in the chapel and have Kevin officiate, even though he would probably go to Vatican prison if anyone found out about his subterfuge. If it had been up to Max, she would have eloped, but her parents wanted their only daughter to marry in the church, at St. Thomas, and in front of their few hundred closest friends. They got their wish.

The wedding reception was at a big catering hall called the Lighthouse located at Chelsea Piers, a mammoth sports complex on the Hudson River. The room, to Max, was pedestrian, and she would have preferred an edgier, hipper location. But when your father is shelling out six figures for you to get married, you get married where he wants you to get married and you're happy about it. She understood that. Had she gotten married in her twenties when she was slightly more headstrong, it might have been more of an issue.

Max, Fred, Crawford, and I arrived in the limousine about a half hour after the guests arrived, due to a picture-taking session in the chapel. We were held in the limo for a moment while the maître d' alerted the band that we had arrived.

I sat next to Crawford, who had thawed a bit since we had last seen each other. I attributed that to the short memory that most men have. Slighted women hold grudges much longer, in my opinion. I was a little happier now that we had polished off the bottle of Veuve Clicquot champagne that was in an ice bucket in the backseat. As far as Max and Fred were concerned, they were the only ones in the limo and they made out the whole way from the Bronx to Manhattan, a thirty-minute trip. That left plenty of champagne for me and Crawford, and we made short work of it, passing it back and forth between the two of us and drinking directly from the bottle since the limo company had forgotten to stock glasses. I'm nothing if not a classy dame.

While we were waiting in the back of the limo, I handed Max a lipstick from my purse. "Here. You might want to freshen up," I suggested. Her hair, which she had let grow a little longer for the wedding, was a mess, and she had a giant lipstick smear across her cheek. Crawford let out a little snicker next to me and I shot him a look.

She put on some lipstick, and smoothed her dress down. "Better?" she asked, turning to Fred and rubbing his bald head.

"You look great," I said and took the lipstick back from her. I didn't think I'd be able to reapply my lipstick; I couldn't feel my lips. I put the tube in my pocketbook and snapped it shut.

Fred stared across at me. "I forgot to tell you how nice you look," he said in his deep baritone.

"Thanks," I said. "You look handsome in your tuxedo."

Crawford piped up. "What about me? Don't I look handsome?" he asked.

"If you weren't an asshole, I would have sex with you right now," Fred said. "That's how handsome you look."

The maître d' arrived and opened the door to the limo. Crawford jumped out and offered me his hand, which I took. He helped me out of the car and steadied me as I landed on the curb, slightly drunk from the champagne and in the highest heels I had ever worn. He grabbed me around the waist. "Are you okay?" he asked.

"Never better," I said and put one foot in front of the

other as we made our way into the reception hall. I held on to his hand in a death grip. We stood at the bottom of the stairs that led to the dance floor and waited for our cue; both of us had done this before and knew the drill. Wait for the bandleader to announce your name, go onto the dance floor, smile, and then go to your table while the happy couple dances.

The dance floor was a raised, parquet affair, surrounded by railings made out of steel tubing. The seating for the guests was lower than the dance floor and surrounded it on three sides. The whole place overlooked the Hudson and the view was spectacular, the twinkling lights of Manhattan visible to the north and south out of the windows.

The bandleader called out for the matron of honor and I cringed. "And best man, Bobby Crawford!" he screamed and we made our way up the metal steps and onto the dance floor, still holding hands. After our appearance, I started off to the right, but Crawford pulled me slightly to the left. "This way," he whispered and we made our way to our table. We stood beside it as Max and Fred entered to thunderous applause.

The band struck up "More Than a Woman," by the Bee Gees. Leave it to Max to pick a song for her first dance with Fred that would center on how extraordinary she was. We stood to the side of the dance floor and watched them dance—the giant behemoth and his tiny bride.

The bandleader called out again to the matron of honor and the best man, commanding us to dance. Crawford followed me out and held his hand out. I took it as the rest of the wedding goers clapped politely for us. I'm not sure why people clap when the participants called by the bandleader take the floor; they're just following directions, after all.

"Get your hand off my ass," I said, as we assumed the

dancing position. Right hands together and up, left hands around each other's waists.

Crawford moved his hand up to my back and looked down at me. "Better?" he asked. "You only allow ass-holding during 'The Girl from Ipanema,' right?"

"Yes, thank you." In my heels, we were almost nose to nose. He held me a little close and I got a whiff of his clean laundry smell, hoping I wouldn't swoon right there on the dance floor. Pheromonally, we were very well suited to each other. "My priest is here. I don't want to look like a loose woman."

Crawford, in normal clothes, was handsome enough. In a tuxedo, he was spectacular—broad shouldered, tall, and sexy. I focused on the table of wedding guests that were in view directly over his shoulder and tried not to think about him, me, or us. One of the guests had a porto-bello mushroom on his lapel and that grounded me.

"Stop leading," he said. Max and Fred glided by, their eyes locked on each other.

"I'm not leading."

"Yes, you are," he protested and steered me to the edge of the floor. The bandleader called the rest of the wedding guests onto the floor and it became flooded with dancers. We were no longer the center of attention and that was good; fighting about who was leading in front of a room full of guests was not the right thing to do at a wedding. "Are we having fun yet?" he whispered in my ear.

"Don't whisper in my ear."

"I'm sorry. I didn't get the rule sheet before the wedding." He spun me toward the middle of the floor, nearly taking out two other couples. I hoped that his lack of rhythm didn't creep into any other aspects of his life—namely, ones that might include me in a prone position later on in our relationship. "What else is on there?" He leaned in and put his lips to my neck.

"No neck kissing," I said halfheartedly, almost defeated. "And no hair touching."

He put his hands into my coif. "Does this count?"

I nodded. "Yes," I said weakly.

"How about a real kiss?" he murmured in my ear.

My resolve weakening, I reminded him that my priest was in the room.

"So what?" he said, and kissed me.

It had been a long time since I had been kissed like that and I attempted a subject change. "Are you wearing a gun?"

He smiled lasciviously. "No, I'm just happy to see you," he said, harkening back to one of our old jokes.

"I'm serious."

He stiffened and we returned to our standard dancing position. "You are obsessed with the gun."

"I just like to know if you have it or not."

"Why?"

I shrugged, and stepped on his foot again; this time it was an accident. "Sorry." I readjusted my feet. "Who knows what could happen at this wedding? Samoans, Irish, a French Canadian . . . a full-scale rumble over fishing rights could break out."

"Yes, I'm wearing it. We're in the New York City limits. I'm required to wear it."

"Is Fred wearing his?" I asked.

He sighed. "Probably."

"At his own wedding?" I asked, incredulous.

Crawford didn't answer.

I looked around the room and picked out several cops. "So, we've got about twenty weapons at this wedding?"

He looked at me, a slight smile playing on his lips. "It would seem so."

I nodded, satisfied. "I've never danced with anyone packing heat before."

He leaned in. "And I've never danced with anyone who talks as much as you do."

I had never realized how long this particular Bee Gees song was, but it seemed to last well into the next day. Finally, the song was over and we were instructed to take our seats at our table. Max and Fred sat at a table at the front of the room, by themselves. Some clever veteran of the wedding circuit began clinking their champagne glass to get Max and Fred to kiss. They obliged, looking like they were about to devour each other. Much applause followed.

I found my seat and stood beside it, looking for the waiter with the drinks. Crawford came over and held my chair out for me. "Thanks," I said, and sat down.

Crawford took his seat beside me, his hand finding my knee under the table.

My usual steely resolve weakened by the romance of the event and my surroundings, I put my hand on top of his and gave it a squeeze, first gentle, and then hard enough for him to reconsider his decision. I looked out the window at the beautiful river behind the hall and decided that I needed some time outside. I asked Crawford if he would join me.

We strolled along the walkway that ran adjacent to the room where Max and Fred's wedding was in full swing. We stopped and gazed downtown at the lights of lower Manhattan and the beautiful Statue of Liberty in the distance, her torch ablaze. I knew that Max had compromised when choosing the location for her wedding, but at that moment, there wasn't a more beautiful or perfect place to be.

We stared out at the river for a few long moments, enjoying our time together, away from the throngs inside the banquet hall. I decided, after a few seconds of contemplation, that it would be the perfect time to ask about Ray's murder investigation. I thought wrong.

Crawford sighed. "Do we have to talk about that here?"

"I just . . . we haven't talked . . ." I sputtered. "I just want to know what you know."

"And you know I can't tell you what I know," he said slowly, in case I didn't understand. The way he figured it, we'd been over that point a thousand times. I didn't think it hurt to try.

"Did you talk to Terri and Jackson again?"

He stared down at me but didn't say anything.

"Well?"

He chewed on the inside of his lip. "If I tell you a little bit, will you back off?"

Maybe. "Yes."

"I don't think it's them. I'm more interested in the Micelis right now."

That's what I thought.

He put his hand on the back of my neck. "But you," he said, kissing me, "are to do nothing on that front." He kissed me again, a knee-weakening lip-lock that I was powerless against; I decided to go with the flow because I didn't know how long it would be until I got to kiss him like that again. "Understand?"

I nodded. I understood. Completely. But I couldn't promise that I wouldn't do anything with that information.

Crawford awoke to knocking. Confused at first, he couldn't tell if it was the banging in his head or someone actually at his front door. He stumbled out of bed and took stock—he had on boxer shorts and nothing else, his tuxedo was in a heap at the foot of his bed, and his head was pounding. He pulled on the tuxedo pants and buttoned the top button, half walking, half staggering toward the door of his apartment.

The knocking was unrelenting and matched the brass band playing John Philip Sousa in his head. "Hold on!"

he called, making contact with the edge of the coffee table on his way to the door. "Shit!" he said under his breath and grabbed his knee. He narrowly missed falling over his dress shoes before crashing into a chair at the dining table. Finally, he made it to the door without further incident and opened it. His wife, Christine, stood on the landing, half turned toward the stairs like she was about to leave. In her hands were the set of keys that she had kept after moving out of the apartment with the girls a few years earlier. "Wait," he said. "I'm here."

She turned and took a look at him, an eyebrow raised. "Rough night?" she asked, looking over his shoulder to see if there was anyone else in the apartment. She had a bemused smile on her face as she took in his unzipped tuxedo pants, bare chest, and bloodshot eyes.

He pushed his fingers through his hair and stepped aside to let her in. "The wedding." That was enough of an explanation. She had been to enough cop weddings to know what went on and how most of them felt the day after a night of celebrating. He left out the part about the four hundred beers and celebratory tequila shots; the odor emanating from his pores probably gave some indication of that.

"Right," she said. She hooked a finger toward the door. "Is Bea going to church in a limousine these days?"

"What?"

"There's a limo parked outside your front door. Did Bea hook up with a millionaire?"

He shrugged. "This neighborhood's gotten fancy in the past couple of years." He asked her to wait while he grabbed a shirt. He came back out a few seconds later, his pants zipped, wearing a plain white undershirt. He had taken a few seconds to brush his teeth and hair as well.

Christine was still standing close to the doorway, a paper bag in her hands. Sometimes, he forgot how small she was, a full foot shorter than his six and half feet, to be exact. And after all of the years since they had first met, he still found her beautiful, her short black hair, blue eyes, and pale skin exactly the same as when she had been a teenager. "I brought breakfast." She walked to the round table that resided between the galley kitchen and the living room and spread out some bagels, coffee, and a couple of cheese Danish. "Plates still in the same place?"

"I'll get them," he said, and went into the kitchen. Sleep finally released its hold on him and he realized that he had no idea why she was in his apartment. "Were we . . ." he asked, pointing between the two of them.

"Supposed to have breakfast?" She finished his sentence. "No. I needed to talk with you so I figured I would come down and drop off the girls. They're having breakfast in the coffee shop on Ninety-sixth. I told them that we'd meet them in about an hour."

He put the plates on the table and held a chair out for her. He took a seat across from her and opened one of the bagels, wrapped in paper and slathered with cream cheese. "I need this. Thanks."

She handed him a cup of coffee. "Here. Looks like you need this, too." She opened the wrapper that held her bagel and took the lid off the other cup of coffee. "How was the wedding?"

He took a huge bite of bagel. "Great," he mumbled.

"The girls said that Fred married your friend's . . ." She hesitated, blushing slightly. "Alison's friend. Max?"

He looked down and studied his bagel. "Right."

"Do you like her?"

He thought for a moment. "Max? She's an acquired taste."

She laughed. "That doesn't really tell me anything."

"How do I describe her?" He looked up at the ceiling, thinking. "She's smart, gorgeous, and adores Fred. That alone makes her suspect."

She took a sip of coffee. "Give Fred my best."

He nodded. "I will."

They sat in silence for a few minutes. He started to come back to life after half a cup of coffee and the bagel. He looked at her and smiled sadly, sensing a little distress beneath her calm exterior. Her eyes filled with tears.

"I have to let you go," she said quietly. She put her hands around her coffee cup and looked down at the table. "I can't do this anymore. I can't do this to you anymore."

He reached across the table and took her hand. He felt tears pressing at the corners of his eyes. "What do you mean?"

She swallowed and choked back a sob. "I'm sorry, Bobby. I'm not going to stand in your way anymore. I've talked with Father Kevin and told him to forget about the annulment."

He was stunned. "What? You don't want an annulment?"

She waved her hand dismissively. "Only if you want it. It doesn't matter to me."

He didn't understand her change of heart and didn't want to pry. He didn't know if she had met someone else and that precipitated her decision, and he didn't want to know. "Do the girls know?"

"I told them," she said. "They'll be fine." She took a sip of her coffee, more of a time killer than anything else. She wiped her eyes with a napkin and blew her nose.

"Christine, I don't know what to say," he said.

She gave a sad laugh. "Just say that you'll help me put them through college and everything will be fine," she said, smiling. "Meaghan's decided she wants to go to

Stanford, so unless she gets a basketball scholarship, you and I will be living on peanut butter and canned soup for the next four years." She turned the empty bagel wrapper into a ball and held it in her hand. "Just help me with that."

"Of course," he said, nodding. "That goes without saying."

She nodded. "I know it does. You always do the right thing, Bobby."

He let go of her hand and got up from the table. He went over to her and knelt beside her, putting his arms around her small body. She started crying, seemingly unable to stop. "I tried so hard to keep you, and you tried so hard to love me, but it just wasn't meant to be," she said, her voice barely audible.

He put his head on her shoulder and began to cry. "I'm sorry." He took a deep breath, a shudder. "You were always my best friend."

They held each other for a long time. He had tried to love her and, in a way, he did love her, but he had never been in love with her. And now that he was in love with somebody, he knew what that felt like and was sure that he never felt it with her.

She stopped crying long enough to get up and clean off the table. After years of attending to her father's needs, both at home and in the bar, she was always in constant motion, always picking up, wiping tables, washing dishes. He told her to leave everything. She turned and laughed. "Old habits." Christine had been a virtual scullery maid in her father's Upper West Side bar before marrying Bobby and escaping. Her nervous habits ran from obsessively wiping countertops until they gleamed, to washing the same stemware over and over. She came out of his kitchen. "You should take a shower. That will give me a chance to get myself together before we go get the girls."

He stood for another minute, stuck in place. Now that he had a chance to move forward, he didn't know what to do.

Chapter 13

I spent the night at Max's because it was closer to Chelsea Piers and I didn't want to face a drive home after a few martinis. I got out of bed and took a shower, using some kind of exotic shower gel and shampoo that came out of a dispenser shaped like a flower. When I was done, I got out and dried off, running into Max's bedroom naked and rooting through my overnight bag to find an outfit to wear home; I was determined to catch the 10:20 local to Dobbs Ferry and I had to rush to make it. I stood up suddenly and got a major headache—payback for last night's festivities. I went back into the bathroom and found some Excedrin, taking three and washing them down with good old New York City tap water.

Crawford and I had parted ways after the wedding with his vague promise to call me later in the week. A call was fine, but I knew that I couldn't see him again until his life was straightened out. I didn't think that bore repeating, so I gave him a kiss on the cheek and a little wave as I took off in a cab to downtown Manhattan.

I blew-dry my hair and put on a little makeup. I had dark circles under my eyes and my skin looked a little like parchment; I could practically feel the olives floating around in my stomach, vodka having replaced any stomach acid. I needed a strong cup of coffee and some food; a nap at home later would help round out the antihangover trifecta.

I put on a sweater, jeans, and a pair of boots. I packed up all of my things and left Max's apartment. Down on the street, the limousine idling in front of the building barely caught my attention as I wrestled with my bags and scoured the street for a cab to Grand Central.

When the back passenger door to the limo opened and I saw who was inside, I nearly collapsed on the street.

"Alison! Hi!" Peter called from the car. "Going somewhere? I'll give you a lift!" He waved me into the car with his little stubby fingers.

I stood on the street, a garment bag weighing me down. I thought about dropping it and running, but all thoughts of escape were thwarted when the driver of the limo got out, came around to the curb, and motioned me into the car. He took the garment bag and my small tote from my hands and waited while I got inside. I recognized him as the same guy who waited outside my house while Peter disconnected my phone line and force-fed me biscotti. Resigned, I got into the car.

I sat across from Peter in a stretch limo, my back to the driver's back. Peter took up a good deal of the bench seat, what with his wide ass and tree-trunk thighs, but I was compressed into as small a space as possible, afraid to move.

Peter guffawed. "You always look so scared when I see you, Alison." He apparently found this very funny.

"You scare me, Peter. You didn't use to, but you do now," I said as directly as I could.

He looked chagrined. "I hate to hear that." He opened a small refrigerator next to his seat and waved a hand in front of it. "Orange juice? Iced coffee? Soda?"

I shook my head. "No, thank you."

"How was Max's wedding?" he asked.

I had gotten over the shock of knowing that Peter

Miceli knew everything I did and every place I had been; I was actually becoming bored by it. I sighed. "It was fine, Peter. What is it that you want?" I asked, out of patience.

"Why didn't you ever have children, Alison?"

That question did shock me. Not having children was something that I had made my peace with a long time ago, but hearing the question come from him made me feel sad and vulnerable all over again. I decided to keep the truth from him—that I wanted children desperately but had married a man who would go to great lengths not to have any—and offered a noncommittal shoulder shrug.

"Every woman wants children, don't they?" he asked, studying my face for some indication of the truth.

"Some do. Some don't. I'm one of the ones who don't." Tears were pushing at the back of my eyes, but through sheer force of will, I kept them there. He had hit a nerve and, emotional terrorist that he was, he knew it.

He nodded slowly. "I see."

I stared back at him, holding his gaze.

He rubbed a hand over his bald head. "Well, as hard as it is for me to admit this, Alison, Kathy was pregnant when she died."

I knew exactly where he was headed with this.

"Cut to the chase, Peter." I lurched slightly to the right as the limo took a corner at a sharp angle.

He shot me a look, unhappy at being instructed as to what to do. "And as hard as it is for me to say this, Alison, I have become convinced that your ex-husband, Dr. Stark, was the father of Kathy's baby."

Now it was my turn to laugh. "Oh, no, Peter, you've got that all wrong," I said. "That's not possible."

In his expression was the apparent surprise that someone had questioned his judgment. Apparently, nobody ever told him that he was wrong. "I don't think so, Alison."

"Peter, Ray had a vasectomy while we were married."

He looked confused. "Why would he do that?"

"Because we didn't want children," I lied. Ray was the one who didn't want children.

It was Peter's turn to laugh. "Alison, nice try, but that's a ridiculous story. You don't strike me as the career woman type."

"What does that mean?"

"You know, career woman, all job, no kids. Not you, Alison. No way."

This guy was good. He could see right through my lame story. But how could I make him believe the truth: that Ray had waited until I left for a teaching position overseas, had a vasectomy, and never told me?

Peter leaned forward and put his hands on his knees, staring at me. "You're a terrible liar, Alison." He put a hand on my knee and gave me a little squeeze. "Now why don't you own up to the fact that your ex-husband was a sleaze and got a nineteen-year-old girl pregnant?"

I got a little panicky; we were treading in very dangerous waters. I looked out the window and saw that we were indeed heading toward my destination, but I knew that one false move, one transparent lie, and I would end up in the South Bronx with no way home again. Or worse.

Peter looked at me, his black eyes glistening slightly at the corners. "Cat got your tongue?" he asked, his voice getting hoarse.

"Here's the deal, Peter," I said, knowing that nothing was worse than an angry Peter Miceli. I decided to tell him the truth. "Ray didn't want kids, but I did. He knew that from the day we got married. I went to Ireland one summer to teach and he had a vasectomy. He never told me until we were getting divorced." I was babbling. Even

I didn't believe the story despite the fact that it was the truth. "It was a horrible betrayal. I'll never forgive him. For years, I thought I was infertile." I finished but wondered, at this point, did it really matter what Peter Miceli thought? Ray was dead and one of Peter's minions had probably killed him.

Peter watched me, his eyes narrow and dark. He took his hand from my knee and leaned back on his seat. He interlaced his fingers and let his hands hang down between his knees. Looking out the window, he suddenly exclaimed, "That's the most ridiculous story I ever heard!"

He was right. It was a ridiculous story, the kind that fell into the "truth is stranger than fiction" category. I let the tears behind my eyes slip out. It was almost as if Peter wanted someone to blame, and Ray was the most convenient person around.

"Is that the best you can come up with?" he bellowed. He threw his hands up. "That your husband had a vasectomy and didn't tell you?" He looked at me directly. "That is ridiculous!"

"It's not ridiculous, Peter. It's the truth," I said. I asked the next question, born of a courage I didn't know I had. "Is that why you killed him, Peter?"

He looked at me with a pained expression, but didn't answer me. He hit a buzzer on a panel next to his seat. "Where the fuck are we, Franco?"

Franco's disembodied voice flowed through the speaker with such clarity it was almost as if he were sitting beside me and not behind four inches of Plexiglas. "Thirty-second and Madison, Mr. Miceli."

He looked at me. "Where are you going?"

"I can get out here."

"That's not what I asked you."

"Grand Central," I whispered.

"Grand Central, Franco," he yelled into the speaker.

He took his finger off the button and looked at me. "I have to go back home to go to church. Do you go to church, Alison?"

"Sometimes." Hardly ever.

He pulled a cigar out of his jacket pocket and stuck it in his mouth. "Mind if I smoke?"

"Go ahead."

"They talk a lot about life after death at church. Do you believe in that?" he asked, pulling out a lighter and taking a few long drags on the cigar to get it lit.

"I'd like to." It would make the thought of my departed parents that much easier to accept.

"You should," he said quietly, puffing on the cigar. He took it out of his mouth and blew on the glowing tip to make it light. "Believing that makes things a lot easier." He looked out the window as we approached the Forty-second Street entrance to Grand Central, the beautifully etched doors beckoning to me, the inside of the building a sanctuary. If I could just get out of the car.

I wiped my hands over my eyes to clear my vision. I looked at him as we sat, idling, in front of Grand Central. He looked at me sadly, his eyes conveying some kind of conflict.

"If you just tell me that you killed him, Peter, we can all move on," I said. "Just tell me."

"I didn't kill him," he said softly.

"Okay, then, one of your people—"

"I didn't kill him!" His rage in full view, I concluded that this conversation should end and wisely didn't say anything else.

He pushed a button and the door locks popped up. I put my hand on the handle.

"Wait," he said, and leaned over again. He was calmer than just moments before. He grabbed me and embraced me, putting his lips to my neck. "It's okay that he's gone, you know," he whispered into my hair.

I didn't want to know what that meant, but I felt more confident than ever that I had stared into the face of Ray's murderer.

Chapter 14

I leapt from the car and onto the street, half falling, half running to the doors of the transportation hub. As soon as I was inside, I realized that I had left all of my luggage in Peter's car: my overnight bag with my clothes, my garment bag with my matron of honor dress, and all of my makeup. Fortunately, my purse was strapped crosswise over my chest and I had money and my cell phone. I turned and saw that the limo was gone, so I took a few deep breaths and collected myself. I smoothed my hair down and walked back outside onto the street, busy even for a Sunday morning.

I looked around, afraid I was making a spectacle of myself, but nobody gave me a second glance. I was just another New Yorker on the street.

My legs were like rubber as I made my way down the steep ramp to the main part of the train station. People were rushing past me, trying to make trains, and I realized I was standing still in the middle of the great room. I took a seat on one of the steps on the grand staircase in the main part of the terminal, trying to figure out what to do, when my phone rang.

I pulled it out and flipped it open, the device nearly flying out of my shaking hands. I didn't take the time to read the screen to see what number was displayed. "Hello?"

Max guffawed into the phone. "Hi!"

"Max . . ."

"I'm on my honeymoon!" she screamed. Technically, her honeymoon location was Bali and she was still in New York, but I wasn't one to quibble. "Did you have fun at my wedding?"

"I had a wonderful time," I said, scanning the crowd in Grand Central. She moaned slightly in response and let out a little breath of air, audible even over the din at the train station and with the crappy cell phone reception. "Max?" It occurred to me that while technically she wasn't yet on her honeymoon, she was still in the midst of her wedding night. "Are you having sex while you're talking to me?"

She giggled. "Sort of."

"Sort of?" I asked. "How do you 'sort of' have sex?"

All I got was another moan in reply.

"I'm hanging up," I said.

"Wait!" she screamed.

I stayed on the line.

"I'm going to be gone for two weeks."

"I know."

"I'll miss you," she said, and hung up. Max isn't one for sentimentality; hearing what I had to say in response would have made the conversation go on much longer than she could stand. I wasn't surprised to hear the phone go dead and mouthed "I'll miss you, too" into the mouthpiece.

I sat for another moment, considering whether or not to call Crawford. I decided against it. There was nothing to tell. Once again, I had been picked up by Peter Miceli, but this time, I had been dropped off at my destination. Peter had seemed pretty adamant in his denial, but then again, he was a professional criminal; he probably had honed that skill long ago. Was it easier to say that you hadn't done something when you had had someone do it for you? Or was he truly blameless in this? It was hard to tell. I had known Peter a long time ago, and even coupled with our recent close encounters, that wasn't enough to allow me to adequately judge his motivations.

Thanks to Peter's car service, I managed to make an earlier train than the one I originally planned on taking. Safely ensconced in a window seat on the river side, I leaned my head against the cool glass and dozed until I heard the conductor call my stop.

I got off the train and looked around; no limos. I breathed a sigh of relief. Without the bag that I had left in Peter's car, I was not weighed down and trudged up the hill from the train station in record time. Although I was sort of hungry, I was more tired than anything else, and decided to go home and crawl into bed for the remainder of the day.

I reached my street without incident and made the turn that would take me straight to my house. My legs felt like lead, but I kept my pace quick so that I could dive into bed sooner rather than later. As I approached the house, I spied Terri on her front lawn playing with Trixie. Trixie spied me first and took off down the street, bounding with unbridled joy at seeing me.

I braced myself for the inevitable Trixie love fest. She jumped on me and started licking my face, which, while not as lovely as being licked on the face by Crawford, was pretty damned enjoyable. I tried to keep my mouth closed because I drew the line at doggie French kisses.

Terri approached tentatively and commanded Trixie to heel, which, amazingly, she did. She sat patiently at Terri's side, watching me.

"Hi, Alison," Terri said in her breathy voice.

"Terri," I said, barely disguising my disgust at seeing her.

"Listen, can we talk?" she said, holding my eye.

"Do we have to?" I said, whining. I had almost made it home, I thought. And then this.

She looked disappointed and more than a little bit taken aback by my rudeness. "Well, okay, then. I guess I'll just say what I have to say out here."

I waited.

"I just wanted to say that I may have been just a little bit, you know, teensy bit, maybe, just a bit overly . . ."

Yes, I get it. "Little bit" would have sufficed.

She took a deep breath and regrouped. "I may have accused Jackson of doing . . . Ray's . . . you know . . . prematurely and unnecessarily."

A Dale Carnegie graduate she was not. I continued to look at her. "Got it," I said. "Jackson didn't do it. Not that you know of."

"Well, you know, the police came back again," she said, a little outraged. "They questioned us once and then they questioned us again. It was very upsetting."

Boo-hoo. I've been accused of murder, so I know it's upsetting. Something occurred to me, so I decided to ask her. "You didn't kill him, did you, Terri?" Feeling a bit peckish, I decided to push her buttons a teensy bit, as she would say.

The look on her face was one that I had never seen before. It took a few seconds before the rage that immediately registered in her eyes after my question softened into mild anger. "What?"

"You know, kill Ray. Did you do it?"

Tears appeared behind her thick, mascaraed lashes. "I'm going to forget that you ever asked me that and walk away, Alison. In case you've forgotten, I loved Ray."

Well, that makes one of us, I thought. I wondered how long it would take her to realize that professing your love for another's husband—albeit another's *former* husband—was really not acceptable in polite society. She turned and walked away, pulling at Trixie's collar. Trixie turned back one last time to look at me sadly.

I watched them walk away and looked at the fifty feet that separated me from the interior of my house. If I can just make it up the driveway, I thought, I'll be home free. I went in through the front door—the back door, which opened up into the kitchen, was still a bit of a roadblock for me—and stood in the hallway, gazing at the hall closet door, which sat ajar.

Hanging in the closet were my garment bag and overnight bag, the two items that I had left in Peter Miceli's limousine.

Chapter 15

I'm a big believer in napping to cure all ills. That is, when martinis are either unavailable or not appropriate, given the hour. I was out of vodka and it was just after noon, so a nap was the next best thing.

Although I was distressed that either Peter Miceli or one of his cohorts had been in my house, it was clear that they had only entered to return the stuff that I had left in the limousine. That was actually kind of polite, when you stop to think about it. If they had really wanted to cause me harm, they would have been waiting for me upon my return, right? That's what I told myself. So, after my heart stopped racing, I went straight to my bedroom, where I stripped down to my bra and underpants and dove under the covers, pulling them over my head in an attempt to block out the rest of the world.

I probably would have slept straight through to the next morning had the phone not started ringing at around five o'clock. Groggy from my five-hour nap, I picked up the receiver and held it upside down against my face. After attempting to speak to the person on the other end through the mouthpiece, I finally figured out what was wrong and turned the receiver the right way.

"Alison? It's Jack McManus."

Oh, boy.

"Alison? Are you there?"

I cleared my throat. "Uh, yes. Hi, Jack." I closed my eyes and lay back on the pillows.

"Kevin said it would be okay to give you a call. I'm at the Rangers' practice facility and was wondering if you might be available for an early dinner? It's not far from you."

How much more complicated could things get? I had a sort-of-married boyfriend who was a homicide detective, of all things (I was starting to appreciate my mother's decision to marry a UPS man—regular hours and no dead bodies); I had a gangster following me around; my deli guy wanted to marry me; my neighbors were psychotic; and now I had a completely available, gorgeous man interested in me. While I should have been jumping for joy, I was dumbstruck.

"Alison?"

"Uh, yes." I meant that response as an affirmative, that indeed, I was Alison, but Jack took it another way.

"You're free? Great!" His cell phone crackled. "I'm losing you. I'll be over in about fifteen minutes. See you then."

He was gone before I could make up some excuse for not going. Fifteen minutes? I studied my reflection in the mirror across from my bed. I needed more like fifteen hours. My hair was a virtual rat's nest and my eyes were bloodshot from a nap that went on about four hours longer than it should have. I would never be able to re-create the Barbra Streisand hairdo in fifteen minutes. I threw my legs over the side of the bed and hung my head while I straightened out my thoughts.

"Your boyfriend is still unavailable," I reminded myself. "You're not doing anything wrong." I got up and stood for a moment, trying to quell the feelings of guilt and paranoia that bubbled in my gut. My internal monologist is not a very good debater and even I couldn't convince myself that going out with Jack again was the right thing, or even a good thing, to do.

But I don't have caller ID, so I couldn't call him back to tell him that I couldn't go. And when I hit *69, I was told that his number was unavailable. He probably blocked it so that Kevin couldn't bug him about Ranger tickets constantly.

After brushing away the fuzz that had taken up residence in my mouth during my nap, I decided on my outfit. What does one wear to a casual dinner with a friend? I erased the word "date" from my mind and started getting dressed. I settled on a pair of jeans that Max had bought me and which I was sure cost a few hundred dollars. They sure didn't look, or fit, like the jeans I buy at Target and a quick check revealed that my ass had never looked better. I pulled on a clean T-shirt and a suede blazer from my closet to complete the look. I decided I didn't have the strength for the *Funny Girl* coif and ran a brush through my hair enough times to flatten it down against my scalp. After a couple of swipes of mascara and some lip gloss, I looked and felt better than I had just moments before.

I sat on the bed and was pulling on my shoes when I heard the doorbell ring. I stood and confronted myself in the mirror. Channeling my inner Max, I gave myself one last look and tried to get excited about going out with a handsome, single man, but again, all I could come up with was a feeling of guilt. With a side order of guilt. Would you like some guilt with your guilt?

Jack had a bouquet of flowers at his side when I opened the front door. And yes, he was as gorgeous as I remembered him. What was wrong with this guy? Why hadn't some intrepid female Ranger fan found and lassoed him? I had never asked if he was the Chewbacca costume–wearing brother, but it didn't matter. He was a catch, and I couldn't figure out why, at close to forty years old, he hadn't been caught. He had a big smile on his face and seemed genuinely happy to see me. I opened the door wide and let him in. We embraced awkwardly and I was grateful to have the excuse to get the flowers in water to break the hug.

Jack followed me into the kitchen. "How have you been? Have things settled down?"

I found a vase in one of the cabinets and put it in the sink to fill it with water. I didn't want to go into the more sordid aspects of my life, like how a chubby mobster followed me around and made vague threats to me, so I just shrugged and smiled. "Sort of."

"Kevin said that the wedding was nice."

I kind of had a feeling that Jack knew more about me and my situation than he was letting on. I'm sure Kevin had filled him in on the whole thing. "It was lovely," I said noncommittally.

When it was clear that he wasn't getting any more out of me, he turned to the subject of dinner. "Where would you like to go for dinner? You're more familiar with Westchester than I am so whatever you suggest is fine."

It was early so I suggested that we go to a popular waterfront restaurant by the train station. When we got there, only a few tables were taken, so Jack asked for one that had a river view. After we settled in and ordered drinks, we sat and made small talk. After a few minutes of conversation ranging from "who's the next Ranger on the trading bloc?" to "how about those Devils?" Jack became a bit more candid.

"I have to be honest with you."

Uh-oh. I hate honesty on the second date. I took a sip of my perfectly prepared martini and braced for the worst. I knew it. He was the Chewbacca costume brother.

"Kevin told me that you wouldn't go out with me again

unless I just dropped in. I normally wouldn't do that . . . but . . ." He stopped, looking at me sheepishly.

So he did know more than he had let on. "It's fine, Jack. I'm happy to see you." And that was the truth. I just knew in my heart that what we had couldn't go any further with the relationship despite my single status, his good looks, and my burgeoning attraction to him. However, if I let my hormones do the talking, all of that was bull crap and I would be making out with him by dessert. A little making out wouldn't be so bad, right?

Jack opened his menu. "What's good here?" He perused the offerings.

"The Crawford appetizer is wonderful."

He looked up from his menu. "The what?"

Damn. Damn, damn, double damn. I looked down at the menu. "The crawfish. The crawfish appetizer. It's great. Pretty much everything is great." I studied the list and gave some thought to the stuffed flounder.

"I presume you'll be having the rabbit?" he asked, a smile on his lips. He continued looking at the menu.

"Now, why would you say that?"

"I know a thing or two about French Canadians. And if I know one thing, they love their roadkill."

I raised an eyebrow. "They do, do they?"

"Oh, yeah. The roadkillier the better."

" 'Killier' isn't a word."

"Oh, yes it is. See *Ulysses,* page four hundred and three."

"I've read *Ulysses* several times and I don't remember the word 'killier' being in there."

"You've memorized the whole book?" he asked, daring me.

I shook my head. "Of course not. But I would have remembered a word like that. It's not in there."

He put his menu down. "Wanna bet?" He held out a pinkie. "Loser has to take the winner to dinner."

From his perspective, that was a win-win, but I didn't mention that. "You're on." I linked pinkies with him and pulled lightly.

He took a sip of his drink. "Messier and I used to eat at some pretty wild places when we traveled."

I dropped my menu. "*Mark* Messier?"

He nodded casually, resuming his study of the menu.

"The Messiah? The Captain?" Mark Messier was my favorite Ranger and the man responsible for the Rangers winning the Stanley Cup—the Holy Grail of hockey—after a forty-odd-year drought. Any insult I could have taken by his suggesting that all French Canadians ate roadkill was mitigated by his mention, and apparent friendship, with Mark Messier. And if Mark Messier ate roadkill, well, then by God, I would eat roadkill, too.

He looked up, giving me a sly look. "Impressed?"

"Just a bit," I stammered.

"Next time he's in town, I'll make sure we get together."

My heart almost stopped beating. Now he was playing hardball. "Really?"

He nodded. "Sure. We go way back."

Okay, I admit, he was a bit cocky. But he also had a jocularity and casualness that suggested the personality of a border collie. Border cocky?

He closed his menu. "I'm sorry. I hope I didn't offend you. Kevin always reminds me that I'm not as funny as I think I am."

And self-aware. The package just kept getting better and better.

I reached across the table and touched his arm. "No offense taken. If I had to be completely honest with you, I would have to admit that I ate my fair share of wild game on summer vacations in Quebec. I just didn't think I'd ever have to admit that to anyone."

We ended up having a great time and I wondered more than a few times how I had ended up in a situation whereby I had two men interested in me at the same time. This was Max's domain and I didn't even have her around to counsel me. We arrived back at my house in his car, and I turned to tell him what a great time I had. He surprised me by leaning in and planting a long, lingering kiss on my lips.

"Make sure you look up page four hundred and three in *Ulysses,*" he whispered, his arms around me in a snug embrace.

"You know as well as I do that I'm not going to find the word 'killier' in there," I whispered back.

He smiled before kissing me again. "So where do you want to go to dinner next time?" he asked, admitting defeat.

I pulled back a little bit, which took every ounce of strength and will that I had. "Jack, listen. Things are a little complicated right now . . . I kind of have someone in my life—" My protestations were cut off by a very long and very involved kiss that incorporated tongues, lips, necks, and a few other body parts. My God, I thought. I've just gone to second base on the second date. Perish the thought of what might happen after a third, and heavens, a fourth date.

"How about we do this?" he asked, pulling away, his face still close to mine. "Why don't we give this a try while you're waiting for that other thing to sort itself out?"

Completely flustered, I swallowed hard and pulled back. "I have to take out my garbage. Tomorrow's garbage day."

He looked at me, confused. "Is that a yes?"

That was my way of saying no, but I didn't know how to convey that without sounding like I was rejecting him.

"We'll see." I regretted saying the words the minute they were out of my mouth.

Jack's face brightened at my noncommittal response and he gave me another kiss. "Good night," he said.

I let myself out of the car and stood in the driveway, watching him drive away. I couldn't have fouled that date up more if I had tried. What did this guy see in me? What did any guy see in me? I looked up at the sky, now dark, and wondered about the laws of attraction.

I turned to go up the driveway and was startled to see Terri standing on her driveway. "Hi, Alison."

"Hi, Terri." I didn't know how long she had been standing there but I had an inkling that she had been watching my make-out session with Jack. I smoothed my hair down self-consciously.

"Nice car," she said, referring to Jack's very new, very expensive BMW. She started toward me. "A friend of yours dropped by while you were out."

I turned toward her. "Who?"

"She didn't tell me who she was. She said that you knew her husband." Terri raised an eyebrow while conveying that piece of information. I wanted to remind her that I know plenty of women's husbands, but the difference is, I don't sleep with them. "And she left this." She handed me a slim, cream-colored envelope. She waited, expecting me to open it, but I thanked her, turned, and continued up the driveway. Why in God's name did that woman think that we had anything to talk about? And, more importantly, why was she always standing on her driveway?

I went into the house through the front door and sat on the stairs in the hallway. I looked at the envelope, which had my name printed on the front in a beautiful, hand-written script. The note inside was short: "Alison, I hope you enjoyed the biscotti. Gianna."

I dropped the note on the floor as if it had caught fire. So, she knew about Peter's visit. If that was the case, she probably knew about him driving me to Grand Central that morning. Although the note held a seemingly innocuous message, it was clear to me that Gianna wanted me to know that she knew what Peter was up to.

And, I inferred, she was not happy.

Chapter 16

The next day I had two hours to kill, so I drove to the Fiftieth Precinct.

I was still processing everything that had happened over the weekend: the wedding, my ride with Peter, my date with Jack, the note from Gianna. My conclusion was that I needed to stay far away from anyone named Miceli or McManus.

Even though I knew I had to see Crawford to fill him in on what had transpired after the wedding, I still had myself worked up about my date with Jack. I tried to adopt a casual posture and expression so that when I did see Crawford, "I made out with a guy in his car last night!" didn't slip from my lips or broadcast itself from my rosy cheeks.

Crawford, on top of being great looking, kind, and responsible, is also extremely perceptive. His bullshit detector is more finely honed than that of just about anybody I've ever known. Nothing gets past him. Not revealing the previous night's actions was going to prove extremely taxing to me, I was sure.

Before I left for the precinct, though, I had taught my two morning classes, including the Modern Lit class. There was no sign of Ms. Podowsky and there hadn't been since I had run into her at the bookstore. I wondered if she had dropped the class. But for now, I had more pressing matters to attend to so I didn't drop by the registrar's office to find out.

I pulled my car up to the front of the building into one of those diagonal spots that I always had trouble backing out of. I figured if Crawford was there, he could help me back out without smashing into anything, such as a person.

I had never been to the precinct before and I was more than a little curious about where Crawford worked. I had been in another precinct earlier that year and it was horrendous; I couldn't imagine going to work in a place like that every day. The Fiftieth was a little bit better—a teensy bit, maybe?—and I took heart that he worked there instead of in a more dicey neighborhood.

It was an atypical fall day in New York when I arrived at the precinct, located a mile or so south of St. Thomas. Usually, the weather is slightly warm, sometimes with a chill in the air, and sunny. Today, the weather matched the precinct building to a tee—gray, dull, and dark. I went through the heavy metal doors and into the main area of the precinct.

I walked to the switchboard area where a very attractive female officer was manning the phones. Crawford had described his colleagues as fat, smelly, and definitely unattractive; Officer Gorman (as her name tag identified her) did not fall into any of those categories. And when she stood to greet me, I could see that not only was she not fat, she was built like a brick shithouse. And I don't even know what that means.

"Hi," she said, smiling. "Can I help you?" Gorgeous and friendly. Great.

"Is Detective Crawford here?" I asked.

She smiled again, still friendly, but this time with a slight curl to her lips and an arch to one eyebrow. "Sure. Can I tell him who's calling?"

I gave her my name and waited while she plugged a couple of numbers into the phone. "Detective Crawford? Ms. Bergeron to see you?" She waited a minute to hear his answer before hanging up, and then motioned that I should go up a flight of stairs to the squad room. I got a few feet away from the desk and heard her whisper, "You got it, Hot Pants."

Detective Hot Pants was Max's name for Crawford before she really knew him. I realized now that she had probably told Fred, and this little tidbit had made its way into the precinct vernacular. I wasn't sure having a gorgeous fellow cop of Crawford's knowing the name made me feel all that comfortable, but I tried to let it go.

Before I walked away, a ruddy-faced man wearing a short-sleeved shirt and equally short tie stopped next to me; he had been eavesdropping on Gorman's phone call to Crawford, announcing my presence. He gave me the once-over, lingering a moment too long on my legs. Gorman took notice and cleared her throat.

"Can I help you, Moran?" she asked.

"Is this the lovely Dr. Bergeron?" he asked, holding out his hand.

I was surprised that he knew who I was since we had never met. I took it and allowed him to hold it a little longer than he should have. "Yes."

He bowed at the waist. "Arthur Moran. I saw you on television."

Good Lord. And they say the ratings for NHL games are at an all-time low. You'd never know that, judging by how many people had seen me on television.

He pulled me a few feet away from Gorman and dropped his voice. "I've been working with your boyfriend on your ex-husband's case." He let go of my hand and pulled up to his full five feet seven inches, pulling at the waistband of his Sansabelt pants.

"Thank you, Detective Moran. I appreciate your hard work on this. I'm sure Ray's family does, too."

"I'm very sorry about the circumstances of his death,"

he said. "You know," he said, pulling me close so that he could whisper in my ear, "this has Miceli written all over it." He drew back and raised an eyebrow at me.

"Really?" I said. Since Crawford wasn't giving me any information, I decided that pumping Moran for information was the next best thing. "Do you think it was Peter Miceli or one of his men?"

"Oh, Miceli doesn't get his hands dirty anymore. Got to be one of his foot soldiers. Someone who's trying to get 'made.'" He gave me a knowing look. "Let's just say your ex was a little indiscreet and that did not serve him well."

I gave him a knowing look back. "Gotcha."

He kept going. "And, having a pregnant daughter who's still technically a teenager would make the most sensible father crazy."

So they did know. This was like taking candy from a baby. "I agree. So, will you keep working it until you locate the Miceli henchman or will it close?"

He crossed his arms over his broad chest. "This guy is in the weeds, so unless we can come up with something, that's a dead end."

That was unfortunate, but I wasn't surprised. I figured it was harder to locate a professional killer than someone who killed in a fit of passion or by accident. "So, my neighbors really aren't suspects?"

Moran laughed, a throaty chortle. "Nah. They never were. Crawford had focused on them for a while, but I told him he was wasting his time. Concannon is sick of using man hours for the case because he doesn't think we'll find the Miceli who did it."

"What about the other women that Ray had relationships with?"

He laughed. "We're still working through that list." The way he said it let me know that list was using up the most manpower.

He paused and shook his head. "Crawford's still working the Miceli angle. Hard. Man, he's thick," he said, pointing to his head with one finger. "Once he makes his mind up . . . oh, hey, Crawford!" he said.

I turned to see Crawford ambling down the steps from the squad room upstairs. There was a little hitch in his step when he realized that I had been talking to Moran and his mouth turned down into a frown. "Alison." His greeting was flat, not that I really expected him to feel me up in the lobby of the precinct. In that split second, I imagined that he knew all about my second date with Jack, even though intellectually, I knew that couldn't be true. I tried not to look too guilty as he approached and I flashed my best smile at him. I was happy that I had worn my slutty pumps and a skirt that fell just above my knees for him. Moran had noticed, but it didn't look like Crawford did; he focused on his colleague. "Moran. Don't you have somewhere else to be?"

Moran moved off; he wasn't that clueless. Crawford looked like he was going to wipe up the floor with him.

Crawford said hello to Gorman and then turned to me. "You weren't doing what I think you were doing, were you?"

I smiled innocently. "Just a chat with a new friend," I said.

He threw a look in the direction of Gorman who had busied herself counting paper clips. "She heard the whole thing." He took my elbow and steered me out of the precinct. We stood on the street, him staring down at me with a hard look on his face. "Is it that you think we're not doing enough to close this case?" he asked.

Aha, so that was the problem. It was less about me poking around for information and more about him wondering if he was letting me down. I decided to ignore his question and throw the blame back on him. I shook my arm free from his hand. "Listen. I came here to take you to lunch, but you're obviously in a pissy mood." I turned and started to walk toward my car, trying to put as much righteous indignation into my gait as I could. However you do that without killing yourself on a cracked sidewalk in heels.

He stood outside the precinct, watching me, until it was clear that I wasn't fooling around. When I beeped the key tag to unlock the car, he called out, "You're parked in a 'cruiser-only' spot."

I smiled, in spite of myself and my righteous indignation. I looked around and, indeed, every car there was a blue and white NYPD cruiser. And the sign right in front of my car indicated that parking where I did would end up with my car being impounded. "You told me the guys at work called you by your first name. Gorman clearly called you 'Crawford.' You lied to me." I turned and faced him.

"Apparently 'Hot Pants' is my new name." He glared at me as he closed the gap between the two of us and I felt two spots of pink in my cheeks. He leaned down and whispered in my ear. "I don't know whether to wring your neck or handcuff you to your bed and have my way with you."

I swallowed hard. "I don't know either."

He stared at me for a few seconds, apparently deciding.

"Are you done being mad at me?" I asked.

His reverie interrupted, he looked at his watch. "Have you eaten?"

I shook my head.

He walked back to the front door and called in, "Gorman! Lost time!" He walked back to me and held his hand out. "Give me your keys," he commanded, and instead of arguing with him, I complied. "Please," he added, the gentleman returning. He walked around to the passenger's side and opened the door for me.

He jackknifed himself into the driver's seat and fiddled around with the seat controls until he was practically sitting in the back seat. He pulled the car out of the spot and headed south. After a few minutes, he pulled up in front of a deli and wedged the car into a spot right in front. I got out and waited for him on the sidewalk.

The deli was warm and smelled like garlic. I was sure my next class of students would appreciate that when I began my lecture on Kerouac. The counter was on the right side of the deli, behind it the kitchen, and on the left side, a bank of booths. Crawford asked me what I wanted.

"What do they have?" I asked, my mind-reading skills not what they used to be.

He shrugged, still unsure of whether or not he was mad at me. "Food. Drinks."

"That narrows it down," I said. "Then get me some food. And a drink." I turned on my heel and sat in a black Naugahyde booth, wrestling myself out of my leather jacket. I didn't know if he was being oblique just to bug me, if he really didn't have a clue, or if low blood sugar made him disoriented.

He returned a short time later with two Cokes and a couple of sandwiches. He put them on the table. "Chicken salad or ham and cheese?"

"What do you want?" I asked politely.

"I don't care." He looked at me expectantly.

I took the chicken salad.

"Whew. I wanted the ham and cheese," he said sarcastically.

I took a long drink of soda and picked at the crust of the sandwich. After just a few minutes in the Fiftieth, I was unable to eat, having seen human flotsam and jetsam go by while I was talking to Arthur Moran. Watching Crawford eat his sandwich, I marveled at how inured you could become to such unpleasantness. He wolfed down half of his ham and cheese before coming up for air. He looked at me. "What?"

"You were hungry," I remarked.

"I'm always hungry," he said. "I never get to eat at regular intervals so I'm always a meal or two behind. You know that."

If I was supposed to feel sorry for him, I did. I stopped short of inviting him over for dinner because I knew what that would lead to: a burned pot roast and missing underpants. "I have to tell you something."

He started on the second half of the sandwich. "Go."

I didn't go for the preamble. "I took a ride with Peter Miceli yesterday."

He maintained his grip on his sandwich but looked up at me. "What?"

"Peter Miceli. I saw him again yesterday," I said.

His face turned hard again; boy, was he in a bad mood today. "He picked you up again? Jesus, Alison, you have got to stop getting in that guy's car!" he exclaimed, a little too loudly for the surroundings. A couple of diners looked up from the food to see what the commotion was about.

"What do you suggest I should have done?" I whispered, leaning in close to his face.

He looked around. "I don't know . . . run?" he asked, his tone patronizing. "You're tall, you have long legs. Hit the pavement and don't stop until you can't see him anymore. And if you happen to run into a cop, tell him that you're being harassed and have him shoot the bastard's nuts off." He looked chagrined, having lost his cool for a moment.

I ignored that comment and gave him the details of my conversation with Peter. "He told me that Kathy was pregnant."

"What?" He seemed surprised that I knew this detail.

I looked down at the table. "He thinks Ray did it."

I could see his mind working. He knew Ray was physically incapable of impregnating anyone—in my usual "reveal everything way too soon" manner, I had told him about Ray's secret vasectomy soon after we had met.

I looked away. "Let's do this another time."

He let that go and put the sandwich down. He wiped his hands over his face, clearly exhausted by everything. "I'm sorry." It took him a few seconds to form his next thought. "I worry about you."

It wasn't exactly "I love you" but it was close enough. I felt hot tears burn in my eyes. "I worry about you, too."

He took my hand. "I promise you that I will find who did this," he said. And for about the fiftieth time in our relationship, he reached in his jacket pocket and took out a clean square handkerchief. Crawford always has on a clean, white undershirt, and he always carries a nice pressed square of linen, seemingly for my use only. He handed it to me. "Listen, this is my last handkerchief. I'm going to have to switch to tissues if this keeps up."

I wiped my eyes and blew my nose before commencing with the story of my postwedding Sunday. I told him about running into Terri, too, and the note from Gianna. Although I wasn't sure what that conversation with Terri amounted to, I thought it was worth mentioning; I knew that Gianna's note was a warning to me to stay away from her fatso husband and told Crawford so.

He listened to my story while he finished his sandwich, and when I saw him eyeing mine, I pushed it across at him. He worked on the chicken salad and wiped his hands on a paper napkin when he was finished. He pulled out his notebook and a pen and started asking me questions. "Tell me everything you talked about with Peter. And Terri." I answered as thoroughly as I could and tried to hold my tears at bay, none too successfully. I didn't want to be married to the asshole anymore but I had never wanted anything bad to happen to him, either. Okay—so that's kind of a lie. I had wanted bad things to happen to him, only I wanted to be the perpetrator of said bad things, not some crazed Mob capo.

He collected all of the debris from lunch. "Please do your best to stay away from Peter Miceli. Got it?"

"Got it." I was relieved now that I had told him everything. "Thanks, Crawford."

He got up and pushed all of the garbage into a long, cylindrical garbage can by the door. We left the restaurant and stood on the street, facing each other under the elevated subway. "If I close this case, you'll owe me," he said suggestively, cupping his hand to my cheek. "And I'm bringing my handcuffs."

I blushed deep red.

"Oh, Jesus, I was just kidding," he said, exasperated. He held his arms out. "Come here." I walked into his arms and stayed there for a few minutes, drinking in his clean laundry smell; I didn't know when we were going out again, but I figured it would be a while until I got this close to smell it again.

I looked up at him and leaned in to give him a kiss but his cell phone rang, interrupting us.

He answered the phone and listened to the person on the other end. "Four-fifteen?" he asked. "Make it four-thirty. If I'm not there, wait for me, Alex. Don't leave. I'm not kidding." He waited a few seconds. "If you leave, Alex, I'll find you. And it won't be fucking pretty when I do. I'll kick your fucking ass." He looked over at me, again a little chagrined at the cursing and loss of composure. I looked down at my shoes. "Fine. Four-thirty." He hung up and looked at me.

"Good friend?" I asked.

"Informant," was his one-word answer. A train rumbled

overhead, passing by slowly. Crawford started to say something else, but I couldn't hear him because of the squealing train brakes. It sounded like "Christine," but I couldn't imagine what he would need to tell me about his wife. I pulled away and looked up at the train to see how long it would take before we could resume normal conversation; the sound obliterated everything else.

But when I screamed as the bullet tore through my upper arm even the train couldn't drown out the sound.

Chapter 17

When I awoke, I was on a stretcher and the big, giant face of Arthur Moran wavered in front of me. I waved at him, and tried to smile. Crawford stood next to him, peering down at me with a concerned look on his face, his hands on his hips and his gun back in the shoulder holster. There was blood smeared across the front of his starched white oxford shirt. When he saw that my eyes were open, he leaned in to talk to me. "They're taking you to Mercy. I'll meet you over there."

I was wheeled out and put into the ambulance for a bumpy ride across the Bronx to Mercy Hospital. I was in pain, but not as much pain as shock at the fact that someone had tried to shoot me. I think. I may have just been an innocent bystander, but even to me, that explanation sounded pretty thin.

Embarrassingly enough, my wound, a graze, was only serious enough to warrant ten stitches. From the way I had been crying and carrying on, and the amount of pain I was in, I was sure it was an amputation situation.

I was sitting in the emergency room in a curtained-off area, looking at the pile of gauze that wound around my upper arm. I begged the doctor for a painkiller and he finally relented and gave me a prescription for something called Vicodin. He handed me two in a tiny Ziploc bag and instructed me to take one now and one later. He then told me to fill the prescription at home, warning me not to take any unless I was in severe pain. Otherwise, I was to take Tylenol. I didn't mention that I take four Advil at a time when I have cramps. A bullet wound? Bring on the hard stuff.

When he had left the room, I swallowed both of them with a gulp of water from a flimsy paper cup.

I saw Crawford's shadow on the other side of the curtain. "You decent?" he called in.

I was rather indecent, truth be told, but I didn't think that was the question. I told him to come in.

"Ten stitches, huh?" he asked, and came over to survey the wound. The doctor had cut off the sleeve of my sweater to stitch me up, so the gauze was clearly visible. Crawford gingerly took my arm in his hand and turned it so he could get a full view. "I was expecting you to have a prosthetic arm with the way you were carrying on." He smoothed my sweat-soaked hair from my forehead. "Good news. We found the slug on the street. Ballistics has it now."

"That's good news?" I asked and attempted to slide off the bed. "What would bad news be?" The Vicodin was already taking effect and my legs felt a little wobbly. He grabbed me before I slid all the way to the floor. With all of the drinking I had done in the last several days, you'd think a painkiller would be a day at the beach. But I had the feeling that my body was filled with helium and that I'd float away if I didn't hang on to his arm for dear life. "Can you take me home or do you have to go see Alex?"

"Who?" he asked.

"Alex. The guy you were cursing at on the phone and threatening with an ass-kicking."

"Oh, him," he said, the synapses firing again. "I'll call him and cancel. He wasn't going to show up anyway. And then I'd just have to find him and kick his ass. I'm too tired for all of that." He looked at the wound again. "Are you in any pain?"

"Not since I took painkillers," I admitted, my tongue thick and virtually unusable in my mouth. I held on to him and walked through the emergency room and out into the parking lot. I didn't have a jacket anymore—it had been bagged as evidence, even though I wasn't sure what kind of forensics could be performed on a ripped-up jacket—so Crawford took off his blazer and put it around my shoulders. The temperature had dropped by a few degrees and I was now shivering, so I was grateful for his act of chivalry. He grabbed my good arm as I wandered off in another direction.

"This way," he said, and pointed to my car. He pointed the key tag at the car and unlocked it. After I was safely inside, my seat belt across my chest, he started the car and drove out of the lot and onto the highway. "Do you remember anything about what happened before the shot was fired?"

"I remember thinking that I love . . ." I started and then stopped. "The way you smell," I said, not meaning to say anything but hearing the words come from my lips. "And did you say the name Christine?" My head lolled to the side of the headrest.

He changed lanes and didn't respond. "Did you hear anything? See anything? Like a specific car? Someone suspicious looking?"

"I remember you telling me that I would owe you something if you helped me find Ray. And about your handcuffs. I stopped thinking after that. That's what I remember." I closed my eyes and ran my tongue over my lips. "What do I owe you?"

"How many painkillers did you take?" he asked.

"Two," I mumbled. "But they were good ones."

He pulled his cell phone out of his pocket.

"Aren't talking and driving against the law?" I asked.

He dialed a number and waited a moment for someone to answer. "Yeah, it's Crawford. Clock me out for the day. I won't be back in." He waited a few more seconds. "I don't know . . . sick leave . . . lost time . . . a vacation day? Whatever you want." He flipped the phone closed and looked over at me. "Do you want something to eat?" he asked, almost relieved when I said that I wasn't hungry. I had thrown up on this man more than anyone in my life— even my own mother.

We pulled into the driveway at my house about a half hour later. Crawford had been here several times and knew which key opened which lock on the front door, so he got out, opened the door, and then came back to get me, a virtual vegetable in the front seat. I took his hand and got out, a strung-out-on-Vicodin, high-heel-wearing college professor. I stumbled up the path to the front door.

"First thing we're going to do is take off those shoes," Crawford said when we got into the house. He sat me on the bottom step of the staircase, knelt in front of me and took off my pumps. "How do you teach in these things?" he asked rhetorically, holding up and examining my beautiful, black suede pumps.

I shrugged. "I don't know. I'm used to wearing heels."

"They're a little sexy for school, don't you think?" he asked, his eyes narrowing.

"You know me," I said. "I'm all about the sex," I said, trying to snap my fingers to convey a hipness that I did not possess.

"That's what I'm hoping," he muttered, putting my shoes to the side of the stairs.

I started up the stairs, holding on to the railing. I got into my bedroom and flopped onto the bed facedown, careful not to fall onto my stitched arm. Crawford followed me up and came into the room.

"Do you want to get undressed?" he asked.

I rolled over. "I don't know. Do you?" I tried to sit up, but the room turned upside down in front of me, and I lay back down on the bed. I put my good arm over my forehead.

"Do you want a glass of water?" he asked, leaning over me and studying my face.

I nodded. "You didn't answer my question!" I called after him as he went into the bathroom and ran the tap to fill a glass of water for me. He came back out and told me to sit up, handing me the cup of water. I took a long drink. "You should give Vicodin to your suspects. It's like truth serum."

He turned my face to his and kissed me lightly on the lips. "You need to get some sleep." He put his hand on the back of my neck. "If I promise not to look, can I help you get undressed?"

I sighed again. "You can look all you want. There's really nothing to see."

He stood. "That's what you think."

I lay back on the bed again, unable to stay sitting if he wasn't propping me up. "Crawford?"

He took off his jacket and threw it across the foot of the bed. "Yes?"

I decided to take a different tack. "What happens now? With us?" I asked.

He leaned against my dresser and crossed his arms. "What do you want to happen?"

"I don't know."

"You already know how I feel about you. I guess you need to figure out how you feel about me." He looked at me. "For all I know, you're still mad at me."

I tried to sit up again. "How could you know how you

feel about me? We had this whirlwind relationship for a few weeks in the spring that culminated in . . . nothing," I said. It had actually culminated in my broken heart, but he already knew that. It would do no good to revisit that. I was slurring my words, but felt pretty clear of head, so I kept going. "Do you even feel like you know me?"

He nodded. "I know you." He walked over and unbuttoned my cardigan sweater. He pulled the remaining sleeve—the one that hadn't been cut off—down the length of my arm and gingerly took the other, sleeveless half off, careful of my bandage. I had a camisole underneath it and he pulled that over my head. "You're smart, you're funny, you're beautiful . . ." he said, pausing to kiss me. He pulled me to my feet, reached around my back and unzipped my skirt. "You know the difference between a cruiser and a regular car," he said and kissed me again, "and you're tall. What more could I want?" he whispered as my skirt fell to my feet. "Oh, wait. And you're smart. A heck of a lot smarter than me, but hopefully you won't hold that against me."

"And I know for sure that 'killier' is not a word." Whoops. As soon as I said it, despite my drug-addled state, I realized that I was having the wrong conversation with the wrong man.

He looked at me quizzically. "What?"

I decided that mounting a good offense was my best maneuver. I put my good arm around his waist and tried to pull him closer. "Do you want to sleep over?" I asked.

He looked down at me and I could see his mind working. Finally, he shook his head. "No." He smiled.

I sat back down on the bed and attempted to take my stockings off by myself. "A little help, please?" I asked.

He helped me roll them down and pulled them off my feet. "This isn't what I had in mind."

"I didn't really expect that the next time you jumped

me we'd be on a dirty city street under the el, but we all adjust. What exactly did you have in mind?" I asked.

He sighed and turned back around to my dresser, not answering. "What do you like to sleep in?" he asked.

I told him that my pajama pants and T-shirt were hanging on the back of the bathroom door. The T-shirt was police issue, navy blue, and he had given it to me shortly after we had first met. He came back with them and helped me get my pants on. "What did you have in mind?" I repeated.

"Well, for one thing, you wouldn't have a Vicodin monkey on your back."

He had a point. I saw his eyes drop to my black bra and then come back up to my face. Thank God I had worn some decent underwear; when I had gotten dressed that morning, it never occurred to me that anyone would see me half-naked. He helped me put the T-shirt on and sat down next to me on the bed. He fished a small Ziploc bag from his pocket and handed me another pill. "The doctor gave me these. He said you could have another one to help you sleep." He put it in my hand and got the glass of water, which I drank down in one gulp after swallowing the pill. "I'm going to call Dobbs Ferry PD and get a car out front. Then I'm going to go home, put some things in a bag, and come back. Will you be all right for a few hours?" he asked, pushing a piece of my hair behind my ear. He pulled a piece of paper out of his pocket. "I'll also get your prescription filled."

I nodded. "What's the bag for? Are you staying awhile?"

He smiled. "I'll stay at least as long as the Vicodin doesn't wear off. When you're sober, you're going to change your mind about everything. I know you well enough to know that." He pulled the comforter out from under the pillows and helped me get into bed. He folded the comforter down across my chest. "Go to sleep," he said, kissing my forehead. He stood up, thought for a moment, and then leaned over me again, this time kissing me on the mouth for a lot longer than I would have expected, given our conversation. Although my lips were numb and my tongue was stuck to the roof of my mouth, I enjoyed it.

I drifted off to sleep, caught in that space where nagging doubt is replaced by unending hope.

Chapter 18

I awoke with my tongue still stuck to the roof of my mouth, but fortunately, in no pain. I turned to look at my clock and caught sight of a figure—Crawford, I assumed—framed in shadows, in the corner of my room. I smiled, happy that I wasn't alone, and fell back to sleep.

I dreamt of Ray. I don't know why, but he kept appearing, an annoying phantom, messing up my peaceful, drug-induced slumber. I kept asking him to leave but all he did was smile, hold his hands out to me, and disappear, only to reappear after a few minutes. Finally, in my dreams, I asked him to go away for good, and he did.

When I awoke, although I couldn't remember what time I had gotten into bed, it was dark in the room. My limbs were heavy and I stayed on my back with my head heavy on my pillow, my thoughts jumbled and confused. Still doped up on my new favorite drug, I fell back to sleep for a few more minutes, thinking about how I could con my gynecologist—the only doctor I ever saw—into giving me a refill of Vicodin.

I awoke to the sound of a dog barking. I reached across the bed to the nightstand and grabbed the clock, squinting to see the time: eight-thirty in the evening. I kicked the covers off and pulled myself into a sitting position, which wasn't as hard now that the Vicodin had worn off and I was more in control of my limbs.

I stood. My arm was sore, but the pain wasn't unbearable. I gingerly touched the covered wound with my good hand and was relieved to find the gauze dry and soft. I left the room and started down the stairs.

Crawford's back was to me; he was standing in the kitchen, looking down. When he heard me, he turned around, and I noticed that he was standing with Trixie, which gave me pause. Maybe I was still asleep. Trixie gave me a short "woof" in greeting and a big golden retriever smile: tongue hanging from the side of her mouth, drool pooling on my kitchen floor. Crawford looked at me, confused.

"What's Trixie doing here?" I asked, making my way down the hallway and into the kitchen.

"That's what I was going to ask you," he said, wrapping the leash around the knob of the back door. "She was in the backyard tied to a tree when I got back." He handed me an envelope. "There was a note taped to the back door."

I opened the note. The envelope was lavender and the note inside was, too; the paper was thin, lacy, and scented. It had the markings of Terri all over it. I read it out loud.

Dear Alison, thank you so much for agreeing to take Trixie. The move has been very hard on us, but particularly because our new accommodations cannot accept pets. I am devastated. But knowing how much you love Trixie and what good care you'll take of her makes us feel better. Terri.

I looked at Crawford. "How long have I been asleep exactly?" I asked, feeling suddenly like Rip Van Winkle.

Crawford stood and looked at me. "Long enough for you to inherit a dog, apparently."

"Where did they go?"

Crawford shrugged. "Not a clue."

I looked at Trixie. I did love her but I wasn't sure that I wanted to live with her. I made a couple of noises of protest but they were weak.

He pointed to a bag on the counter. "I don't know what she eats, but I went to the grocery store on Route 9 and got some dog food."

I pushed my good hand through my hair. "This is weird." I looked out the window at the house next door. "Do you think maybe they finally split up and went their separate ways?"

He shrugged. "Hard to tell. You think she was lying in her note that they went together?"

I didn't know. I started for the back door.

"Where are you going?" he asked.

"Next door," I said.

He put his hand on the door. "No you're not."

I gave him an impatient look.

"I already went over there. There's nobody there. It's locked, no cars in the driveway, all lights are out. They're gone." He waited a beat watching my face and recognizing that I had a joke that just had to come out, said, "Okay, just say it."

I let out a laugh. "They don't call you Detective Hot Pants for nothing."

He bowed at the waist. "Thank you."

I thought for a moment. "I don't want a dog," I said, almost whining. "And you can't take her. You're never home."

Crawford looked at me with his sad face. "You could always give her to a shelter."

I looked at Trixie, who seemed to be wearing the same sad face that Crawford was. "I don't want a dog," I said again, this time with less whining but with much less conviction. Crawford and Trixie seemed to sense my weakening resolve and continued to look at me with their pathetic faces. "Okay. She can stay. Until I track them down."

Crawford sighed, relieved. "This will be great for you. Dogs are wonderful. And Trixie seems like she's very special."

I sat at the kitchen table, contemplating the decision I had just made. I thought about Jackson and Terri. "We have to find out where they went," I said. Although I never talked to either of them unless I had to, it seemed odd to me that they had left without telling me. There had to be more to this story than met the eye.

Chapter 19

When I was a child, my parents, concerned that I was an only child, bought me a dog. "Dog" actually was a dubious characterization: Coco was five pounds, furry, and looked like a cat. But my father swore that she was a teacup Yorkshire terrier and really a dog. I had Coco until I left for college. She wasn't there when I returned for my first Thanksgiving break, having succumbed to a rare blood disease that had set my mother back three thousand dollars.

Coco wasn't a ton of work for me; she was walked four times a day by either my father or mother. Because in addition to being an only child, I was spoiled rotten and not expected to have to do any heavy lifting, so to speak. So, when I awoke the next morning, Crawford in bed beside me, snoring like a buzz saw, and Trixie licking my face, I wasn't exactly sure what that meant. After a few moments of staring into Trixie's sad eyes, it occurred to me that she probably had to go out.

I stuck my foot into Crawford's side, interrupting a long, wheezing snore. He sat up, grabbed for the gun on the nightstand, and looked around. "What?"

"I think the dog has to go out," I said, touching the gauze on my graze. Again, it was dry, a good sign. I yawned. "Can you take her?"

He lay back down and put his hand to his heart. "I forgot where I was for a minute."

"You don't usually wake up with someone sticking their foot into your side?"

He shook his head and rolled over onto his side. "I don't usually wake up with someone next to me at all."

That's what I wanted to hear.

"How are you feeling?" he asked.

I sat up and took stock. "Not bad. I think I have a Vicodin hangover, but other than that, I'm good."

"Any more nightmares?" he asked, rolling onto his side and putting an arm over my waist.

"Nightmares?"

"You don't remember?"

I shook my head.

"You woke me in the middle of the night because you thought Ray was downstairs. You heard noises. It was Trixie," he explained. "I don't think Trixie's ever been told to put her hands in the air."

I pondered that. Time to lay off the Vicodin. The pain had subsided to a dull ache and I had to pretend, at least, to be a little bit tough and deal with whatever pain the wound would deliver. The crying, fainting, and general kvetching had to be getting on Crawford's nerves. Hell, I was starting to annoy myself.

"We have to figure out where Terri and Jackson went and how I ended up with this dog," I said.

Crawford moaned. "Can we eat breakfast first?"

I rolled over and looked at him. "Of course we can." Did he remember who he was talking to? "I just think this whole situation is extremely odd and I want to get to the bottom of it."

He sat up and looked at the gauze on my arm. "Looking good." He threw his legs over the side of the bed and stood after a minute, naked except for a baggy pair of red plaid boxer shorts. Every other time he had slept over, he had slept in his clothes. I guess we were making progress.

"Nice boxers, Crawford," I commented. I lifted the comforter and was relieved to find that I was fully dressed. If we were going to be intimate at some point in the relationship, I at least wanted to remember it. I gave him another look; he had gotten thin. He was on the thin side to begin with, but since the last time I had seen him this undressed—in the spring—he had clearly lost some weight.

He dug into a D'Agostino's shopping bag next to my dresser and pulled out a pair of jeans and a sweatshirt, both of which he put on. "Why don't you get up and we can both take Trixie for a walk?" He pulled a pair of low hikers onto his feet.

Trixie bounded over to my side of the bed and gave me a look that told me I wasn't getting off the hook. I pulled myself out of bed and found a cardigan sweater in the closet that I could pull on over my bad arm. I slipped my feet into clogs. "Ready."

Crawford gave me the once-over. "You're going outside in your pajamas?"

"More disturbing is that I haven't brushed my teeth or hair, but what the hell?" I took his hand. "Let's walk this animal."

Trixie followed us downstairs and into the kitchen. I found an old *New York Times* home delivery bag to pick up whatever present Trixie left us and we headed outside. The day was bright, sunny, and pleasant. Crawford came out behind me, Trixie on her leash, and we started down the driveway. The sound of bagpipes came wafting through the light breeze.

"Is there a parade today?" Crawford asked.

I pointed to Bagpipe Kid's house. "No, the kid over there plays the bagpipes. Badly."

"How can you tell?" he asked. Trixie sat down on the driveway and looked over at her former abode. She whined softly and looked up at the two of us. "Everyone who plays the bagpipes sounds awful." He walked Trixie to the front of my house and let her stroll around, looking for a spot that suited her. After a few minutes, she squatted and took care of business. "Good girl, Trixie," he said, and scooped everything up in the plastic bag. He turned to hand it to me. "Here you go."

I stepped back, crinkling my nose in disgust. "What do you want me to do with that?"

"Put it in the garbage?" he suggested.

I took the bag between my thumb and index finger and walked back up the driveway to put it in the garbage can. When I came back to where Trixie and Crawford were standing, he handed me the leash.

"I'll walk into town and get us some coffee. Are you hungry?" he asked.

What kind of question was that? Of course I was hungry. I'm always hungry. "There's an Italian deli in town," I said, figuring it was safer to send Crawford to Tony's alone than to accompany him and risk Tony's wrath. "Go there. He's got espresso and cappuccino and muffins. Tony's. You can't miss it." I gave him general directions.

"Got it." He started down the driveway. "Do you think you can stay out of trouble until I get back?" he asked, calling back over his shoulder.

"I'll try," I said, and knelt down to rub Trixie's head. I watched him amble down the street, waiting until he was out of sight before starting back up the driveway.

I gave Jackson and Terri's house another look. There were still curtains hanging in the windows, and the lawn furniture—a leftover vestige from the summer—was still on the back patio. It looked like they still lived there, but there was clearly no sign of them. The minivan was gone and, apparently, so were they.

Something occurred to me. When Jackson and Terri

had first moved in, I remember him giving me his card. Something about "if you ever need anything." Yeah, I need you to leave me alone and mind your own beeswax, had been my first thought; I had been going through a particularly rough patch with Ray and was kind of cranky. But I thought about that card now and figured if I could find it, I could call his work number to see what the message was on his voice mail.

I ran up to the bedroom that doubles as an office. Ray had used this room mostly, but I had an old table that served as a desk with old checks, bills, letters, and the like strewn across its oak top. I rummaged through a bunch of the papers. "Oh, there's my diploma!" I said happily. I had been looking for that. I finally found the card, stuffed between a stack of my mother's old recipes on the right side of the desk: "Jackson Morrison, Graphic Designer."

Well, well. I picked up the phone on the desk and dialed the number. Instead of ringing two or three times before going to voice mail, it went directly to a recorded message. "Hi, this is Jackson Morrison. I'm on an extended leave of absence. If you need immediate assistance, please call Rick Felter, who'll be handling my projects in my absence." Click.

"Felter? I hardly know her," I said, cracking myself up.

So they were going to be gone for a while. I called again, jotting down Rick Felter's number.

I might just be in the market for some graphic design, I thought.

Crawford strolled off in the direction of Main Street, Dobbs Ferry, feeling better about things than he had in a long time. The circumstances surrounding his visit to this bucolic town were still frightening and disturbing, but he was happier being with Alison than living his somewhat safe existence in Manhattan. He rounded the corner and caught sight of the Hudson, glimmering in the autumn sun, and smiled. Everything would be fine.

He found Tony's deli right away and stocked up on coffee and breakfast food. If he knew anything about Alison, it was that she had a tremendous appetite, and if he didn't buy enough food, she would eat what was rightfully his. Her lack of appetite the day before was an anomaly and he wanted to make sure he was prepared.

Tony was a friendly guy who communicated in heavily accented English. He asked Crawford if he was new to town, and Crawford told him he was visiting a friend.

"A friend? In Dobbs Ferry? Who?" Tony asked, throwing four muffins into a brown paper bag.

Crawford hated small talk and didn't want to go any further with the conversation but didn't want to appear rude, either. "Alison Bergeron." Crawford thought he detected a slight hesitation in Tony's actions, but brushed it off.

"Nice girl," Tony said, turning and giving Crawford the once-over. "What do you do for a living, my friend?"

"I'm a police officer," Crawford said.

Tony turned back to the coffee maker but didn't respond. "Milk and sugar?"

"Black."

Tony turned back around and put the two coffees on the counter. He punched some numbers into the cash register and told Crawford the total. Crawford handed him a twenty and waited for his change.

Tony counted out the change and put it in Crawford's hand, grabbing his wrist. "Listen, my friend. You be nice to her."

Crawford pulled his hand away and put the money in his pocket. He wasn't sure what kind of response was appropriate so he gave Tony a steely look, one that usually had perps shaking in their boots. Tony surprised Crawford by holding his gaze as Crawford backed away from the counter and out the door.

So, Alison could count an elderly Italian deli owner among her conquests. He'd have to ask her just how serious she was with Tony before investing any more time in their relationship. He started down Main Street and hung a right onto her street.

His cell phone rang and he pulled it out of his pocket, looking at the caller ID: the precinct. He flipped the phone open and sat on the curb, his bag of food beside him.

"Crawford? Moran."

"Hi, Champy. What's up?"

"We've got a girl here, a St. Thomas student. Came in on her own; wants to help. Her name is . . . Julie Ann Podowsky."

Crawford waited through Champy's pregnant pause.

"Says she had a relationship with Dr. Stark," Champy said, and by the way he said "relationship," his tongue rolling around the syllables, Crawford knew what that meant. "She's a senior; broke it off last winter with him. He was getting kind of clingy, she said."

Crawford shifted on the curb. "Clingy how?"

"Wanted a long-term thing. She was just having fun, she said." He paused again. "And let me tell you something: this is a girl who looks like she knows how to have fun. I'm just saying."

Crawford didn't even want to think about that; his girls weren't much younger than Julie Anne and he told Champy so. "She's someone's daughter, Champ. Just keep that in mind."

"Will do," Champy said. "She's a big girl, too. She's gotta be six feet if she's an inch."

Crawford looked down toward the river and considered this. None of this was terribly meaningful to him; Ray had slept with countless women, based on what they had learned in the course of the investigation. "Where you going with this, Champ?"

"Guess what her hobby is, Bobby?"

Crawford didn't have a clue.

"Fencing."

Chapter 20

Medical technology has become so advanced that I only had my stitches for about a week. Okay, that's only half true: the wound didn't warrant them staying in any longer than that. After I got them out, I had a nice scar on my arm. Talk about street cred. I looked like I belonged in a girl gang. If girl gangs counted middle-aged college professors among their ranks, that is.

Crawford and Champy continued to work the shooting, even though, thankfully, it didn't fall into the "homicide" category. I really didn't think that I was a target for anyone and went with the "innocent bystander" explanation, but that even sounded thin to me. I didn't think any of the Micelis wanted me dead but what did I know about the mentality of any of those people? Maybe Gianna still saw me as a link to Kathy's death and wanted me gone. I didn't dwell on any scenario too long because I was convinced that I would drive myself mad.

Although Jackson and Terri's departure gave me great joy, I continued to ruminate on where they had gone. Nothing makes you look more suspicious than leaving town and not coming back. When I tried to think about where they might have gone I couldn't come up with anything; I really didn't know them. How do you go from accusing your husband of murder to recanting that accusation to disappearing with the lunatic? None of it made sense.

I had called Rick Felter at Jackson's office, but he was

as clueless as I was. And I was pretty clueless. He told me that nobody had had any idea that Jackson was leaving, nor where he had gone. He suspected that human resources might have more information but he said that they were especially tight-lipped when it came to giving out details. I thought about that and concluded that I would wait for Max to concoct some kind of lie about why I needed information about Jackson and his whereabouts. She works in a corporation and knows the ins and outs of human resources. But more importantly, she also knows how to lie better than anyone I know.

I lay in bed listening to the rain fall early the following morning. Crawford was working a day tour and then was with his girls for the day; I knew that I wouldn't see him for at least another twenty-four hours. Crawford had given up on trying to keep information from me. At this point in our relationship, he actually had started using me as a sounding board and tossed a few ideas my way every now and again. He told me that he wasn't entirely convinced that one of Peter Miceli's henchmen had murdered Ray, and wanted to look into Jackson and Terri a bit more now that they had done the highly suspicious disappearing act. Right now, all he had was that Jackson was well liked and well respected at work and that didn't really leave him with anything to go on. Terri, he said, was a blank slate.

I could have told him that.

Trixie was lying in the new bed that I had bought her and looked up at me, surprised to see me at this hour. I noticed that she had taken one of my suede pumps to bed with her and that the heel was chewed beyond repair. I gave her a stern look.

"Trixie, what did I tell you about eating my shoes?" I said, giving her a gentle tap on the nose. She hung her head for a split second and then looked up at me again, her tongue hanging out. She looked at me expectantly. "Okay, I'll take you out," I said, and went into the kitchen. Crawford had nailed a fancy hook inside the back door which held Trixie's leash and a flashlight for nighttime walks. I fastened the leash to her collar and went outside, realizing, too late, that I needed an umbrella.

Between the rain and the fact that it was a little after four-thirty in the morning, darkness enveloped the backyard. I switched on the flashlight and shone it on the spot where Trixie had chosen to do her business. I yawned loudly, looking around to see if anyone else in the neighborhood was awake. I turned toward Terri and Jackson's vacated abode and watched as a dark-clothed individual made his way around the side of the house to the back patio. Trixie peed quickly and stood at attention at my side, waiting to see if the person in the yard adjacent to mine was friend or foe.

I walked toward the hedgerow that separated the two yards and peered over the prickly shrubs. The person in the yard swung around suddenly and trained a very powerful flashlight on me, temporarily blinding me. I put my arm to my eyes. Trixie let out a loud bark, something that I had never heard; she sounded very, and uncharacteristically, menacing.

"Police, ma'am," the flashlight owner called out to me. He swung the flashlight to the ground and approached me holding out a badge.

I patted Trixie's head. "It's okay, Trix," I said, keeping the hedgerow between me and the cop. After all, I was still in my pajamas; no need to get arrested for indecent exposure. "What's going on?" I asked him.

He didn't respond directly to my question. "Is there anybody in this house?" he asked, swinging his flashlight in the direction of Terri and Jackson's house.

I shrugged. "I think they left. There hasn't been anybody there for several days." Trixie tensed again, and I rubbed the top of her head. "Why?"

"A 911 call came from inside," he said, a bit perplexed. "But if there's nobody living there, then that's impossible." As if to punctuate his puzzlement, he took off his hat and scratched his head. "Happens sometimes. The system gets quirky when it rains."

Well, that's comforting, I thought. I hoped I never needed a cop during a thunderstorm. "Did you look around?" I asked, the rain beginning to soak through my pajamas.

"Yep," he said. "Nothing going on. Looks deserted. I'll write it up but it must be the system. It gets quirky when it rains."

So I've heard. Well, I'll keep my eyes and ears open, I thought, not as content with the quirky-system explanation. I looked over at the house. It certainly seemed empty. I watched the cop amble down the driveway, spend a few minutes in his car, and drive away. I looked down at Trixie. "Are you done?" I asked, and she stuck her nose into my butt. I took that as a yes and went back inside.

"So, what do you think, Bobby? Bobby?"

Crawford looked up from the stack of papers on his desk and turned toward Champy. "What?"

"Diamond stud earrings. For Patty."

Crawford grunted. The precinct was quiet at five in the morning on that Saturday and he was hoping to get some of his paperwork done. It was another one of those Saturdays when he wouldn't be with the girls. Christine had taken them to an all-day swim meet somewhere in Connecticut, so he had decided to come in and do some paperwork in peace; once he saw Champy saunter in, all hope of a quiet morning was gone. "Good."

"Have you heard anything I was saying?" Champy asked.

"Not really," he admitted. "Did it have anything to do with fellatio?"

"No. She hates Cuban food," Champy said.

Crawford sighed. "Blow jobs, Arthur. Did it have anything to do with blow jobs?"

Champy smiled. "Guilty as charged."

"Then I didn't really miss anything, did I?" Crawford said. He stood and refilled his coffee cup from the pot next to Champy's desk. "Did you review the notes on the neighborhood canvass on the Stark case?" he asked, leaning back against the desk that the coffeemaker sat on.

"Nobody seen or heard nothing," Champy said. "It's Van Cortlandt Park, Bobby. Unless you had some middle-of-the-night lovebirds, or someone cruising on the down low, you ain't gonna get nothing." He smoothed his tie down. "I'm just saying."

"You're just saying," Crawford muttered, and made his way back to his desk. He sat down and looked around for the file for Ray Stark's case.

"Champ, who has the Stark file?" Crawford asked when he couldn't find it.

Champy picked a file out of a giant stack on his desk and tossed it over to Crawford. Crawford caught it before the papers inside came spilling out. He reread the interview with the fencer, Julie Anne Podowsky, and came away even more convinced that she had had nothing to do with Ray's death. He wasn't sure why she came in exactly, but he didn't dwell on that too much. Champy, on the other hand, saw her as a viable suspect and kept bringing her name up.

"So, what do you think about the diamond studs?" Champy asked again.

"They couldn't hurt, Champ," he said. "Does she like jewelry?"

"Are you kidding?" Champy asked. "She loves jewelry."

"Then that's a step in the right direction," he said.

Champy walked over to Crawford's desk and leaned down on it, hovering over Crawford. He dropped his voice to an almost-whisper, despite the fact that they were the only two people present in the squad. "Tell me. How do you get some?"

Crawford wiped his hands over his face and let out a loud sigh. "Some what?"

Champy shrugged. "You know." He wiggled his eyebrows up and down, signaling that the carnal conversation was still in full swing.

"I don't get a lot, Champy, so I'm probably not the right person to ask."

"You? I can't believe that." Champy snorted. "You're a big, good-looking guy . . . what's the problem?" He paused for a moment and narrowed his eyes. "You're not . . . you're . . ." he started, dropping his hand at the wrist.

"Gay, Arthur? Am I gay? No, I'm not gay," he said.

"I'm just saying . . ."

"Yeah, well, go say it somewhere else," Crawford said, riffling through the old file, hoping Champy would get the hint and return to work. Crawford kept his eyes on the file, hoping to see something that would pique his interest about Julie Anne. There really wasn't anything there; all they had was a scared twenty-year-old girl who thought her parents would find out that she had slept with a professor if she didn't come to the police first to give a statement.

Poor kid. She was scared to death. And she was under the mistaken impression that whatever she said to the police was kept in the strictest confidence, much like a confession to a priest. Champy had disabused her of that notion, making her the most frightened girl on the St. Thomas campus now. Crawford was sure of that.

Crawford's phone rang. "Crawford. Fiftieth Precinct."

Champy's voice came over the line, still in a whisper. "Because you know, you could tell me if—"

Crawford slammed the phone down with so much force that a piece of plastic flew from the receiver and onto the radiator cover next to his desk. The phone began ringing again immediately, and although he was happy to hear Alison's voice, he wasn't so happy to hear what she had to say.

Chapter 21

I went back into the house and called the Fiftieth Precinct. My plan was to leave a message with one of Crawford's colleagues; I was surprised to hear his voice, sounding cranky, tired, and exasperated. I hoped that my propensity for being involved in murder investigations wasn't taking a toll on our budding relationship, but it had to be getting old.

"Crawford! Fiftieth Precinct!" he screamed into the phone.

"Crawford?"

"Oh, hi. I'm sorry," he said. "It's early. Is everything okay?"

I described my early-morning walk with Trixie, the cop next door, and the 911 calls. "Is it strange to you that the cop just left?"

"That's a career-ending move if I ever heard one."

"What do you mean?"

"Well, in a couple of days, say you smell a suspicious odor coming from the house and the cops go in, only to find a decomposing body with a finger on the phone keypad?" he asked. "Trust me. The captain would fire that cop's ass for not following up on a mysterious 911."

"Gross."

"That's the sort of thing you don't blame on a screwy 911 system. That's the sort of thing you break doors down for." He looked at his watch and then at the stack of files on his desk. "Listen. Don't do anything. I can't come over until late tomorrow. I've got to pick up my girls tonight and I don't want to be late." He let out a loud, exasperated sigh. "Please don't do anything. Please."

"Okay," I said, hesitantly.

"Promise me," he said.

I waited a few beats. "Fine. I'll wait for you."

I am a lousy liar.

I stood in the kitchen, still pajama-clad, considering my options. I could wait for Crawford, but his estimated arrival time was two days from now. I could focus my attention elsewhere—like the junk drawer in my bathroom vanity—but that would only occupy an hour or two after I threw out all of the old hair twisties and unused mascara samples. The choice seemed simple. I would go and look around the house now, before the sun came up and Bagpipe Kid, faithful practitioner of all things requiring hot air and bellows, began his morning vespers.

I looked at Trixie. "Not one word of this when Crawford comes over."

She looked at me in adoration.

"Yes, I'm pretty amazing, Trixie, my girl, but you have to promise me. We must make a solemn vow."

She barked enthusiastically in response.

"I'm not kidding. Any Crawford butt sniffing or whining to indicate that I wasn't true to my word and we're done." She stared back at me, her head cocked to the left; it was the same look Crawford got when I made a joke he didn't get. I shook my head. "Shit. I'm trying to extract promises from a dog." I opened the back door. "I need to get laid."

It was still fairly dark and the mist had changed into a heavier, steady rain. Once again, I was outside with the wrong footgear (slippers) and no coat or umbrella; I attributed this lack of planning on failure to drink coffee before beginning reconnaissance. I tiptoed across the minefield of puddles and pools of mud until I hit the macadam of my driveway. I peered down to the street and was confident that the cop who had been snooping around had returned to Dunkin' Donuts or wherever it was that suburban cops went when there was no action (which was most of the time). I mused on this momentarily, wondering if I should cover my body in powdered sugar to get back in Crawford's good graces, and finally snapped back to reality when I felt the water flowing into my slippers.

I went into Jackson and Terri's backyard and approached the big picture window that exposed their family room, complete with cathedral ceiling and wide-screen television. And there, right where they had left it, was the parasol and toadstool wedding portrait. I shuddered when I saw it again.

They had a classic McMansion and I hated unoriginal architecture; I knew that if I could gain access, I would know exactly where everything was, roomwise. I put my face up to the window and pressed my nose against the glass, leaving a lovely nose print from which some crime scene investigator would be able to get a perfect match, if nose printing was a new form of crime scene technology. I hastily rubbed it off the window, leaving giant, albeit smudged, fingerprints on the glass. Besides the unorthodox and inappropriate outdoor footgear, I really wasn't prepared to be a peeping Tom.

After examining all I could from my position on the back lawn outside the family room, I ascertained that all looked well in that part of the house although I wasn't sure what I was expecting to find. I walked around the perimeter of the house and was unable to see into any of the other rooms; Terri was big on ornate, elaborate window treatments and they obscured my vision of any of the other rooms.

I went back around to the backyard once I was content that the perimeter was secure. I didn't have the clothing or ability to be a second-story man, so I walked far back into the deep backyard and looked up at the second floor of the house where, presumably, the bedrooms were located. Staring up, my face turned into the falling rain, I focused on where I suspected the master bedroom might be; a garden window next to a bank of windows suggested the master bath. It was only a flicker, a moment, but I thought I detected a shadow moving among the darkness of the bedroom. I turned to stone.

I remained on the lawn, my slipper-clad feet sinking deeper and deeper into the muddy sod. I continued to look at the window but didn't detect any other movements; my neck became stiff and I finally changed positions. I pushed my wet hair off my face and thought about my options for the second time that morning. I decided that calling Crawford—despite the consequences—was my best course of action. If the cop that had answered the 911 call earlier was any indication of the caliber of officer on the crack DF police force, I was in trouble.

I gingerly made my way back to my own house, kicking off my muddy slippers when I entered the back door. Trixie came running and took both slippers in her mouth, her tongue rolling around them like they were a fragrant and delicious foie gras. I called Crawford again.

"Fiftieth Precinct. Detective Arthur Moran speaking."

"Good morning, Detective. This is Alison Bergeron. Is Detective Crawford available?" I assumed that I was speaking with my old friend, the infamous Champy. Now I knew why Crawford was so cranky when I called earlier; Champy got on his last nerve.

"I believe he went to see a man about a horse, Ms. Bergeron."

Huh?

"The latrine, ma'am. He's in the head."

"Oh, okay." This guy was on another planet.

"He didn't take his newspaper, so I don't expect he'll be long."

Yuck. Talk about too much information.

"Would you like to hold?" Moran asked.

This would be a great time to get some information. "Uh, no. We can chat," I said sweetly. "What's going on with the case?"

He dropped his voice to a whisper. "Not too much. But we did meet one of your students from St. Thomas."

"Oh, really? Who?"

"Julie Anne Podowsky? Know her?"

Know her? Sure do. "Uh, a little." But I call her Miss Blurry Tattoo Ass.

"Came in on her own. Seems she and Dr. Stark were doing the horizontal mambo."

The what? Ohhh. I played along. "Really?"

"Yep. And guess what else?"

"What?"

"She's a fencer."

I think I had heard that once but had forgotten that little detail. I wasn't entirely sure what it had to do with anything, not really picturing someone hacking off someone's hands with a long fencing sword, but Moran seemed to think it had merit. Had he noticed that she could probably crack walnuts with her thighs? That, to me, was more compelling.

When I didn't reply, he spelled it out. "Swords?"

I tried to sound convinced. "Right!" I wondered who was going to tell him that foils and épées aren't sharp. But he sounded elated at this new development and who was I to ruin his good mood?

"So, anyway, that's where we are. Hey, can I put you on hold for a minute? I've got another call coming in."

"Sure." I sat chewing the skin on my thumb until Crawford came on the line, about thirty seconds later. He startled me with a gruff greeting and I tore off a thick patch of skin from around my nail, blood erupting on the surface. "Hi," I said. "Everything come out okay?" I asked, using a joke my father used to love.

"What?" he asked.

"I hope I didn't get you at a bad time." I put my thumb in my mouth and attempted to stanch the flow of blood.

"It's always a bad time when a special someone is around," he said, sotto voce. "If you get my drift."

I cut to the chase. "Crawford, there's someone in that house."

"And you would know that *how*?" he asked, irritation creeping into his normally calm voice.

"I went over there." I took my thumb out of my mouth and wiped the blood onto my pajama pants. "I didn't break in or anything. I just did a survey of the perimeter."

"'A survey of the perimeter'?" he asked. "Leave the crime scene talk to the professionals."

I rolled my eyes. Will do, Detective Pissy Pants. "Do you think I should call the Dobbs Ferry police again?"

"Uh, yes," he said, as if I were a complete moron. "I told you not to go over there, didn't I?"

"You did, but—"

"But what?"

"You know what? Go back to work. You're cranky and I can handle this myself." I sucked on my bloodied thumb again. "Call me when you're in a better mood if you want to know what happened." I began to put the receiver back on its cradle but heard his voice calling me.

"Wait!" he said.

"Can I help you?" I asked.

"I'll come over later. I'll bring the girls with me."

I looked at my thumb, blood still pooling around the

cuticle; this was going to hurt like a mother later. I hoped one of his kids was premed-bound because I'd be comatose from loss of blood by the time he got here. I walked over to the back door and peered out; the rain was still falling and the sun didn't seem to want to make an appearance. All seemed quiet next door as I half listened to Crawford blather on about the schedule of events for his day. I fixed my gaze on the door of the detached garage of Jackson and Terri's house.

". . . and that's if we don't catch any cases," he said.

"What?" I asked, realizing I had missed his entire monologue about a day in the life of Detective Crawford. Scintillating stuff. I focused on the window of the garage door, seeing movement behind the glass.

"I was just . . ."

"There's someone in the garage," I said.

". . . and that's if we don't catch any cases," he repeated. He paused. "What did you just say?"

The door to the garage began to rise slowly and I stood in the window, mesmerized by its slow and steady progress. A plume of smoke emerged from the car idling behind the half-closed door. "There's someone in the garage." I squinted in order to get a better look. "Someone's in that garage and the door is opening."

"Stay in the house, Alison, and just tell me what you see," he said.

But I had other plans. I hung up without saying goodbye and went searching for a pair of shoes, decided that I didn't have any on the first floor of my house, and stole my saliva-soaked slippers from Trixie's mouth. I ran back into the kitchen in time to see a small red car exiting the garage, slowly, in reverse. I grabbed my keys from the counter, letting out a little shriek as the phone began ringing—Crawford, I presumed—and left the house, running across the sopping grass of the backyard. I hit the key pad and unlocked my car doors, at the same time trying to get a look at who was driving the car. The rain and darkness conspired against my making an identification, so I contented myself with backing down the driveway at fifty miles an hour, hoping to catch the car, which had picked up speed on the straightaway of my block.

I spied my cell phone on the passenger's seat next to me and I turned it on. Moments later, it began ringing.

"Hello?" I said, making a left turn onto Broadway, keeping a safe distance from the red car. I'm sure whoever was driving knew that I was tailing them because when we approached Route 9 the driver ran the red light at the corner and took a hard left.

"What are you doing?" Crawford asked, none too pleased. "You're not doing what I think you're doing, are you?"

"Crawford, whoever this is, I'm not letting them get away." I sped up as we approached the light at the Stop & Shop and sailed through as the light went from yellow to red. I couldn't drive like Jeff Gordon and talk to Crawford, so I put the phone back on the passenger seat and both hands on the wheel. Ashford Avenue led straight to the Saw Mill River Parkway, winding through a residential and business area; I continued behind the red car, speeding along, hoping that I wouldn't lose whoever this was once we hit the highway. I looked at my speedometer and saw that I was going sixty miles an hour in a thirty zone and hoped that all of the cops were either asleep at the station house or getting their morning coffee. If I got pulled over I would (a) lose the driver in the red car, (b) get a hefty summons, and (c) be exposed as being dressed only in pajamas. I sped up and was now tailgating the red car, still unable to identify anyone at the wheel.

We approached the light at the Saw Mill and the red car surprised me by blowing right by the highway and driving straight, heading down the hill toward the next light and the center of Ardsley, the town next to Dobbs Ferry. I stayed with whoever it was, in the center lane, until the driver took a sharp right and headed toward the thruway. We headed south on the thruway, and the red car blew through the toll plaza's E-ZPass lane, not slowing down (as recommended) to the fifteen miles an hour posted. I did the same, not noticing the state trooper waiting for me on the shoulder.

I heard the trooper before I actually saw him. I had just passed the exit for Home Depot when I heard the sirens and looked in my rearview mirror. The red car sped up and pulled out of sight in that instant and I realized that the jig was up, so to speak. I drove a bit past the exit, slowed down, and pulled over onto the shoulder, banging my head on the steering wheel. "Stupid." I realized that my cell phone was still on the passenger seat and that Crawford might still be on it. I picked it up while I waited for the trooper who sat in his car, probably running my plate. "Crawford?"

"Yes?" he said, preternaturally calm. "Is that you, Lucy?" he asked, doing his best Desi Arnaz impression. Not funny.

"I just got pulled over."

"Big surprise." I could hear him sighing over the lousy connection. "NYPD or State?"

"State."

"You're dead," he said. "The only trooper I know retired last year. Where are you?"

"Stew Leonard's." I looked in my mirror again and saw the trooper sitting in the front seat, looking down. I could feel the sob starting in my chest and took a couple of deep breaths. "What should I do?"

"Cop a plea," he said and started laughing.

"This is not funny, Crawford." I bit my lip. "He's coming. I have to hang up."

"Tell him that I—" I heard him say before I flipped the phone closed and put it on the seat beside me.

The trooper tapped on my window, surprising me with the speed at which he had arrived, and I hit the roll-down button. He was a chiseled-jaw Ken doll, kind of cute in a plastic-doll kind of way, with intense blue eyes and, apparently, no sense of humor. His gun was drawn and hanging down by his side. To me, it didn't look like your standard traffic stop, but how menacing could a woman in pajamas be? Judging by his behavior, very. "License and registration, ma'am."

I didn't have either one with me and had to confess that.

"Step out of the car, ma'am."

I let out a little laugh. "I'm in my pajamas."

He didn't seem to care. The trooper stood next to the car, stone-faced, waiting for me to follow his order. When I got out, he asked me to place my hands on the hood of the car. The rain was heavier than when I had left the house and I was soaked instantly. The trooper began patting me down, and unlike my fantasies about being frisked, it wasn't exciting at all.

It was starting to dawn on me that perhaps I was under arrest.

Crawford sat on the edge of his desk, facing away from the squad room, eating a Krispy Kreme doughnut from the box that Carmen had brought him when she arrived in the squad a few minutes earlier. Champy had gone out with a young detective to interview a witness in a homicide from the day before and, once again, things in the squad were quiet. He hadn't heard from Alison in the last two hours and all of his calls to her cell phone went directly to voice mail. He felt guilty that he had laughed when she had sounded so nervous; it was apparent that something had happened since their last conversation. He ate the rest of the doughnut—his third—in one bite and dug into the box for another one.

"Easy, big fella," Carmen said, noticing his excessive eating. She was at her desk, typing a "five" at her ancient computer. "She'll call."

He swung around. "Where do the Staties take you for questioning?"

Carmen shrugged. "Don't know. Where was she when you last spoke?"

"She said that she was at Stew Leonard's. I don't even know who that is."

Carmen laughed. "Not who, baby. What." She stood and tottered over to his desk. Today, her sizable backside was packed into a pair of skintight black pants and four-inch high-heeled boots were on her feet. The buttons of her shiny red top strained across her bosom and she pulled the tail of the shirt down over her hips. "It's a giant grocery store in Yonkers. Right off the thruway. You know, right after the fifty-cent toll?"

"Right," he said.

"You think they took her in?" she asked, grimacing.

He nodded.

She exhaled loudly. "That can't be good. Those Staties got no sense of humor. And you can't reach out to them, they're so fucking insecure, thinking you're going to steal their collar or whatever." She perched on the edge of his desk. "What makes you think they took her in?"

"Well, she was speeding, she probably didn't have her license or registration, and God knows what she said when she got stopped. I think they took her in. You know how they are." Crawford worked on his doughnut, licking powdered sugar off his thumb. "I have no idea where they would take her, though. Any ideas?"

"Not a clue," she said. "I'll call Ricardo and see what he can find out," she said, picking up Crawford's phone and dialing her husband. She put her hand over the receiver. "His cousin Javier has been a trooper for the last couple of years. Dios mio," she said, fanning herself. "What a gorgeous man, that Javier. That man is built like a brick sh—" Ricardo must have picked up because her tone changed in an instant. "Hey, honey." She explained Crawford's situation, waited a moment and then hung up. "He'll call us right back."

Crawford finished the doughnut and took another one from the box. He held it out to Carmen. "Want one?"

"Trust me, Crawford. That will look better on your hips than mine." She put her hands on her hips and wiggled from side to side before returning to her desk and resuming her typing.

Crawford sat at his desk and ate the doughnut slowly, washing down the remnants of it with his sixth cup of coffee. He hoped the doughnut would absorb some of the caffeine in his system, not taking into account how much sugar he had eaten. He opened the Stark case file again and looked at the crime scene photos from both the park and Alison's house.

In the background, he heard Carmen talking on the phone in Spanish. He recognized a few words and determined that she was probably speaking with Ricardo and not on a business call.

After a few minutes, she said, "*Muchas gracias,* baby. I'll see you later." She pulled a piece of paper off her legal pad, the noise startling Crawford. She threw the piece of paper on his desk. "She's at the barracks at the junction of the Saw Mill and 9A in Hawthorne. Do you know where that is?"

He grabbed the paper. "I'll find it."

"Hey, what do you want me to tell Concannon?" she called after him.

Crawford stopped in his tracks. Good point. He turned

slowly. He had used up his "get out of jail free" with Concannon a long time ago and didn't want to push his luck. "I don't know."

She looked at him, her black eyes twinkling. "Get going. I'll figure it out. Maybe I'll give him a lap dance," she said, laughing. "That ought to throw him off. Hell, it will probably put him in the hospital." The phone on Crawford's desk began ringing and she went over and picked it up. "Fiftieth Detective Squad. Montoya."

Crawford watched her face for some indication of who it might be and whether he should wait. She held up one long, red-lacquered fingernail, indicating that he should wait. Finally, she held the phone out to him. "Alison."

Chapter 22

I sat in the barracks of the New York State Troopers, in my pajamas and slippers, looking like a sad homeless person who had been picked up on the side of the road. The only difference between me and a sad homeless person was that they probably wouldn't be handcuffed to the chair on which they were sitting. I sat in the room, alone, watching people go past the window in the door, hoping that I would recognize one of them sooner or later. My stomach growled from hunger, but it was obvious that I wasn't getting anything to eat in the near future.

I heard a loud voice, not unlike Crawford's, coming from outside the room and the door burst open suddenly. A short, pudgy man with eyes and coloring similar to Crawford appeared, his long-sleeved polo shirt half-tucked into khaki pants; he was swinging a beat-up leather satchel. He was Crawford after a whirl in a food processor—same features, but lost in the fat of his face. Everything was compressed and rearranged. "Hey," he said, holding out his hand. "Jimmy Crawford. I'm your lawyer."

"Hey," I said back, waving my uncuffed hand. "I can't shake right now."

His face turned hard. "They've got you cuffed?"

I pointed with my good hand to my cuffed hand, attached to the metal chair on which I sat.

"For fuck's sake," he said, and exited the room. Moments later, he returned with the state trooper who had pulled me over. The trooper knelt beside me and uncuffed me, without speaking a word. I didn't think he was so cute anymore. He gave Jimmy a look as he prepared to exit and it wasn't the "pleased to meet you" look.

"You ever hear of professional courtesy, son?" Jimmy asked.

The trooper stopped and turned to stand over Jimmy, at least a head taller. The scene resembled a terrier squaring off with a Doberman, but my money was on the scrappy ratter, aka my new lawyer. Crawford had told me that his brother was an experienced attorney and quite the legal mind. When I called him with my sanctioned one phone call, he said he would call Jimmy instead of coming himself, given the circumstances of my situation.

The trooper finally left, defeated that he hadn't even remotely intimidated Jimmy.

Jimmy turned to me. "Asshole." He held his hand out.

"Thanks." I held out my hand and shook his. I rubbed my wrist, a little red from the cuff. "Nice to meet you. Although not under these circumstances."

He sat at the table and pulled a legal pad from his bag. "What happened here?"

I started with the bizarre 911 call, the cop at the house, and my seeing someone in the shadows. I ended with the traffic stop in front of Stew Leonard's (shopping for farm-fresh eggs would never seem the same) and my being taken in and handcuffed to the chair.

He looked across at me, narrowing his eyes. "They say you resisted arrest."

I sighed. "I tried to get back in the car to get my cell phone. I wanted to call Crawford . . . um . . . Bobby."

He rolled his eyes. "That wasn't very smart. Trooper thought you were going for a gun. Although I don't know why." He wrote a couple of unintelligible notes on his pad. "You tell them about my brother?"

"About our relationship?" I asked, clueless.

He was still in serious lawyer mode, but he couldn't help cracking a smile. "Uh, no. Did you tell them that my brother is a cop?"

I nodded. Lot of good it did me to drop that nugget of information.

"They also said they got a call from the driver of the red car saying that you were following him or her. They couldn't tell which. Lousy Westchester cell phone reception."

I nodded. "I was following them."

He dropped his pen on the paper. "You're not making this easy."

"Did Crawford fill you in on what's been happening?" I asked.

"Sort of," he said, leaning back and running his fingers through thick, unruly black hair. "You were following the red car because you thought it was either the husband or wife of the couple who used to live next door."

"Correct."

"Aforementioned wife was having an affair with your late ex-husband."

"Right."

He looked at me. "And what were you going to do once you caught up to said husband or wife?"

It suddenly dawned on me what the situation looked like. No wonder I had been handcuffed to the chair. I tried to come up with an excuse. "Ask them if they wanted their dog back?" I offered lamely.

He rolled his eyes. "That ain't gonna work, sister."

I leaned forward. "All I wanted to do was find out who it was, and if it was Jackson or Terri, why they left, where they were going, and yes, if they wanted Trixie back." I relayed the story of the 911 call coming from inside their vacated house, too, but Jimmy still wasn't buying it. It didn't even sound true to me, and based on the look on Jimmy's face, not to him, either.

"The dog."

"The dog," I said, giving him a solemn nod. Sounded reasonable to me.

He drew a couple of lines on the paper and seemed to get lost in thought. After a few minutes of silence, he jumped up. "Wait here."

He left the room and me alone with my thoughts. Now, instead of just dragging Crawford into my increasingly sordid business, I was dragging members of his family into it as well. I had a lawyer now, and he was a chubbette named Jimmy who I hoped was much smarter than his appearance suggested. He clearly was tough in a street kind of way but I wasn't sure if that translated into book smarts. I had a city cop and a lawyer at my disposal but I couldn't seem to stay out of trouble. I licked my lips, chapped and dry after hours in this institutional environment, and waited for him to return.

He came back fifteen minutes later. "Let's go," he said, grabbing his satchel from the table.

"What?" I was a little confused by the sudden turn of events.

"Let's go," he repeated. He leaned in close to me and dropped his voice. "You've still got the speed, but I got the reckless driving, harassment, and resisting arrest dropped. You've got four points on your license and need to take a defensive driving course." He took my arm and steered me out into the hallway. "A little community service probably wouldn't hurt, either. Got any orphans around you could feed or make clothes for? Any nuns at the college need sponge baths?"

I kept my eyes to the ground as we passed the front desk of the barracks, careful not to do anything that would make them change their minds. My slippers made a shuffling noise on the hard linoleum. Once outside, Jimmy handed me a small plastic bag with my keys and cell phone. He had browbeat the trooper into having my car towed to the barracks and it was sitting in a spot right next to his minivan. I thanked him profusely for coming out on a Saturday, for not mentioning my pajamas, and for getting most of my charges dropped. "It was nice to meet you," I said.

He smiled. "You, too." He started for his car and turned when he reached the driver's side door. "Stay out of trouble," he said, chuckling.

The rain began to fall, a light mist that clung to my uncombed hair and eyelashes. "I will. Thanks again."

He stood next to his car, swinging his briefcase back and forth. "So, you're dating Captain America, huh?" he asked, amused.

"I prefer to think of him as Detective Hot Pants," I said.

He started to say something else, thought better of it, and looked at me one last time before he got into the car, a silver minivan with a car seat in the back. He gave me a wave as he drove off, merging onto the Saw Mill Parkway at the base of the barracks' driveway.

I watched him drive off, marveling at my luck at meeting a man who would not only bail me out of jail but who would enlist members of his family to do the same. I was just glad that it was his brother, and not his mother, or sister, who was the crack attorney. Women are far less forgiving of failings in their male relatives' lovers.

Even I knew that it was never good to meet your boyfriend's mother while handcuffed to a chair.

Jimmy called Crawford right before he and Carmen left for lunch.

"Your girlfriend's out on bail," he said, laughing

loudly. "They had her on reckless driving, harassment, and resisting arrest. That's the trifecta of arrests."

Crawford didn't think that was very funny but that was what separated him from his brother—Jimmy's sense of humor. "Thanks, Jimmy. How much do I owe you?"

"I'm just kidding. There's no bail. I got most of the charges dropped but she's got to take one of those moronic defensive driving courses at the local high school. Her and every teenage DUI in Dobbs Ferry."

Crawford felt the tension drain from his body, relief replacing it. "Thanks, Jimmy," he repeated.

"I gotta tell you, man, she's cute. Even in wet pajamas and without her hair combed. I can see what you see in her." His cell phone cut out momentarily. ". . . gotta stay out of trouble. The Staties won't cut her any slack next time."

"Jimmy, I owe you. I'll call you later." Crawford hung up and ran his hands over his face. Owing Jimmy was the last thing he needed; Jimmy had a lead foot and his other car was an eight-cylinder BMW. If he didn't have a brother with connections, Jimmy would have a suspended license from all of his speeding tickets, a fact that didn't stop him from doing eighty on the local highways. He turned to Carmen, still sitting at her desk doing paperwork. "She's out, Carmen."

Carmen took her hands, but not her eyes, off the keyboard of the typewriter and began clapping. "Can we eat now?"

"One second," Crawford said, picking up his ringing phone. "Crawford. Fiftieth."

The breathing was labored and heavy, the voice husky. "Crawford."

Crawford sat down. "Alex?"

"I got something for you, Bobby. On the hands and feet."

Crawford felt his pulse quicken. "Shoot," he said, picking up a pencil.

"Not on the phone." Alex sneezed loudly.

Crawford expected the stalling; Alex had been an informant for the last five years and was known for that as well as his inability to follow a logical thought from point A to point B; years of abusing his body had taken its toll on his mind. Crawford pushed the point of the pencil through the legal pad, agitated. "Alex, I don't have that kind of time. Help me out here. Give me something."

Alex sneezed again. "I'm real sick, man. I've been hiding. I've been outside for a while."

"When I see you, I'll buy you lunch. But give me something to make me come out, Alex." Crawford heard the squeal of train brakes and suspected that he was in front of Maloney's on Broadway, his favorite spot to panhandle. "Why have you been hiding?"

"I'm scared, man. I saw the hands and feet."

"Where? What did you see?"

Alex coughed and mumbled something Crawford couldn't understand.

"What do you have for me, Alex?"

"Well, the guy who got killed was a college professor at St. Thomas."

Crawford rolled his eyes. "I know, Alex. I read the papers. I'm working the case. I saw the body."

Alex dropped his voice to a whisper. "I saw the guy who threw them away. He was with a blond lady. She was little."

Crawford sat up straighter. "What did the blond lady look like?"

Alex paused. "She may have been blond. She might have been a brunette. It was hard to tell. It was dark."

Crawford slumped in his chair.

"Actually, it might not have been a lady at all."

"Don't fuck with me, Alex. What did you see?"

"I'm not sure." He coughed loudly. "I'm real sick, Bobby. I think I have a fever."

Crawford stood. "Where are you?"

"In front of Maloney's."

Bingo. "I'll be over in a few minutes. We can go to the drugstore and get whatever you need. Wait for me, Alex." He hung up and stood. "Let's go, Carmen. We're going to have a guest for lunch."

Carmen frowned. "Oh, Bobby. How we gonna make out if someone else is there?"

They headed over to Broadway and 242nd Street. There was a fifty-fifty chance that Alex would be there and Crawford preferred to take the "glass is half full" approach. Carmen was dubious. When they pulled up in front of Maloney's, there was no sign of their sick, drugged-out informant.

Carmen held out her hand. "That'll be five dollars, Mr. Man."

Crawford got out of the car and looked around. He never worried about Alex; although his word wasn't rock solid, Crawford could tell that he was counting on him for a few bucks and a meal. Alex didn't pass up the opportunity for money or food, and would even make up information just to get both. He put his hands on his hips and looked down at the pavement.

Something wasn't right.

Chapter 23

I went home and took a shower, hoping to wash the day's unpleasantness off along with the mud that had pooled in my slippers and on my feet. I threw the slippers into the bathroom garbage can and took my clothes off, marveling at just how horrendous I looked after my little adventure.

Thank God for Jimmy Crawford. I didn't think going back to school and having to confess to Kevin and Sister Mary that I almost had gotten a criminal record was such a good idea. Reckless driving I could handle, but harassment? Resisting arrest? Those two charges were for real criminals, not for nerdy, rule-following college professors.

I didn't know where this newfound bravado came from or what had possessed me to follow the red car. The car was not one of Jackson's or Terri's; she had a minivan—in preparation for their future spawn, I suppose—and he had an old Nissan Sentra, what we around these parts called a "station car." Everyone who commuted via the railroad had an old junker that they drove the few miles to the station. The red car wasn't theirs. But whose was it?

After my shower, I called Crawford's cell. He picked up after a few rings. "I hope I'm not getting you at a bad time."

"I'm in a Dumpster behind Maloney's. It's not a great time."

Curious. "What are you . . ." Never mind, I thought. "First, thanks for sending your brother. He got me out."

"He told me. You're welcome."

"Second, I thought we should run the plate on the red car. I got the license plate number."

"I'm up to my knees in garbage right now, so maybe we should have this conversation later?" He sounded winded and more than a little perturbed.

I sat down on my bed, drying my hair with a towel. "Do you want to call me when you get back to the precinct?"

"What I want to do is get out of this Dumpster, have lunch, go home, and forget this day ever happened."

Well, alrighty then. "Give me a call later," I said, hanging up. Instead of focusing on Crawford's crabby demeanor, I thought about all of the mysteries I was now involved in: who killed Ray? Who shot me? Where did Terri and Jackson go? And did they have anything to do with each other?

I decided that I wouldn't be able to think clearly until I ate something.

I ended up at the diner in town, one of my favorite hangouts. I figured that if I was going to become an amateur sleuth, I needed a greasy spoon to hang out in where everyone knew my name. Although it had been a hundred years since I had read a Nancy Drew book, I was sure she had a hangout. I remembered that she had a sporty coupe and I vowed to buy myself one of those. Maybe having a sporty coupe would mitigate the fact that no matter how many times I went to the diner, nobody ever remembered me, so I always sat at the counter, slightly dejected that I was that unmemorable.

"Help you?" a young waitress asked, approaching me in my usual spot. Her pencil was poised above her pad, awaiting my order.

"Cheeseburger deluxe and a chocolate milk shake," I said. If the ten thousand calories I was about to consume didn't wipe away the memories of my arrest, I didn't know what would.

"Is that all?" she asked, more out of habit than curiosity.

"I should hope so," I said, cracking myself up. When I didn't get a reaction, I replied, "Yes, thank you."

I stared at the refrigerated case in front of me, elaborately frosted cakes stacked on the shelves. I looked at each one, thinking that I would finish the meal off with a big, gooey piece of chocolate mousse cake. After all, I had been shot at and arrested. I needed something to take the edge off, and I had flushed all of my remaining Vicodin down the toilet. I thought chocolate would be the next best thing. A shape appeared behind my reflection in the glass, and judging by its silhouette—that of a bowling ball—I knew immediately who it was.

I didn't turn around. "Hello, Peter."

He put his hands on my shoulders and squeezed. "Expecting anyone or dining alone?" I didn't answer, so he took the seat to my left. "This is a coincidence, huh?" he said.

I refused to make eye contact with him. "It certainly is." I pulled a napkin out of the holder in front of me and wiped my upper lip. "Do you often come to Dobbs Ferry for diner food?"

"Nothing like a good Greek diner." The waitress approached him and he ordered a cup of coffee.

I told the waitress to cancel my order and threw a ten down on the counter for her trouble. I had lost my appetite but, for some reason unknown to me, I wasn't afraid. Annoyed, yes. But afraid? Not anymore. I knew that Peter wasn't going to hurt me. I was convinced that he had killed Ray and that that had been his ultimate goal all along. I didn't know why he had come; perhaps he wanted congratulations on the murder? Were we finally even? I stood.

Peter grabbed my arm. "Sit, Alison."

"Leave me alone, Peter," I said through my teeth.

He pulled on my arm. "Sit," he said, this time more forcefully.

I looked around the restaurant, not knowing what I was hoping to see. A police officer on a break? Someone I knew? Now would be a good time for Detectives Hardin or Madden, or both, to grab a cup of coffee, I thought. But that didn't seem to be a possibility and I finally relented, sitting back down on the stool. I leaned in close to Peter, with courage born of a near-death experience, jail time, and a peripheral involvement with too many murders. "Peter, I'm only going to say this once. Leave me alone."

I wasn't entirely surprised when he burst out laughing. "You are not a tough broad, Alison. No matter what you think." His coffee arrived, some of it slopping over onto the saucer. He took the cup and dumped the residue on the saucer into it. He set about adding three sugars and a hefty dollop of cream from the metal pitcher on the counter. After a couple of sips, he turned back to me. "I just wanted to tell you that I have come to the conclusion that Dr. Stark was probably not the father of Kathy's baby."

"Then you must feel really bad about murdering him," I spat out.

He looked surprised. "I didn't murder him, Alison." I started to get up, but he pulled me back onto the stool. He put his hand on my knee, his attempt to keep me seated.

"God, Peter. You must think I'm a moron."

He shook his head. "Someone got to him before—"

"Before what? Before you could?" I asked.

He shook his head. "God knows, Alison, I had a few

reasons to kill him. Of course, for Kathy, and then for the way he treated you. But I didn't have anything to do with it. So, I'm here to pay my respects. For your loss."

"For the way *he* treated me? Why would you care about that?" I snapped. "And what about the way you've treated me? You've kidnapped me, threatened to kill my best friend and my ex-husband, had him killed for all I know, and broke into my house not once," I said, my voice getting loud, "not twice, but three times!" I jabbed his chest with my index finger. I took a deep breath and brought my voice back to its normal timbre. "I'd take a philanderer any day of the week over your brand of chivalry, Peter."

Peter moved back a little bit on his stool and regarded me, only slightly amused. "Well." He took another sip of his coffee. "I like you, Alison. I always have. Maybe too much. At least that's what my wife says." He looked down, almost ashamed at the admission. "But I'm afraid that this must be good-bye."

"God, if only," I said, turning back around on my stool to face the dessert case again. I put my hands on either side of my face and looked down, my eyes closed. "Please, Peter. Please leave me alone. We have nothing to bind us anymore. Not Kathy, not the case, not Ray. They're gone and the case is over." I removed his hand from my knee. In the brief instant where our fingers touched, he wrapped his around mine and squeezed. "We may meet again when I testify against you in the trial for Ray's murder, but if they don't get you, then we'll never have to see each other again."

He looked sad. "You never understood what I was about. I wanted to help you. I wanted to pay you back for all of your help. For solving Kathy's murder. I wanted to put us all out of our misery."

"I always understood what you were about, even in

college. You're about intimidation and hurting people. You're about 'the family.' You are the most despicable person I've ever met." When I thought about how he had probably killed Ray, I felt tears pressing at the backs of my eyes, a lump growing in my throat. "You kill people. You killed Ray. And God knows who else. I hope you rot in hell."

He studied my face for a minute before putting his hand behind my head and pulling me close. He surprised me by tilting his head and putting his lips on mine, holding them there for several long seconds. The kiss was gentle, not grotesque, and nauseating all at the same time. Anybody watching us would have seen two people engaged in a tender yet passionate kiss, a couple who had to show their love for each other.

I pulled back from him and let the tears flow freely. I looked around to see if anyone was watching us, but nobody was. It was as if we didn't exist and nothing had happened. My lips were numb and I hoped they would stay that way. Peter caressed my cheek and looked at me sadly until I finally broke his gaze and looked away. I took a bunch of napkins from the holder and placed them over my eyes, trying to compose myself; I was shaking with anger, but the sobs were from sadness. After a few minutes, I took the napkins off and looked around.

Peter was gone.

Chapter 24

Before going home, I stopped in at the local pharmacy and bought the biggest bottle of Listerine that I could carry. The memory of Peter Miceli lingered on my lips and I thought some noxious, alcohol-based mouthwash was precisely what the doctor ordered.

I wended my way home, feeling a little nauseous. If Gianna didn't like that Peter had brought me biscotti, what would she say if she found out that we had kissed? I didn't even want to entertain the thought of how she would react. I flashed back to the destruction she had wrought at Maloney's all those years ago and shuddered.

I walked up the driveway and was just about to enter the house when a voice called out my name.

"Hi, Mrs. Bergerson!"

I turned and looked across the street and saw a strapping young lad, about sixteen or seventeen, calling to me from his front lawn. I had seen him around but didn't know his name. I assumed he was the bellows-challenged Bagpipe Kid. He ran across the street and deposited himself on my front lawn, a six-foot-two bundle of energy.

"Hi!" I said with extra enthusiasm, making up for the fact that I had no name to go with the greeting; I've lived here a long time and I should have known the kid's name. He wasn't offering and I wasn't about to ask at this point in our relationship. He obviously, or sort of, knew my name.

"Can I take Trixie out?" he asked. He was a tall, gangly kid, with a pale face dotted with freckles. His red hair all grew forward and stuck up in places, but judging from the number of teenage girls who came and went from the house, he was either a real Don Juan or had an older brother who was.

"Um, okay?" I said.

He saw the puzzled look on my face and explained. "I used to walk her for the Morrisons."

"Who?"

He pointed to Jackson and Terri's house. "The Morrisons." He shoved his hands in his pockets. "My mom told me that they left and that it looked like Trixie was living with you."

His mom was pretty observant; I, on the other hand, wouldn't be able to pick her out of a lineup, so I was impressed. I started toward the house and he followed me. "Actually, if you want to help me out with her, that would be great. I can pay you what the Morrisons were paying you." I said a silent prayer that the Morrisons weren't paying him fifty bucks a walk or something equally outrageous.

"Oh, they weren't paying me. I was just doing it because I love Trixie."

Even better! And anyone who loves Trixie is a friend of mine. A responsible and free dog walker. How did I get so lucky? Now if I just had an unmarried boyfriend, I'd be all set. I opened the front door and let Bagpipe Kid in. Trixie, sensing a compadre in her midst, bounded down the hall, her leash in her mouth. "Trixie, you learned a new trick," I said, amazed.

The kid blushed. "I taught her that."

"Good work!" I said, and gave him a high five.

"She's been digging a hole in the back of your neighbors' yard," he said, hooking a thumb toward Terri and Jackson's vacant abode. "It's way in the back behind the shed so I'm letting her do it. She loves to dig."

I didn't care. Nobody lived there so it wasn't like anybody else would care, either. I sent the kid and Trixie on their way, telling him to just tie her up in the back when he was done playing with her. They took off down the front walk, a boy and . . . well, a dog he didn't own.

I took my bottle of Listerine into the kitchen and filled a tall glass halfway with the stuff. Damn that Peter Miceli and his roving lips. I took a hearty sip of the mouthwash, looking out onto the backyard and craning my neck to see if Trixie was still working on the hole. She was at the edge of the shed working as hard as she could to dig a giant chasm. I could see her hind legs kicking up earth, great clumps of it flying to and fro. The kid crouched next to her, staring down into the void that she had created, smiling and petting her from time to time, seemingly happy that she was happy.

I gargled a few times, swishing yellow liquid around in my mouth until my tongue had gone numb. When my eyes started to water, I spat out the fluid into the sink, rinsed the glass out, and filled it with water, drinking down the residue that remained in my mouth. I didn't know if I felt any better or if I had completely erased the idea of Peter's lips touching mine, but my mouth felt tingly and clean. I peered out again to check on Trixie's progress, surprised when a flash of red flew past the window over my sink which I recognized as Bagpipe Kid's head. His furious knocking at the back door interrupted my reverie and I opened the door to find him in a tizzy, winded and agitated.

"Mrs. . . . Trixie . . . the hole," he said, finally putting his hands to his knees and taking deep breaths. It dawned on me that he wasn't as winded as he was terrified. When he stood up straight again, I noticed that his face was ghastly white, his freckles standing out against a pallid background.

"Slow down," I said, putting a hand on his back.

He grabbed my hand and pulled me out of the kitchen, the force so hard that it lifted me off my feet. "Come with me."

I could see Trixie standing by the hole, whimpering, her tail between her legs, and her head hanging dejectedly.

The kid reached the hole before I did and he pointed, his arm stiff. He looked away, focusing on the side of my garage, the structure directly opposite from where we stood. A couple of strangled sobs escaped from his throat.

I walked over to the hole and peered in, the bile rising in my throat. I turned away quickly and closed my eyes but the sight of the body, missing its hands and feet, remained imprinted on the insides of my eyelids.

I backed away from the grave, dragging the kid along with me. Trixie started walking in circles, issuing a low, sad moan. I turned and put my hands on the kid's shoulders.

"What's your name?" I asked. I figured now was as good a time as any for introductions.

"Br . . . Br . . ."

"Brian?"

He shook his head, unable to form a complete word or thought.

"Bruce?"

He shook his head again.

"Brady?"

"Br . . . Br . . . Brendan," he finally managed to get out.

I put my face close to his, steadying both of us with the

pressure I put on his shoulders. "Brendan, do you want to go call 911 or stay here with the body?"

He pointed at my house.

"Good. Go over to my house and call 911. I'll stay here."

He started to walk away but when he reached the hedgerow, he turned back. "What should I tell them?"

Poor kid. "Tell them that you found a dead body. They'll know what to do," I said. "Then call your mom and tell her to come over here. You should stay with me because the police are going to want to question you."

The look on his face almost broke my heart; it was a mixture of sadness, shock, and terror. In this one instance, his world had changed forever. I watched his shoulders sag as he walked toward my house.

I sat on the grass, a dozen feet or so from the grave, and waited for the chaos to begin.

Before Crawford left work, he spoke to the desk sergeant and told him to alert all sector cars to Alex's disappearance. Most of the cops in the precinct knew Alex, and those who didn't got a copy of a photograph that Crawford kept in his desk. "Put the word out, Sarge. Anybody who sees him should call me on my cell."

He left work tired and dejected. He got in his car and headed toward Connecticut to pick up his daughters.

The slapping of the wipers on the windshield lulled him into an almost hypnotic state and he drove as if on autopilot, letting instinct and memory steer him in the right direction. He hadn't talked to Alison since earlier that day, when he had been knee-deep in Maloney's garbage in a Dumpster behind the bar. He and Carmen had found Alex's stash—a blanket, a stack of books, and an empty bottle of Wild Turkey—right by the Dumpster and stayed around the area, looking for anything that would give them an idea of where he might be or might have gone. Crawford spied a bloody shirt hanging out of the Dumpster, but Tommy Maloney confirmed that a fight the night before in the bar had produced the rent and soiled garment. A call to the desk sergeant confirmed that there had been a fight the night before and a sector car had responded. He bagged the shirt anyway and asked the sergeant to hold the paperwork on the fight so that he could see it on Monday; he'd want to question everybody involved to see if they had seen Alex.

He arrived on Donald Street about forty minutes after he had left the precinct. He walked up the curving front walk of Christine's small Tudor and rang the doorbell. She answered the door, looking beautiful in a black dress and the pearls he had given her for their first anniversary.

"You look nice," he said, making her blush. She opened the door wide and let him in.

"Girls!" she called from the bottom of the stair.

Meaghan bounded down the stairs with her knapsack and ever-present iPod attached to her jeans. Erin followed close behind, in pajama pants and a tank top. Crawford raised an eyebrow. "Are you sick?"

Erin threw him a snotty look. "No."

"Then why are you in your pajamas? I'm taking you to dinner."

Meaghan laughed. "We always dress like that. Everyone does."

Crawford pointed up the stairs. "Put on some clothes," he said. "Please." She stomped up the stairs, muttering at the injustice of it all. He looked at Meaghan. "You always dress like that? When? Where?"

"When we go to school. Or out."

He shook his head. He didn't have the energy to argue with them about something as trivial as wearing pajamas in public, and fortunately, Meaghan let it go. Erin came down the stairs a few minutes later in baggy jeans with a hole in one knee. He gave her another disapproving look; they weren't a vast improvement over her original pants.

"What?" she said. "You said no pajama pants. These aren't pajama pants."

He looked at Christine and gave her a tense smile. "Okay! We'll be on our way then."

She stood on her tiptoes and kissed his cheek. "They're all yours." She opened the front door. "I'll see you tomorrow?"

He nodded. "Around five."

She ushered the girls outside and put her arm through his. "Can you stay for dinner? There are a couple of things I need to talk to you about."

He smiled. "Does one of them have to do with why you look so gorgeous on a Saturday night?"

She blushed deep red again. "It does."

He leaned down and gave her a long hug. "I'll be here." He started for the door. "Have a good time."

The girls wanted to go to a restaurant in the city, and after much discussion, they decided on Chinese. Crawford dropped his car off close to his house and locked their bags in his trunk. They went to their favorite Chinese place—Hunan Garden—and ordered enough food for six, after which they filled him in on the details of the swim meet.

Crawford took a swig of his beer. "So, how was the rest of your week?"

"Mom's dating a stockbroker," Erin blurted out.

Meaghan punched her sister in the arm. "You are an asshole."

Crawford gave Meaghan a steely look. "Hey!"

She looked down at the table, shamefaced.

"And he's got four kids!" Erin said, obviously distressed. "All under ten!"

"So, if they get married, you'll be the Brady bunch," Crawford said, laughing. "You'll have to hire an Alice, though."

"It's not funny, Dad." Erin pouted, ripping her napkin into little pieces. She looked at him, her face sad. "Does Alison have kids?"

He took another sip of his beer. "No." He set his beer down on the glass-topped table. "She has a dog."

"Does she want kids?"

"I don't know. We've never talked about it." And that was the truth. "From what I know, she didn't even know she wanted a dog." He took in their confused expressions. "Long story."

Erin continued ripping her napkin. "What if she does want children? What if she wants to marry you and have children with you? Where does that leave us?"

Crawford held up a hand to stop her. "You're getting way ahead of yourself. Alison and I haven't actually begun dating. Not in the traditional sense of the word."

Meaghan gave him a sly look. "Dad's a player!"

"No, no, no . . ." he said, shaking his head and closing his eyes. He didn't know when these two had gotten so sophisticated but he didn't like it. He knew what Meaghan was implying and he wanted to set the record straight. "It's not like that. It's complicated. Our lives are complicated."

"Don't flatter yourself, Dad. You're a pretty simple guy," Meaghan said, dipping a crunchy noodle into the duck sauce on the table. "How complicated could it be? As long as she's got beer in the refrigerator, a bag of chips, and knows how to make guacamole, you should get along just fine."

She had a point. "Well, it just is," he said, for lack of a better retort. He drank the rest of his beer and motioned to the waiter to bring another one. It seemed like it was going to be a long night. A muffled phone rang and all three of them checked their pockets for their cell phones. Crawford held his up and saw that it was ringing. "Hello?"

It was Carmen. "Hey, handsome. I miss you, baby. What are you doing?"

"I'm out to dinner with Meaghan and Erin. What's up?"

She let out a long sigh. "Bad news, honey. Sector car just found Alex in the park."

Crawford rubbed his hand over his eyes. If she was calling, it couldn't be good. "Time of death?" he asked.

"Right after he called you." She spoke to someone in the background and then returned to the call. "I think he got in the middle of that drug thing that Casey and Mariano are working on. One of the Brotherhood left his calling card."

The Brotherhood were a Bronx gang and responsible for most of the pot-dealing that went on. Although most people thought of pot as the gentle person's choice of drug, it produced some of the most vicious and deadly turf and gang violence in the city. The Brotherhood were territorial, brutal, and killed without a second thought; their signature was a black bandana left at their executions.

Crawford felt the tears pressing at the back of his eyes and he took a swig of beer to wash down the lump in his throat. He looked down at the table to avoid the girls' gaze; it was clear that they knew something was wrong. "Do you need me?" He mouthed a thank-you to the waiter when his second beer appeared.

"No. I'll handle it. I'm pulling a double so I can go to Ricardo's sister's baby shower tomorrow. That oughta be fun," she said. The noise in the background got louder and she shouted to an officer to cut his siren. "I'll call you later," she said and hung up.

A wave of exhaustion took hold of him. The body count was rising and his energy was ebbing.

Neither one was good.

Chapter 25

I managed to make it through the Hardin/Madden tag team questioning session in just under two hours. Brendan and I spent those two hours answering their questions until it became apparent to them that we had nothing to say beyond "we found a body in a grave and we don't know anything else." They were perplexed as to why not one, but two, bodies missing body parts had been found by me. I reminded them that it was Brendan, not I, who had found the second body. Small but salient point, in my opinion. I was perplexed about the two bodies, too, however, and asked them if they had any theories about that.

We also reviewed the 911 calls of the early morning, and they told me that they would follow up on that. I got a glimpse of the cop I had seen earlier that morning and he didn't have the look of someone who had just gotten the news that he was receiving a commendation in the near future.

But despite everything I told them, they still regarded me suspiciously. Two things about Hardin and Madden: one, they don't find me remotely amusing, and two, they really don't have a clue as to how to conduct a murder investigation. If they did, would they really consider me a viable suspect? If I had any smarts at all, would I have buried a body in the yard next to mine and then allowed my dog to dig up the body? I think not.

I mentioned to them that Peter Miceli had been in the

vicinity that day and that seemed to excite them more than the thought of throwing me in the slammer overnight. I explained to them how the missing hands and feet were a Miceli signature and that the NYPD was working that angle on Ray's murder.

"And what would Miceli's motive be in killing Terri Morrison?" Hardin asked, his hound-dog face sad and questioning.

Hmmm. I hadn't really thought about that. "Give me time. I'm sure I can come up with something," I said, ever helpful. I'm nothing if not gifted in coming up with murder scenarios and told them so.

Their stony gazes told me that they weren't impressed.

When they finally released the two of us, Brendan's mother, Jane, drove both of us back home with a promise to check in on me the next day.

I was worried about the kid; he had become almost catatonic on the short ride home. I was hoping that after a hot meal, a good night's sleep, and the care of his lovely mother, he would be able to function somewhat normally again. Then again, he was a teenager who had seen a dead and dismembered body. It might be a long time before he felt normal.

The next day, I wandered around in a haze, careful not to look over into the Morrison's yard, which would remind me again of what I had seen. I spent the better part of the day on the couch trying to wipe the memory of the day before from my mind and was only partially successful. The only time I wasn't thinking about it was when I was thinking about either who had killed Ray or who had shot me. I was happy when I checked my watch and saw that it was six o'clock and cocktail hour could begin.

There was not enough vodka in the world to erase the memory of seeing Terri, for whom I now had a little sympathy despite our past, in that grave. I thought I would give it a shot, though. I made myself a giant martini with about twenty olives and took it into the living room. Funny thing about finding Terri: I was no longer thinking about Peter Miceli. I had already fixed myself some guacamole from an old avocado I had found along with a plate of cheese and crackers. I was a little catatonic myself. I figured I deserved a quiet night after everything that had happened. And more than one martini.

I hadn't called Crawford; there hadn't been time. I was also sure that the DFPD would let the NYPD know about a second murder where the victim was missing their hands and feet. I didn't expect to hear from Crawford because I knew that he was with his girls and nothing disturbed him when he was spending time with them. However, we hadn't parted in the warmest way on our last phone call so I kind of expected a quick call to let me know that everything was copacetic between us.

Whenever we did speak, I'd have a lot to tell him. Crawford didn't know about my meeting with Peter because our phone call had taken place when he was in medias Dumpster. I knew that if I told him about Peter in the diner, he would go off the deep end more so than when I finally got around to telling him that Terri was dead. He wouldn't have a lot to do with that case, necessarily, unless her hands and feet, like Ray's, were found in his jurisdiction. But me kissing Peter Miceli? In his world, that would be an international incident in magnitude.

The phone rang. Although I expected to hear Crawford's voice, it was Jack McManus. If I had thought that the day couldn't get any more complicated, I was wrong.

"Jack, hi," I said, trying to keep the surprise out of my voice. He wasn't the last person I expected to hear from, but close. Sister Calista was probably the last person I expected to hear from.

"Hi, Alison. I've been thinking about you."

Well, well.

"Kevin tells me you've been kind of busy."

That's for sure. "He's right about that," I agreed.

"How are you doing?"

Good question. "I guess I'm all right." I took a sip of my drink so as not to go into the sordid details of my diner meal and my evening with the Dobbs Ferry police. I would fill Kevin in when I saw him and leave him to spread the word about my latest brush with murder and mayhem.

"Have you been getting your garbage out on time?" he asked.

Oh, yeah. I had responded to his romantic overtures on our last date by running off to take out the garbage.

"Any chance I could take you to dinner in the next couple of weeks?" He laughed. "I'm guessing that by now you've discovered that 'killier' isn't a word."

Oh, silly Jack. Don't you know about my boyfriend, his wife, and our torrid, sexless affair? I thought. After all, your brother is Father Kevin, spiritual adviser and master gossip. But I said, "Oh, Jack, I wish I could, but I'm kind of with that guy that we talked about."

"And that guy doesn't let you have dinner with a friend?" he asked.

He was smooth. Oh, he would let me, all right, and then torture me about it for the next fifty years. Some things just aren't worth the agony. Like Wonderbras. And massive amounts of artichoke dip (long story). Instead of giving him my dissertation on sore breasts and flatulence, I tried to laugh it off. "Thanks, Jack, but I think I'll have to take a pass."

He tried a different tack. "The Rangers are playing the Flyers next week. We can sit in the good seats again."

Geez, why did he have to go there? The Rangers-Flyers rivalry was one of the best in the NHL and one of my favorite games to watch during the season. I was exhausted and I didn't have the energy to run the romantic gauntlet that was Jack McManus and his spectacularly white teeth. "As tempting as that is—"

"Listen, Alison. I have a great time when I'm with you. I like you. I don't get to meet too many women in my line of work."

Right. You work with a bunch of professional athletes, all of whom are known for their inability to meet women and their allegiance to their "he-man-women-haters" club code of ethics. "Thanks, Jack. I had a great time with you, too. And under different circumstances, this would be great. But right now, I'm involved."

He gave it one last shot. "Messier is coming to town next week."

My inner monologist began to speak, but I told her to shut up. "Jack, I wish I could, but I can't."

He sounded disappointed. Who could blame him? It's not every day you get to meet a tall, almost attractive, out-on-bail, single college professor who loves all things hockey. And if you loved being smack-dab in the middle of murder investigations, I was your girl. "Listen, if things don't work out, please give me a call."

I laughed. "By that time, you'll be married to a super-model and raising your kids, Jack. Hopefully, they'll get her looks and your brains. But thanks," I said, leaving out the sarcasm. "I appreciate the call." I hung the phone up and took another sip of my martini.

Trixie, who had been lounging on her bed in the kitchen, sidled into the living room. After gazing at me longingly for a few seconds, her ears perked up and she started to growl way down in her throat. I wasn't surprised when there was a knock at the front door a few seconds later. Trixie was cool with people knocking on the back door, but for some reason, not the front. It was just one of those weird dog things that I had given up trying to understand. She shadowed me as I approached the front door. I pulled the curtain of the sidelight to peer out and was surprised to see Crawford standing there.

I opened the door, happy to see him. "Hi," I said, stepping into the hallway to let him pass.

"I hope this is okay," he said. "You know, just stopping by."

"Boy, do I have a lot to tell you." I launched into my story about Peter Miceli—minus the making-out part—coming to the diner and finished up with how Brendan, aka Bagpipe Kid, found Terri in the grave.

"Missing hands and feet, right?"

I nodded.

He put his hands on his hips and sighed. "Dobbs Ferry called it in to us. What the hell is going on?"

"I don't know, Crawford, but don't you think Peter Miceli had something to do with this?"

"I would if I actually thought he had a motive for killing her."

Killjoy. "Well, maybe he does and we just don't know what it is."

"Doesn't it seem like it's Jackson?"

"Unless we find him somewhere else," I reminded him. "What if he's in a shallow grave in another part of town?"

He thought about that for a couple of seconds. "I can ask some questions about this because it's obviously related to Ray's case, but I can't push too much, Alison. This is a total local jurisdiction case."

"I know," I said. I thought about asking him more about Ray's case and the Julie Anne Podowsky angle, but thought better of it after I took a second to take in his appearance. Although his clothes were in their usual state of neat-and-pressed, he had dark circles under his eyes and his five o'clock shadow had entered its eleventh hour. "Are you all right?" I put my hand to his face.

"I'm exhausted," he said.

I took his hand and brought him into the living room. "Come with me. What can I get you?"

"How about that license plate number?" he asked. When he saw my crestfallen face—I was expecting a beverage request, not police procedure—he added, "And a beer?" He fell onto the couch, clearly out of gas. "You gave the license plate number to Dobbs Ferry PD, too, right? I'm going to run it, too, but they should have this information."

I nodded. "Yep." I went into the kitchen, and when I returned, I had a piece of paper with the license plate number and a cold beer. I handed both to him and sat on a chair across from the couch. "Is this a business call?"

He took a long swallow of beer. "Sort of." He reached over and helped himself to a hefty chipful of guacamole. "This is good," he said, a little awe in his voice.

"I can cook, you know," I protested. While that wasn't exactly true, it sounded good. I didn't think mashing an avocado in a bowl constituted cooking, but if he was impressed, who was I to argue? I moved from the chair to his lap and put my arms around his neck. "Are we still talking?"

He looked at me, surprised. "Yes. Why?"

I shrugged. "You didn't sound too happy to hear from me."

He smiled. "Well, let me recap the last several days." He began to mimic my voice. "Crawford, it's raining.

Crawford, there's someone in the garage. Crawford, I'm following a car with an unknown driver at breakneck speed. Crawford, I'm in jail . . ." He took a sip of beer. "And now you tell me you've found another body? I can't take much more of this," he said, only half kidding.

"I didn't actually find the body," I reminded him. "I was just next to it for a little while."

"Details."

I laughed. "Okay, okay." I kissed him. "Uncle." I pulled at his shirt and put my hand on his stomach. It had been so long since I had seen him that despite today's unpleasantness, I wanted to jump his bones. Bad.

He closed his eyes. "As much as it pains me to say this, I have to go home. Are you going to be okay? Do you want me to call Dobbs Ferry PD and have them send a car around?"

"I think they're already doing that." I wiggled off his lap and onto the couch next to him. "Do you really have to go?"

He took my hand. "I do. It's been a long day."

I suspected that there was something going on, but I decided not to press. "Do you want something to eat before you go?"

He shook his head. "No, I ate." He paused.

"What's the matter, Crawford?" I asked.

"Nothing," he said, a little too quickly. He stood. "I have to go."

I stood and walked him to the front door. "Let me know what you find out about that plate number."

He looked down at me and kissed the top of my head. "I will."

Uh-oh. The head kiss. I got that sinking feeling in my stomach and swallowed hard. The head kiss usually preceded the kiss-off. I had gotten a lot of head kisses from Ray and we were almost the same height.

Crawford left and, instead of watching him walk to his car like I usually would, I closed the door. I looked at Trixie. "This is not the sort of weekend I want to repeat," I said, looking into her limpid brown eyes. She walked over and gave my hand a lick and whined slightly. "I made out with Peter Miceli and got a head kiss from Crawford. What's wrong with this picture?"

She cocked her head again.

I let out a little laugh, almost to prevent myself from bursting into tears. If I kept soliciting advice from a neutered dog and a priest, my love life would be dead in no time flat.

When he got to the stop sign at the end of Alison's street, Crawford banged his head against the steering wheel in frustration. He resisted the urge to turn his car around and drive back to her house; the look on her face when he left was evidence enough that he had behaved like a moron. Once again.

" 'How about that license plate number?' " he repeated to himself. "Smooth."

He drove home in a fog, not even excited when he found a parking spot right in front of his building, normally a cause for great rejoicing. His phone trilled on the seat beside him and he picked it up before getting out of the car.

"Crawford."

"Hey, it's Kenny James."

Crawford sat up in his seat. "Kenny, hey. Thanks for calling me back."

"So, you got another Miceli murder?"

"Or maybe two," Crawford said, watching the inside of his windshield fog up. "I just want to check something . . . that hands and feet thing is always Miceli, right?"

"Here's the thing about the Micelis: they are consistent.

Missing hands and feet are a signature Miceli move, and they don't change method. Ever. Miceli family members and soldiers do everything the same way they've been doing it for fifty years. Some old Miceli hacked off some guy's hands and feet in Brooklyn during World War Two, and that's how they do it now. I can't explain it, but I've seen two dozen Miceli . . ." He paused and laughed. "*Alleged* Miceli murders and they are all the same. They must have a school where they teach these guys messy murder techniques."

Crawford sat in silence.

"You there?" James asked after a few seconds.

"Yeah, I'm here." Crawford opened his car door. "We've got a couple of other suspects. One's a girl from St. Thomas who had a relationship with the vic."

"She come in on her own or did you pick her up?"

"On her own, which is always suspicious. Funny thing is, she's a fencer."

"She deals in stolen goods?"

"No, a fencer. You know, the sport?" Crawford clarified.

James started laughing. "I've been on the job way too long." He paused. "Well, you know, she probably knows how to wield swords pretty well."

"Yeah, that's what one of the other detectives is thinking. I'm still not sure."

"Well, good luck, Bobby. Let me know if I can help."

"Thanks, Kenny. Maybe we can hook up and look over these files? It'd be great to get some fresh eyes on this but even better if those eyes have studied all things Miceli."

"You got it. I'm out next week, though. Taking the wife to Vegas to renew our wedding vows at some tacky chapel. Not my thing but she's got her heart set on it."

"Well, good luck," Crawford said, chuckling.

He walked inside and slammed the front door, not giving any thought to disturbing Bea. She opened her apartment door and took in his disheveled appearance, the bags under his eyes, and the stubble growing on his cheeks. "Get in here," she said, and took his arm.

He went into her apartment and fell onto her couch, exhausted. Bea went into the kitchen and came back with a chocolate pudding pie, two spoons, and two cold bottles of beer. She put the pie on the coffee table and handed him a spoon and a beer. "Have some pie."

The last thing he wanted was pie and a conversation with Bea, but for some reason, he found himself digging into a mound of whipped cream and chocolate pudding and spooning it into his mouth. He washed his first bite down with a swallow of beer and nearly gagged. "I don't think chocolate pudding pie needs a beer chaser," he said.

Bea didn't agree and drained half of her beer in one swallow. "Give it time; it's an acquired taste." She took another hunk of pie. "You look like hell. What's going on?"

Where do I begin? he thought. He was so tired and spent that he found himself pouring his entire life out to Bea. He ended with his visit to Christine's. "She asked me to dinner. I didn't think she was going to ask my permission to remarry."

Bea's eyes were big behind her bifocals. "She's getting remarried?"

Crawford leaned back on the couch and took another swig of his beer. "Seems that way."

"So, that's good, right?" Bea asked. She toddled off into the kitchen and returned with two more beers, one of which she handed to Bobby. "This is a six-pack conversation, if ever I heard one."

He drained his first beer and started on the second one.

"You know she came by the day after Fred's wedding and told me to forget about the annulment," he said.

Bea's sharp intake of breath told him that she didn't know. And how would she? He hadn't told her.

"I thought that was about us. I thought that was about her doing the right thing." He looked at Bea. "What it really was about was her getting remarried."

Bea drank her beer in silence. She leaned over and scooped up another piece of pie, deep in thought. "Does it really matter?" she asked.

"Huh?"

"Does it really matter why she's moving on? Does it matter to you?"

That was something he hadn't considered. He thought for a moment. "Does it?" he asked, not sure.

Bea stared at him. "No, it doesn't." She clinked her bottle against his. "Congratulations." She took in his crestfallen face. "You can't tell me that you're upset about this."

"I'm not," he said, not too convincingly. "I just thought . . ."

"You just thought what? That she was letting you go out of some unselfish desire to see *you* happy? Who are you kidding, Bobby?" Bea finished off the pie and wiped her mouth with a napkin. "Listen, Bobby. It really doesn't matter why it's over now instead of before. It's over. You can move on. That's all that matters." She tipped her second beer to her lips. "Bobby, let's remember one thing: you liked that girl, loved her like a sister, but you were never really in love with her."

Crawford looked at his aunt.

"You took that girl out of a dreadful situation. That father of hers was no good, and neither were the brothers. You saved her." She finished off her beer. "And that was a good thing to do, Bobby. But you can't tell me that you were ever in love with her."

He hung his head. She was right.

"So, get moving. Start living the life you were meant to live."

Chapter 26

I didn't realize how much I had missed Max until she came to my office after returning home from what seemed like the longest honeymoon on record.

I was surprised when she came straight to my office the day after she arrived home, late on a Friday afternoon. Her beautiful tan was highlighted by a crisp white shirt, open at the neck, and a flowered skirt under which she wore no pantyhose. Manolo Blahnik slingbacks on her feet, she strode into my office, bypassing Dottie in the reception area, her shoes making a rhythmic click-clack on the wood floor. She threw open the door and flew into my arms, grabbing me in a giant bear hug.

"I missed you!" she screamed, throwing her purse onto one of my guest chairs. She kissed my cheek.

I was as happy to see her as I had ever been in my life. I held her close. "Max." I felt tears spring to my eyes; the absence of any close family relations in my life made her dearer to me than anyone. "I'm so happy you're back."

She flung herself into a chair and threw her legs over the side, the posture she always assumed when she visited me in my office. "Sounds like you've had a hell of a time since the wedding. How's the gunshot wound?" she asked.

"Healed," I said. "I've got a scar but the doctor said it would fade."

"So much for sleeveless blouses," she said, smiling sadly. "Fred's downstairs. Do you want to have dinner?"

she asked. "We're going over to City Island for oysters." She smiled slyly. "You have to admit. A man who eats raw oysters shows a lot of promise as a lover, don't you think?" She let out a throaty chortle.

"If you say so," I said. I started to make the connection in my head but stopped. "Sure. I'd love to have dinner," I said, pushing a file of papers to the side of my desk. "These can wait." I stood, pulling my briefcase off the floor. I looked out the tall windows that faced the back courtyard of the building and spied Crawford jogging down the steep steps that led to the back door. He looked like he had just come from work, wearing his usual uniform of dress pants, shirt, tie, and blazer.

Max saw him, too. "Let's take a rain check." She stood and grabbed her purse. "Seems our friend, the trusty Detective Hot Pants, might have had the same idea." She hugged me again and gave me another kiss, whispering in my ear, "Remember what I said about raw oysters." She left my office and, judging from the muffled voices out in the main office area, ran into Crawford on the way out. I heard her tell him that they would get together the following week to have dinner, if he was free. I couldn't hear his answer.

The sight of him in my office door was even better than the sight of Max, but several days had passed since the head-kiss incident and it seemed like we had to reacquaint ourselves with each other. He shuffled a little awkwardly from one foot to the other, his hands in his pockets, looking at me. Finally, he stepped all the way in and gave me a tentative kiss on the cheek. Better than a head kiss, but not much.

"Hiya, Crawford," I said.

"How are you?" he asked.

I nodded. "I'm good."

"I have that information on the license plate number," he said. RoboCop was back.

I kicked the door to my office closed with my foot and decided to take matters into my own hands. I grabbed his belt and pulled him close, planting a long, wet kiss on his lips. "Don't ever kiss my head again," I whispered.

He laughed. "Oh, that."

"You can explain later," I said, kissing him again.

He took my hand and interlaced my fingers in his. "Let's start over, okay?"

He wouldn't get any argument from me.

"Hi, I'm Jerry." He reached over and shook my free hand.

"Candy."

"What do you do, Candy?"

"I'm a stripper."

"Perfect," he said. "I'm a buffer." He laughed. "I think that makes us perfectly compatible." His hands found my bare skin beneath my blouse; suffice it to say that I had never been felt up in my office. I was hoping that Sister Calista didn't take this opportunity to drop off her syllabi. "Are you free for dinner?" he asked.

"I am," I said. "What did you have in mind?"

"I don't know," he said. "How do you feel about oysters?"

I feel very good about oysters.

We set out for City Island, a quaint village in the Bronx situated on the Long Island Sound, arriving just as the sun was setting.

At this time of the year, most of the restaurants, which closed after the high season, were still open, and Crawford knew of a small place on the water that he said was one of his favorites. He pulled his car into a spot in the front and turned to me.

"I'm sorry I haven't been around," he said.

"Any breaks in Ray's case? In my case?" I liked to think of my shooting as a "case;" the word itself provided a little distance from what had really happened, which was too gruesome to think about.

"No," he said. "The slug we found in your shooting didn't match any known weapon from in the system, so we're at a loss. The license plate number came up from a car stolen in the Soundview section of the Bronx. We questioned the owners and they check out. Just unlucky. And the Ray thing . . ." he said, pausing. "Well, there's nothing. I've checked with your local police and they've got less than nothing. There's nothing on Terri, either. But Hardin told me that they've got the Feds involved looking for Jackson. He probably won't get very far."

I turned to him. "They'd better find him."

He put his hand to my face. "Come here," he whispered. I scooted closer and he wrapped his arms around me, burying his face in my hair. I put my head on his shoulder and breathed in deeply.

"Just so you know, I don't kiss on the first date," I whispered to him.

He put his lips to mine and kissed me. "But I do," he said, taking his mouth off mine for a few seconds and studying my face before kissing me again.

I groaned slightly when he slid his tongue into my mouth and ran his hands down my back. He moved to my neck. "I thought you promised me some oysters?" I said, giggling.

He pulled away. "Are you one of those women who prefer food and sleep to sex?"

"Is there any other kind?"

He thought for a moment. "Well, there's Max."

"Touché," I said, laughing. "But you're going to have to buy me dinner if you want to get to second base." Even Jack McManus had had to obey that rule when I had dated him but I left that part out.

He sighed and hoisted himself out of the car, going

around to open my door. When he arrived, I was already out of the car and standing on the sidewalk. We walked to a small bar and restaurant and went inside; the atmosphere was dark and intimate. We took a table in a corner near the fireplace.

Crawford ordered a bottle of German Riesling from the young waitress who approached our table; before she walked away he also asked for two dozen oysters.

I raised my eyebrows at him. "White wine? Won't you be fired from the police department for ordering such a sissy drink? Aren't you guys supposed to drink straight bourbon or something like that?"

"I'm six foot five and carry a gun. Who's going to call me a sissy?" he asked. "Besides you, of course."

The oysters arrived within minutes, artfully arranged on a large plate. The waitress explained each different type on the plate, and left them with lemon wedges, hot sauce, and horseradish. Crawford immediately set about doctoring up a few on his side of the plate and noisily slurped the first one down. He had another six eaten in a few minutes' time.

"God, I love oysters," he said. He leaned in close to me. "They're one of my favorite things."

I ate one and put the empty shell on the plate. "Are we still talking about seafood?"

He didn't have time to reply; the waitress arrived with the wine. He tasted it and gave it his approval. He waited until she left to resume our conversation. "I have something to tell you," he said.

I hate it when conversations start with that sentence. They usually end with "I don't love you anymore" or something equally disturbing. I braced myself.

"No, no, it's good," he said. He reached across the table and took my hand. "My divorce is final."

"What?"

He told me how Christine had come to his apartment after the wedding and then how she told him about her re-marriage. She had since signed their divorce papers and everything was legal and official. "So, that night I came to your house, I was . . ." He searched for the right phrase.

"Out of sorts?" I filled in.

"That'll work."

"I'm happy for you," I said. "How do you feel about it?"

He closed his eyes for a minute and thought. After some moments of silence, he opened his eyes again. "I'm re-lieved. Happy." He took another sip of wine. "This has been going on for too long and it was time for it to come to an end." He loosened his tie. "The funny thing is that I think you and Christine would really like each other. She's a wonderful person." He looked closely at me. "For some-body else," he amended, careful not to make it sound like he had any regrets over their split.

"So," I said, "this is the beginning."

"That's what I'm hoping." He leaned across the table and kissed me lightly on the lips. "Do you want to see my apartment?" he whispered.

"I don't know. Do I?"

He nodded. "You do." He kissed me again. "Do you want to sleep over?"

I thought for a moment even though I knew what my answer would be. "As long as you promise me one thing."

"Anything."

"No sleeping."

Chapter 27

I haven't had sex in about three years.

Well, that's not exactly true.

I haven't had sex with *anyone else* in about three years.

My stomach was a mass of knots, slimy raw seafood, and acid as I climbed out of Crawford's car and waited for him on the sidewalk. Every nerve ending I had felt exposed and tingly and I looked at the people passing by wondering if I appeared as tense to them as I felt. If any of them were to look at me, I was sure the look on my face would scream "I'm going to have sex!" and they would run off scared. We were two blocks from his house, and his big hand wrapped around mine was the only thing preventing me from falling to the ground in a mess of nerves and paranoia. I hadn't started the day thinking that it would end like this; I tried to recall what underwear I had donned at six that morning and whether or not my legs were shaved. After doing mental gymnastics for most of the ride to the city, my silence bizarre and certainly not encouraging, I'm sure, I finally let it go. The man loved me, for God's sake, and probably hadn't had sex in at least as long; by the time we got around to the nitty-gritty, he wouldn't care if he found an extra leg or a nest of squirrels under my skirt.

I thought the "no sleeping" comeback to Crawford's proposition was inspired and conveyed a bit more confidence than I had. Ray was a pretty slick lover (tons of practice) and I guess I knew a thing or two about the goings-on of the bedroom. Crawford was the kind of guy who made me feel safe and I tried to focus on that as we approached Ninety-seventh Street and his apartment.

He opened the door to a brownstone tucked back from the street. He ushered me inside, holding a finger to his lips. "Don't make a sound," he whispered, pointing to a door at the bottom of the stairs. "My aunt—I'll explain later."

We tiptoed up the stairs and he opened the door at the top. When the door opened and I got a peek at what lay beyond the small foyer, I was a little stunned but pleasantly surprised. I wasn't sure what I was expecting, but since he had lived alone for so long, I didn't expect a beautifully decorated, impeccably clean interior that smelled of potpourri. He took my hand and led me into the living room, offering me a seat on a leather couch. He took my coat and draped it over a chair. He took his blazer off, draped it over my coat, and removed his tie. He opened the first few buttons of his shirt, offering me a view of the ubiquitous undershirt that I loved so much.

"Do you want something to drink?" he asked.

"Ummm . . . sure," I said, not exactly knowing what I should have.

He stood, looking at me. "Do you want me to guess?"

"Wine?" I offered.

"Red or white?" he asked.

I shrugged. "You pick."

I heard him rustling around in the kitchen; he came back a few minutes later with a couple of glasses and an open bottle of cabernet. He poured me a glass, and sat down on the couch next to me, holding his glass. He took a sip and waited while I sipped mine.

I put my glass down on the coffee table and took his from his hands, pushing him back on the couch. His face was a mixture of surprise and amusement. My nervousness left me and I felt empowered enough to take charge of the situation. "Enough of the small talk," I said, kicking off my shoes and getting on top of him. "I don't think I can wait any longer," I said, laughing. I pulled off my turtleneck sweater and looked down at the white cotton bra that I had put on that morning. "Sorry about this . . . I didn't know what today would bring in terms of nudity."

He reached up and unhooked my bra. "There's only one way to solve that," he said, and threw the bra across the room. "Get rid of it." He reached up and touched my breasts. "Where's Trixie?"

"You see breasts and you think 'Trixie'? I'm going to have to change that." It took me a minute to think of where she was. "Bagpipe Kid. I'll call him later and tell him to walk her tonight and in the morning."

"You really are sleeping over?" he asked, surprised.

"Can I?"

He kissed me, his tongue tickling my lips. "Of course you can." His fingers slipped inside the waistband of my skirt. "I just can't believe my luck."

I leaned down and unbuttoned his shirt. "Go easy, Crawford. It's been a while." I tried to sound lighthearted but in reality I was terrified. I'd been thinking about this man for the last several months, but now that everything I had dreamt and fantasized about was here, I was a wreck. Figured.

He put his hands on either side of my face and looked at me. "For me, too."

I sat up. "Really?"

He nodded, a little embarrassed.

"How have you made it through all these years?" I asked. "Because, frankly, I've been going a little insane. I think that's why I'm so cranky all the time." Or maybe not. Maybe I'm just a bitch.

"I fantasize. A lot," he said, and burst out laughing. "It's the only way to survive sitting in a car with Fred for hours at a time."

"You don't fantasize about Fred, I hope?"

He reached around, unzipped my skirt, and pulled it down, getting more serious. "I think about you all the time."

I managed to get my skirt off without having to get off him. All that was left were my panty hose and panties; the lights were on and I felt a little exposed. "Do you think we could dim the lights?" I asked.

He reached up and clapped loudly and all of the lights went out instantaneously. I started laughing and couldn't stop. "You have a Clapper?" I said, dropping my head onto his chest.

"A gift. From my aunt Bea," he said, choking out the words between guffaws. "Sexy, huh?"

We got up off the couch, and I took off his shirt. I fumbled with his belt buckle, got it open and put my hand on his zipper, thinking that if we didn't consummate this relationship soon, his pants would rip apart by the force of what was underneath. If that happened, it would be like having sex with the Incredible Hulk. He shook his pants off, leaving them somewhere between the living room and bedroom. We made our way into the bedroom, and I sat on the bed, taking off my panty hose. The room was dark, but I could see his outline as he made his way over to the bed, his boxer shorts hanging off his slim hips. He pushed me back and lay on top of me, his body covering mine. He put his hand to my breast and his other hand behind my head, bringing my face as close to his as he could. "I love you," he whispered. "I've loved you since I first laid eyes on you."

I opened my mouth to speak but he covered it with his own. "Crawford, go slow," I said, wrapping my arms around him and holding him close.

He stopped for a second or two and answered me. "I will," he said, his voice deep and husky. He kissed me, his lips soft on mine.

I opened my mouth to speak but the trill of the phone on his nightstand cut me off. It rang six or seven times before the sound of it registered in our lust-filled brains. The machine clicked on and he dropped his head to my breast and moaned. "No," he said, rolling off me. "No."

"Detective?" the voice on the machine inquired.

Crawford sat up and stared at the phone.

"Detective. I've got your aunt. She's with me."

I recognized the cadence, if not the voice, as Peter Miceli's.

"It would be in your best interest to meet me at Morella's junkyard," he said. "East 229th Street . . ."

Crawford moved to the edge of the bed and lifted up the receiver. "Hello?" It was dark in the room, but by his body language, I could tell that something was wrong. "What? Who is this?" He stood, his bare back to me, and he grabbed his boxers from the floor, pulling them on. "What do you want?"

I pulled the comforter from the bed and wrapped myself in it, feeling as though the evening were going to end on a very bad note. I stood, going around to face him. The look on his face was confused, frightened, and angry all at the same time. "What is it?" I mouthed.

His face went white and he dropped the phone receiver. "He's got Bea." He raced from the room, picking up his pants on the way out.

I stood in the doorway of the bedroom, confused.

"Peter Miceli kidnapped my aunt."

Chapter 28

After Crawford left, I stood for the longest time staring at the closed door of his apartment.

Once I got my bearings, I grabbed the phone and called Max; thankfully, she and Fred were home. "Max, I need Fred."

"I haven't been married long enough for you to be hitting on my husband," she said, laughing. "You're a slut."

"Max, this is serious. Crawford may be in trouble and I need Fred's help."

Hearing the fear in my voice, she handed the phone off to Fred. The minute I heard his gruff voice, I knew I had done the right thing. I told him what had happened and that Crawford was on his way to some junkyard in the Bronx.

"Does that idiot have his cell phone with him?" he asked, furious that Crawford had gone to the junkyard by himself.

I looked around the kitchen where Crawford had re-assembled his arsenal after being naked with me. I didn't see the phone. "I think so."

"I'll call you later." He hung up and I was left with a dial tone in my ear. He had obviously picked up Max's phone manners in the few weeks in which they had been wed.

I was incapable of movement and I stood at the counter next to the kitchen, not sure what to do with myself. I chewed on a nail, praying silently that Crawford didn't get himself killed trying to save his aunt. I was glad that I had called Fred and knew that Crawford would respond better to his help than to anyone else's.

I realized that I needed to call Brendan. His mother answered on the third ring. "Hi, this is Alison, your neighbor. I need some help with Trixie."

"Are you out tonight? Do you need us to walk her?"

"That would be great," I said. "Please tell Brendan that I'll see him tomorrow."

"Brendan! Ms. Bergerson needs you to walk Trixie tonight!" she called to her son.

"And in the morning!" I called, hoping that my yelling would reach Brendan.

"And in the morning!" she called to him. "We're all set. If we don't see you later on tomorrow, we'll take care of her into the afternoon."

"Jane?"

"Yes?"

"How's he doing?"

I heard her sigh on the other end. "Let's just say that taking care of that dog gives him more pleasure than anything else right now."

Enough said. Glad I could help.

After a few minutes of standing naked, wrapped in Crawford's comforter, I went around the living room and bedroom and collected all of my discarded clothing, stopping to sit on the couch and trying to understand what had happened. It made no sense for Peter to kidnap Bea unless Crawford had done more than I knew to piss him off. Was Crawford getting close to solving Ray's murder and implicating Peter for the crime? Was Peter still mad at Crawford for previous transgressions like not solving Kathy's murder and for threatening him at his house, a little tidbit that Max had relayed but which Crawford had never confessed to me? I couldn't figure it out. I was the one Peter was obsessed with, not Crawford. I shivered slightly and wrapped my arms around myself to ward off the chill that enveloped my body.

I took my clothes into the bedroom and got dressed. When I was done, I made the bed, restoring it to the order it was in before we started thrashing around on it. I buried my face in one of his pillows, picking up his scent. I felt at loose ends, and I looked around the room, worried about Crawford's aunt, but curious about his life at the same time. Signs of Crawford were everywhere: a pair of jeans strewn over a wing chair in the corner, the tweed blazer that he had worn the first time we met hanging on the closet door, a pair of giant (and probably dirty) socks stuffed in the corner. As bachelors go, he was pretty meticulous about the space, but no man is that meticulous unless he's gay. I was thrilled to see an indication that he was straight (not that that was ever in doubt), he lived alone, and he forgot to put his stuff away sometimes.

I ran a hand over his cherry dresser; not a speck of dust anywhere. Cleaning lady, I deduced. There was a picture of him and the girls at the beach, he in a bathing suit— thankfully, not a Speedo—and the girls wrapped in towels. I looked at the cologne on the dresser, trying to figure out which one made him smell like clean laundry, the smell of him every time I got close. I opened a few bottles, but nothing approximated the scent that came off his skin. I guessed it was just his own personal scent.

I went into the kitchen and looked around in the cabinets for coffee. Didn't characters in movies always make coffee to calm down in stressful situations? It didn't make sense, just as it didn't make sense to drink coffee to sober up, but I figured I would give it a try. I laid my hands on a canister of beans in the second cabinet and I took it out, opening it up and smelling the rich aroma of fresh coffee.

A knock at the door startled me and I choked back a scream. The coffee beans flew from my hands and scattered all over the Formica countertops and tile floor.

"Bobby?" a woman's voice called on the other side of the door. "Are you all right?"

I went to the apartment door and peered through the peephole. A little woman, pudgy with a wide, bespectacled round face, peered back at me.

"Bobby?" she called again.

I opened the door. She took a step back, looking shocked by either me or my appearance; I couldn't tell. "Hi," I said. "Can I help you?" I asked, taking in her snow-white Dorothy Hamill haircut, leggings, tunic top, and the religious medal around her neck.

She seemed taken aback at my appearance. "Hello . . . who . . . I'm sorry . . . where's Bobby?" she finally asked.

"He had to go out," I said. "I'm his friend, Alison."

She smiled broadly. "Oh, yes. Alison." She gave me a hug, her head hitting my boobs at a weird angle. To an outsider, it would have looked like I was breastfeeding a senior citizen.

Now I was the one to be taken aback. She seemed to know me, yet I had never laid eyes on her. "Yes. Alison." I beckoned for her to come in. "And you are . . . ?"

"Bea McDonald." She held a hand out.

I took her hand in mine, but apparently the look on my face compelled her to elaborate even more on her relationship to Crawford.

"I'm Bobby's aunt."

And you're Gianna Miceli, I thought, as I stared at the woman coming up the stairs behind Bea.

Gianna came into the apartment and put a gun to my temple. Peter's goon, Franco, stood in the doorway of the apartment in his usual attire of black suit, black shirt, and shiny tie, his hands folded in front of him. Gianna pulled

Bea into the apartment and instructed her to sit on the couch. Bea's eyes were wide behind her round glasses.

Gianna looked at Bea. "Mrs. McDonald, I presume?"

Bea nodded, holding Gianna's gaze, tough old broad that she was. I had no idea Gianna knew who Bea was, but if she had been planning this for a while, she was smart enough to have done her homework on me, Crawford, and his extended family.

"How did you get in here, Gianna?" I asked.

She snorted derisively. "That was the easy part, Alison. Franco here has a whole set of, shall we say, 'skill sets' that come in very handy in these kinds of situations."

That really didn't answer my question but I let it go. "What the hell do you want with us, Gianna?"

My first reaction to seeing Bea was that while I thought Crawford had been set up and could possibly be in danger, the call had been made to get Crawford out of the apartment. And when I saw Gianna coming up the stairs, the giant gun in her tiny hand, I realized that I was the one who had been set up. Gianna was here for me and she wanted Crawford gone. I came to the conclusion that it had been Franco who had made the phone call, sounding enough like Peter for Crawford to believe that Bea was in trouble.

Gianna had always been impeccably dressed in college and today was no different. I remember that she always had the best and most expensive clothes and what she was wearing now was evidence of that: impeccably cut black pants, black leather boots, and a butter-soft black leather jacket. To me, it had always seemed that Peter had gotten the better end of the deal when he married Gianna; it was the proverbial *Beauty and the Beast* scenario with mafiosi. Gianna waved the gun in my direction. "I understand you've been spending a little time with my husband, Alison."

I looked back at Gianna, the realization dawning on me slowly. The night at St. Thomas where she told me that Peter sent his regards, the note . . . it was all coming together. Oh, jeez, I thought; now I'm caught in the middle of a Mafia love triangle. "Gianna, Peter has this habit of either breaking into my house or kidnapping me. Believe me," I said gravely, "and I mean this with all due respect, I have no interest in your husband." As a matter of fact, he makes my skin crawl, I thought, but I left that out. I also left out the part where we made out in the diner.

Gianna looked at Franco and then back at me. "I don't believe you," she said.

I sighed, more out of frustration than anything else. "Gianna, believe me." I shot Bea a look. "I'm in love with someone else. I have no interest in Peter whatsoever." I was dancing, and dancing that fine line between denial and insult: if I denied an attraction to Peter too much, I would end up insulting Gianna. I had to tread carefully so that I didn't end up with a bullet in the face.

I looked over at Bea, who had a huge grin on her face. "In love?" she mouthed silently.

"Oh, this Detective Crawford character?" Gianna asked, her voice dripping with sarcasm. She motioned around his apartment. "You're in love with a guy who makes a dollar ninety an hour and will retire with a city pension? Spare me, Alison." She looked down at my feet. "The shoes you're wearing cost more than that guy makes in a week." She tossed her blond mane over her shoulder and smirked.

She was right—about the shoes, that is. They were expensive, but I never would have bought them for myself, good old-fashioned French-Canadian thrift being part of my makeup. "They were a gift, Gianna. From Max." I knew they cost a lot. More than Crawford made in a week? Highly doubtful. But Gianna was on a tear and I wasn't going to stop her. She was the one with the gun.

She grabbed me by the collar and pulled me toward the door; I was surprised by the strength in this petite woman. "Let's go." She turned and looked at Bea, who was hunched over on the couch, her hands between her legs. "Are you going to join us or do I need to have Franco"—she searched for the right word—"*persuade* you?"

Bea hoisted herself off the couch and resignedly walked to the door. I noticed a piece of paper flutter to the ground before Bea walked away from the couch. Gianna tightened her grip on my collar and pulled me out into the hallway and down the stairs. The limo was idling by the front door of the house.

I looked around before Franco pushed me into the car, but nobody on the busy street seemed to find it unusual that Bea and I were getting into the limo or noticed our obvious distress. "Where are we going, Gianna?" I asked her.

"Don't worry about that," she said, and tapped on the glass for Franco.

I thought about the situation. It was hard for me to believe that this woman—someone with whom I had only a nodding acquaintance fifteen years ago—was back in my life, accusing me of being attracted to her husband, and threatening my life. But she certainly meant business. My heart was thumping in my chest, and I reached across the seat to grab Bea's hand. She curled her chubby little fingers around my own and squeezed.

We hurtled down the West Side Highway, through the Brooklyn Battery Tunnel, and onto some highway I was sure I had never traveled. We passed acre after acre of warehouses and rundown apartment buildings and houses and it finally occurred to me that we were probably in Brooklyn. We sat in silence for the entire ride, me casting a glance at Bea every now and again, noticing that her face revealed nothing. She didn't look scared, but twenty minutes or so into our trip, I noticed her lips moving in silent prayer. After traveling for about a half hour, we crossed the Verrazano-Narrows Bridge, paid the toll, and traveled farther on a road I knew I had never been on in my life. We finally turned into a landfill and my heart stopped thudding and seemingly ceased to beat. Unless we were on a scavenger hunt, this was going to end badly.

Franco pulled into a spot between two heaping mounds of refuse about two miles into the landfill and cut the engine. He got out of the car and opened the door, motioning for the two of us to get out. Once Bea and I were out of the car—our noses filling with the stench of garbage—Gianna got out, the gun still in her hand. It drooped a bit, not pointed directly at us, and it occurred to me that she was finding it heavy. She waved it at us and told us to move away from the car.

"This time, I'll make sure the shot hits you," she said, smiling slightly. When she saw the puzzlement on my face, she elaborated. "I almost got you the first time, Alison. Under the el?"

I instinctively put my hand to my injured arm.

"You know that saying? 'Good help is hard to find'? Very true. The kid I hired to take you out couldn't hit the broad side of a barn," she said, shaking her head. "Let's just say we've given him a desk job." She chuckled. "I'm afraid we're also turning into the gang who couldn't shoot straight. Right now, we're the gang who can't shoot, maim, or dismember with any efficiency at all. When all of this is over, I'll be cleaning house."

I rubbed my scar from the gunshot wound.

"I almost don't mind Peter having his fun with anonymous sluts. But you? That was too much to bear." A tear ran down her face.

"Gianna, I can't impress upon you enough how wrong you are," I said. I ducked as a seagull flew dangerously close to my head.

"She's in love with my nephew!" Bea exclaimed, still apparently delighted with that news.

"Right. I'm love with her nephew," I agreed, nodding enthusiastically.

"First, my daughter is found, like trash, in the trunk of your car. Then you start spending time with my husband. Is there anything else you can do to make my life more miserable than it already is?" she cried, the gun falling down to hip level.

Franco stood behind her in his usual stance, hands folded in front of him. He didn't seem fazed by this psychodrama and watched everything with a robotic detachment that I found more disconcerting than Gianna's meltdown.

"And to learn that Kathy had been pregnant, probably by your pig ex-husband . . ." She drifted off, her mind elsewhere.

"I told Peter, Gianna. It wasn't Ray. He'd had a vasectomy." I paused. "I promise you, it wasn't Ray." No use going into the whole stupid story again. "You killed him for nothing."

She smirked. "It was really you that I wanted gone, Alison. And I didn't want you to have any warning that it would happen. I will never forgive you, Alison," she said, and raised the gun. "Even after you're gone." The gun dropped again.

Part of me felt sorry for her. I had known her daughter and knew what a lovely girl she had been. I had buried two parents as a young adult yet I had no idea what it might be like to bury a child. I almost understood Gianna's insanity, but I couldn't figure out why I had become the object of it. "Who killed Ray, Gianna? Did you do it or did you have someone do it for you? Who was it?" I don't know why it was so important for me to know, but it was.

She looked at me and smiled. "Oh, some stupid kid. He was supposed to kill you, but when he found Ray, he did him instead. I got sick of waiting around for you, Alison. I figured that I'd do it myself."

So, it was me she wanted. Not Ray. When the cold reality of having cheated death twice entered my consciousness, I shuddered. "Why do you want me dead so badly, Gianna?"

"If you can't figure that out, Alison, then you're not as smart as Peter gives you credit for." Her lips quivered as she fought the urge to cry. "And if it wasn't for Peter, you'd have been dead six months ago."

It was all starting to dawn on me. "Peter didn't have anything to do with any of this?" I asked, not really understanding any of it but coming to the conclusion anyway.

"No," she said.

I decided to go for broke. "What's he going to do when he finds out that you've been ordering hits on your own?" Peter was in charge of the family and, if I had my Mafia rules straight, only he could order a hit.

A look passed across her face, but I had no idea what it meant. "Why would you think that I couldn't order a hit?" she asked.

"Because Peter's in charge," I said.

"You think Peter had something to do with all of this? You think Peter's in charge?" she asked, wonder in her voice. "Huh," she said, amazed that I had drawn that conclusion. She regained her composure. "I'm always amazed that nobody has figured this out. And especially you, Alison. Peter's always talking about how smart you are. Let me fill you in on something, Alison: Peter is a moron." She blessed herself—the name of the Father, son, and Holy Spirit. "God forgive me."

I knew that he was a moron but I wasn't convinced it

made him any less deadly. "I have a hard time believing that, Gianna. He runs the largest organized-crime family in the tristate area. He couldn't be that much of a dope."

"Oh, he is." She laughed, and it was one of those moments where, if she wasn't going to kill me minutes later, we would have had a great chuckle over all of it. Peter the moron. The imbecile.

I had one of those moments of clarity that usually only happens in the seconds prior to waking up. Where it seems like everything is crystal clear but you come to find later that you were really sleeping, almost dreaming, and not quite awake. I waited a few seconds to see if I would wake up and all of this would be forgotten, but I was still in the same place and confronted with the same horrors. I felt my energy start to flag and I grabbed Bea's hand for support.

Gianna let the gun drop to her side. "I'm in charge, Alison. I always have been. Do you think my father would have turned the family over to Peter Miceli?" she said, amazed that I would have thought otherwise. "But it's still a man's world in the family. We needed a figurehead. And that's how I ended up married to Peter. He really was the logical choice given my father's loyalty to Joe Miceli."

"It was an arranged marriage," I said, stunned.

She nodded. "Of sorts. I have a soft spot for the guy, but nothing approximating passion," she said. "I had passion once. For Sal Paccione." I remembered Sal from our college days; he had disappeared one day, never to reappear. She picked the gun up and pointed it at me again. "And we know what happened to him."

Yes, we do, I thought.

"Of course, that's not to say I like the thought of Peter being in love with someone else," she said pointedly. She held the gun chest high and steadied it.

"Why did you kill Terri?" I asked.

She looked confused. "Who's Terri?"

"My neighbor. Terri Morrison. I found her a few days ago."

"That is something that I know absolutely nothing about."

"But the hands and feet . . ." I didn't have the energy to protest so I dropped it. I would be dead and nobody would know whether or not I had gotten Gianna's confession. In what I assumed were my final moments on the earth, I thought of Max and Trixie. An image of my father in his UPS uniform flashed before my eyes as did my mother in all of her incredible Gallic beauty. And I saw Crawford, shaking his head sadly, but smiling at me. I choked back a sob. "Please, Gianna. I'm begging you. Let us go."

"Alison, I might have considered that but now you know way too much." She shook her head, chagrined. "Way too much." She leveled the gun at me and I felt my knees go weak. "How far we've come," she mused.

Bea squeezed my hand.

Franco finally spoke and Gianna turned to the sound of his voice. I had never heard him speak, so I was surprised to find he had a Southern accent. "Mrs. Miceli, put the gun down." He pointed a gun, produced magically from a back pocket, at her.

She trained the gun on him. "Franco, you know why we're here. Now let me kill them and then we can go home."

"Put the gun down, Mrs. Miceli."

Gianna turned and looked at us and then back at Franco, deciding what to do. "I'm not putting the gun down, Franco. Get in the car, please, before I call Mr. Miceli and tell him what a pain in the butt you've become."

"I'll say it one more time, and then I'm going to shoot you, Mrs. Miceli: put the gun down."

Crawford got back to the apartment in record time, thanks to his police escort. Fred was already there, as well as just about every cop from his local precinct. He burst into the living room and found the lead detective, John Galvin, a guy he had gone to the academy with, organizing the other detectives.

"Anything, John?" he asked, panting from the exertion of running up the stairs.

The detective put a note in front of Crawford's face; Crawford wasn't wearing gloves, and Galvin didn't want to taint the evidence with another set of fingerprints. "Does this mean anything to you?" he asked.

There was only a name on the slip of paper, written in Bea's looping, Catholic-school handwriting: "Gianna Miceli."

Crawford looked at Galvin, confused. "Gianna has them?"

Fred walked in at that moment and looked at the note. "What the hell does that mean?"

Crawford walked over to the kitchen. "There must have been a struggle. There are coffee beans everywhere."

Fred looked around. "Yeah, but nothing else." He ran a hand over his bald head. "Why would either of the Micelis kidnap Bea and Alison?"

Crawford had no idea. He shook his head sadly. "I don't know." He looked up at Galvin. "Do we know anything else?"

"No." Galvin handed the note to the crime scene technician who appeared beside him. "Give me a full description of your aunt and the woman with her." Galvin jotted some notes as Crawford described Bea, then Alison. He smiled when Crawford finished. "I think I'll leave 'beautiful' out of Alison's description. With this crew," he said, hooking a thumb at the uniforms, "that'll be open to interpretation. Johnson over there might bring back a Twelfth Avenue hooker," he said, attempting to joke Crawford out of his black mood.

Crawford got up from the couch. "I feel like I should be doing something. Anything." He looked at Fred. "What should we do?"

Galvin held up a hand. "You're going to stay here and do nothing. We've got it under control. Every cop in the city will have these descriptions in about two minutes." He reached up and put a hand on Crawford's shoulder. "Don't worry. We'll find them."

Crawford ran his hands over his face and looked at Fred. Fred didn't say anything, but the intensity of his gaze let Crawford know that he was worried, too.

"Fred," he said, his voice cracking, "if anything happens to them . . ." Then he stopped. He didn't know what he would do if something happened to them and that was the saddest reality of all.

Chapter 29

Franco repeated his request but didn't make good on his promise to shoot her if he had to ask again.

Gianna looked at Franco, her back to us. "What?" she asked.

"Put the gun down, Mrs. Miceli." He hesitated for a moment and then said, "You are under arrest."

Gianna's face was a mixture of surprise, anger, and shock. The gun waved back and forth in her hand and she put her left hand under it to steady it, pointing it now at Franco instead of me and Bea.

"You're under arrest, Mrs. Miceli," he said, keeping his gun pointed at her chest. He reached into his pocket with his free hand and produced a badge. "I'm with the FBI."

Gianna let out a breath of air that sounded like the air coming out of a balloon. "Don't be ridiculous. I think I would have known if you were with the FBI. You've worked for us for five years."

"And I've been with the FBI for twenty," he said. "Put the gun down."

Bea reached over and grabbed my hand, pulling me away from the scene. We slipped around to the front of the limo and crouched beside the front driver's side, our eyes barely over the hood so that we could see what was happening.

"You have got to be kidding me!" Gianna screamed.

"You've worked for us for five years. Why are you pulling this shit now?"

"Because I'm a federal agent, ma'am. And I now have enough to put you and Mr. Miceli away for a long time."

She was obviously as confused as we were. I could almost see her mind trying to process what Franco had revealed, what he had seen in five years, what would happen to her and Peter as a result. And her children, still young. After some time, I could tell that she had made her decision as to how this was going to go and it didn't include her in an orange jumpsuit. She started toward Franco, ten feet separating them, and attempted to squeeze the trigger of the gun.

Franco coolly fired a shot directly into her chest and she crumpled to the ground without uttering a sound. I grabbed Bea and put my head into her chest.

Franco walked over to Gianna and stood over her, the gun pointed at her lifeless body. Convinced that she was dead, he crouched beside her, took the gun from her hand, and put his finger to her neck. "It's all right, ladies. You can come out," he said and stood up.

I stood first, leaving Bea by the side of the limo. "You killed her," I said, stunned. I looked down at Gianna, a lump at the foot of a heap of garbage, a gaping hole in the middle of her chest. I put my hand to my mouth. "Why did you do that?"

"Because she was going to kill you." He reached into his pocket and took out a cell phone, telling someone what had happened and giving them our location. When he was done, he flipped the phone closed and looked at me. "I'm sorry you all had to see that."

"You could have maimed her!" I cried.

"We aren't taught to shoot to maim, ma'am," he said, smiling slightly.

I started crying. "Who are you? And why didn't you try to stop her from having Ray killed? Or me?"

"Franco Castellano. FBI. I've been undercover in the Miceli family for five years." He pulled out his badge and showed it to me; it looked real. "And I didn't know about the hit on you. When I saw that your ex-husband had been killed, I tried to get information, but it's a large family, Dr. Bergeron. A lot goes on. And I spent more time with Mr. Miceli than with Mrs. Miceli."

Bea appeared at my side. "Where are you from?" she asked.

"Alabama, ma'am."

"I didn't know there were any Italians in the South." She looked down at Gianna and whistled her amazement. "You're some shot, my friend." She looked back up at Franco. "Do they have some kind of protection program for guys like you?"

"Ma'am?" Franco asked, unsure of what she meant.

"You know, guys like you. You just killed the wife of a capo in New York. Or a sort of capo. Or the capo herself. I don't know which end is up anymore," she said, confused. "You're a dead man," she finally concluded.

Franco smiled. "I think I'll be fine," he said. He took off his black jacket and placed it carefully over Gianna's face and most of her body; her legs had folded beneath her, so her frame was compressed into a tiny ball under the fabric of his jacket. "Despite the fact that he was a figurehead for the family, Peter Miceli has his hand in a lot of illegal activities. He's going away for a long time. This investigation has unearthed a lot of evidence that the government needed to put him and several of his soldiers away."

"Are you the only one?" I asked.

"The only one?"

"The only undercover agent," I said. "Or are there more of you?"

He smiled again. "If I told you that, I'd have to kill you," he said, in a weak attempt at joke making.

I gave him a wan smile in reply. Seeing how he had just shot Gianna in cold blood, I thought perhaps he was only half kidding.

"Seriously, though, this investigation has been going on probably for as long as you've known the Micelis," he said, and pulled a pack of cigarettes from his pocket. He cupped his hand around the match as he lit one. "Mrs. Miceli's hatred of you and her suspicion of her husband's adultery was really just a nuisance. I couldn't blow the case but I couldn't let her kill you, either. Fortunately, a series of indictments will come down tomorrow and Mr. Miceli will be making funeral arrangements from jail."

His detachment in telling us the details of the story chilled me to the bone but he had saved our lives. Who was I to judge?

I felt as if the ground below me were shifting, unsteady. I put an arm around Bea and turned away, wiping my eyes on the arm of my sweater. In the distance, I heard the persistent wail of sirens and relief flooded my body.

Franco put his hand in his pocket again and pulled out my cell phone. "You'll probably want this back," he said and tossed it to me.

It started ringing the minute it hit the palm of my hand. Crawford. "Hello?"

His voice crackled over the bad connection but I could tell that he was frantic. "Alison? Is Bea with you? Are you both okay?"

I filled him in as best I could and told him I would call him back when I got to the station house; I knew, from experience, that being the witness to a homicide meant a long night. The police cars that had been in the distance sped up to our location, spewing dust and decomposing garbage into the air. I covered my mouth and tried not to gag. Dozens of cops jumped from the six or more cars that had pulled up and immediately sized up the scene. Franco pulled his FBI badge from his pocket and began detailing what had happened over the past hour and a half.

I took one last look at Gianna's form before getting into the police car and said a silent prayer for her tortured soul.

Chapter 30

The week passed without incident, a new and joyful experience for me. Work returned to the mundane, and after having been shot (sort of) and kidnapped (for real), the back-up of papers, phone calls, and student visits was overwhelming. By the end of the week, I was frazzled, but in a good way. Work had helped return my life to normal and that was a good thing.

Sister Calista had begun eyeing me warily every time I set foot in the office area. I wanted to walk up to her and say, "You want a piece of me, lady?" because the events of the past weeks had obviously given her pause when it came to me. Maybe that would make her reconsider her recent recalcitrance.

Franco's promise to put Peter away was kept: a day after Gianna's death, Peter was picked up at a social club in Little Italy and arrested. Franco apparently wasn't the only undercover member of the Miceli family; there were four in total and they had amassed quite a file of information. The number of indictments against him and several of his closest "family" members was staggering and the story filled the paper. Several local newspapers called me for interviews, as did most of the morning programs, but I declined all comment and sent them to my new lawyer, Jimmy, a man I had grown very fond of in the last few weeks. He was a nutcase, and obviously had terrible eating habits and high blood pressure, judging from his potbelly and florid color, but I felt secure knowing that he was fielding all of my phone calls, even if I couldn't be sure of how he was characterizing the situation.

Jimmy was circumspect about the possibility of my testifying at the trial but promised he would do everything to keep me out of it.

Jimmy was also true to his word in getting my resisting-arrest charge dropped along with the harassment portion of the charges. Crawford had continued looking into the stolen-car part of the case on his own time but couldn't come up with anything. He had, however, found out that the person driving the car and who had called the New York State Troopers to report that I was following them was a man. So, it could have been Jackson. Or not.

My money was still on a Miceli but I still hadn't figured out the motive part of things.

Regarding the state troopers, however, I had to pay a fine for driving without my license and registration, had points put on my license for the speed, and had to enroll in the defensive driving class. I sent them a fruit basket just for good measure. All in all, not too bad. But I would never go to Stew Leonard's again without thinking about getting arrested in my pajamas.

I had spoken with Crawford a few times, but we hadn't seen each other since the week before. Our last conversation had held the most disturbing news of all: Franco had gone missing, and when Crawford had called the FBI to get contact information on him, they professed to never have heard of him. That gave me pause. Either he was under such deep cover that that was the FBI's story—a theory Crawford leaned toward, given the fact that he had spent a few months undercover in narcotics and knew a bit about these things—or Franco was a member of another "family" and had been hired to take out Gianna, or a combination of both, an FBI informant and member of the "family." I tried, along with everything else I knew, to put the fact that he was missing in my own brain's deep cover.

I had also talked to Bea two times; nothing brings you closer together than being kidnapped and having your life threatened. We decided to get together for lunch in a couple of weeks to get to know each other outside of a threatening situation.

I was surprised when Crawford stopped by my office unexpectedly on a Friday afternoon. He had just gotten off work and was hoping to catch me before I left.

"Hey, handsome," I said, standing up behind my desk.

He leaned over the piece of furniture separating us and gave me a peck on the cheek. "I was thinking."

"Always trouble," I remarked, shoving some papers into my briefcase.

He smirked. "If you're not doing anything tonight, do you want to come over to my place? I'd like to make you dinner."

I walked around my desk and closed my door, putting some space between the two of us and Dottie's prying eyes and ears. I lowered my voice. "Let's call a spade a spade. We both know what we're talking about here. A pizza, a bottle of cheap red wine, and sex. No interruptions. How does that sound?" I asked him, slipping my finger into the waistband of his pants and pulling him close.

He sighed. "Can we at least have the illusion of romance here?" He looked at a spot over my head. "Does everything have to be so cut-and-dried with you?"

I smiled, holding my hands up as if to say "you knew what you were getting yourself into."

"Fine. Have it your way," he said and shoved his hands into his pockets. "We'll do it your way: come to my place. Seven o'clock. Leave your underwear at home."

"Now you're talking." I wrapped my arms around his waist. "Did you leave your handcuffs at work?"

He flushed a deep red. "Nope. They're in the car."

I kissed him. "Good. Make sure you bring them inside."

He pulled away from me. "Great," he said, exasperated. "Now I can't leave." He looked down at his belt buckle, his zipper lying not quite as flat as when he had arrived. "Talk about James Joyce or something so I don't feel quite so"—he searched for the right word—"happy."

I laughed. "Get going. I'm going to go home and pack some things, call Bagpipe Kid, and I'll meet you in a couple of hours."

"What do you want for dinner?" he asked.

"Pizza, cheap red wine, and sex. I thought we covered that."

He smiled. "I couldn't remember if it was cheap sex, pizza, and red wine. Thanks for putting the adjectives in the proper order. You got it." He put his hand on the doorknob. "I'll see you in what? Two, three hours?"

"Two if I don't shave my legs," I said.

"Don't bother," he said. "I spend all of my time with Fred. Anything less than the 'missing link' look will be an improvement."

We both left the office and I bid Dottie good-bye. She gave me a sideways glance, which made me think she had heard our whole conversation. Did she have the entire office area bugged? She knew more about what was going on in the department than anyone.

He walked me to my car and we parted ways. I was past being nervous about consummating this relationship; it had been way too long in coming, so to speak. I raced home and set about taking care of everything that needed attention before I spent the night away from home.

Trixie greeted me with her usual butt sniff to welcome me home. I checked her dishes and saw that she had been fed by Bagpipe Kid and had fresh water. "God bless you, Bagpipe Kid!" I proclaimed and reached for the phone. I dialed his number; his mother answered after a few rings. "Hi, this is Alison across the street. Is Brendan home?"

"Hi, Alison. No, he's not. He went to a bagpipe festival in the Catskills this weekend," she said.

Shit. "Good for him!" I said, trying to sound happy that Bagpipe Kid had a life outside of being my personal manservant. "I just wanted to thank him for feeding Trixie today," I lied. She informed me that she had another son but he was out of pocket, too, something about a basketball tournament. I looked down and Trixie stared up at me, a pool of drool forming at our feet. We chatted a few more minutes about Brendan's love for Trixie and I asked her how he was doing before I hung up. She said that he was really getting back to being his old self and that made me happy. "Well, Trixie, my friend, it looks like you're going on a sleepover," I said. She responded by wagging her tail vigorously. "At least you don't need to pack a bag."

I did everything I needed to do in record time—including shaving my legs—coaxed Trixie into my car, and started off for Crawford's apartment. I headed south on the Saw Mill, smiling more than I had in over a year. I looked in the rearview mirror and took a look at Trixie, who seemed happy to be out of the house and embarking on some adventure with me. I felt a pang of guilt that I left her alone so much.

I found a parking spot a few blocks west of Crawford's building and wedged myself into the space. I took my bag out of the backseat and grabbed Trixie's leash, the two of us trotting down the street.

The river was at my back and the sun was setting, casting a purple glow over the city streets. I didn't look out of place in this residential neighborhood; several people

who passed me were also walking dogs and we acknowl-
edged each other as members of the secret world of people who like each other only because we all own dogs.
Trixie stopped to sniff the ground a few times and I pulled
her along, anxious to get to our final destination.

We arrived at Crawford's building and I pressed the
buzzer outside the front door. He buzzed me in and stood
at the top of the stairs, waiting and watching as I let myself in.

"Trixie?" he asked, and I let go of the leash, allowing
her to bound up the stairs to greet him. She licked his face,
something I was hoping to do shortly. I followed behind.

"Brendan's got a bagpipe festival in the Catskills this
weekend, so I had to bring her." I made my way up the
long flight of stairs and threw my bag at him. "Thanks for
the help with my bag."

He laughed and picked it up from the floor. "Come
on in."

I went into his apartment; he had lit candles all over
the room and set the table with wineglasses and nice
dishes. A pizza sat in the middle of the table, as did a
nice bottle of red wine. "Crawford," I said, "you've out-
done yourself."

He put his arms around me and kissed me. "I spare no
expense when it comes to you."

Trixie began exploring the room, sniffing in different
corners and wandering into the bedrooms. She came out
of Crawford's bedroom with a dirty gym sock in her
mouth and set about chewing it.

Crawford handed me a glass of wine. "Thanks for
coming."

"Isn't that a little presumptuous?" I asked. "We haven't
done anything yet."

He burst out laughing. "I have high hopes." He poured
more wine into my glass. "I have cannolis again."

I perked up. I love cannolis and he knew it.

"It has been my dream to watch you eat a cannoli," he said.

"Oh, and I won't disappoint, my friend," I said, and took another sip of wine. The heat went through me, settling into a nice, warm glow in my stomach.

Crawford got up and went over to the stereo in the corner of the apartment. "How about some music?" he asked and turned on the receiver. Loud strains of music with a Latin beat—Santana's "Oye Como Va"—blasted through the speakers, surprising him. He jumped back, seemingly moved by the sound of the music.

I jumped up and started to dance. "No, leave it!" I called over the din.

"This isn't what I had in mind!" he shouted back.

I continued to dance toward him, singing along with the music. "Oye como va . . . Hey, mister . . . I'm not wearing a bra . . ." I sang, the words that Max had made up to cover for the fact that she didn't understand Spanish coming back to me.

He walked toward me, laughing. "'Hey, mister, I'm not wearing a bra'?" He pulled at the top button of my blouse and peered in. "Not true and not the words."

I put one arm around his waist and took his hand, making him dance. "I only speak French. No Spanish."

He led me to the stereo and turned it down so that we could talk without shouting. "Speaking of which, you've never spoken any French to me. I think it's about time."

I stood on my tiptoes and whispered some very dirty French into his ear.

"I have no idea what you just said."

"I said I want more pizza."

"No you didn't."

I whispered the translation in his ear.

"Okay," he said slowly, and took my hand, leading me

into the bedroom. He took a final look at Trixie and closed the door. The lights were off, but he had arranged candles around the room so that a soft glow was cast over everything. He took my face in his hands and kissed me, his lips and tongue tasting like wine. "I love you."

I touched his cheek. "I love you, too."

He looked relieved. "You do?"

"Of course I do. What did you think?" I asked.

"I don't know. You're not exactly an easy read."

"How about this? You take off all of your clothes and I'll show you how much I love you. How does that sound?" I led him over to the bed and pushed him down. I got on top of him and ripped his shirt open, buttons making pinging sounds as they hit the walls and floor. "Then, I'm finishing the pizza."

Chapter 31

Crawford and I had settled into a nice routine: Friday nights were spent at my house and Sunday nights we stayed at his apartment. He arranged his schedule so that he didn't have to go to work until ten on Monday mornings, and my classes didn't begin until a little after that, so we got to spend part of the morning together, with him dropping me off at work on his way to the station house. From Saturday morning to Sunday evening, he was in the city with his daughters. He hadn't introduced me to them yet and I was fine with that; although they were sixteen and sounded pretty mature, we were still in the early stages of this relationship and wanted to wait for the right time to unleash the second new relationship in their lives, their mother's new one with the divorced neighbor being the first. I had spoken with his almost-ex, Christine, on the phone a few times, and she was exceedingly nice—almost saintly—in her support of our relationship. She confided to me that her wedding would be the following summer. The girls liked her fiancé which was as much of an endorsement as she needed.

I was actually looking forward to officially meeting her at some point. Crawford was right: she was someone with whom I could be friends.

Bagpipe Kid let me know that he had gotten into Notre Dame, early admission, and would be leaving the following summer to spread his bagpipe love in South Bend, In-diana. Well, actually, I made that last part up—he told me he was excited about going to the school to study prelaw. In the days since we had discovered the body, he had come out of his shell a little bit, and when he came over to play with Trixie, we chatted and I learned more about him. He was still traumatized by finding the body but he seemed to be getting over it as the days passed.

He introduced me to his little brother—whom I dubbed "Accordion Boy"—a sophomore at Stepinac, a local all-boys' Catholic high school. He played piano accordion (apparently, there is more than one type of accordion, which was news to me) in an Irish ceili band and was only unavailable on Thursday nights, which was when the band rehearsed. This all meant something to Crawford, even though it sounded to me like they were always speaking Gaelic. Accordion Boy, whose name continues to escape me, was more than willing to take over Trixie duty in several months and began to learn the ropes. He figured out what made Trixie tick and seemed to enjoy his time with her. If I hadn't gotten so attached to Trixie myself, I would have given custody of her to the boys, but I just couldn't bring myself. Seeing her every night when I came home from work was the best part of my day. Unless, of course, Crawford was in the picture.

Everything was perfect.

One weekend before Thanksgiving, Crawford's daughters were spending the weekend with their mother in Boston, so when we woke up one of those rare Saturdays when we could be together, we had a whole day to spend with each other, uninterrupted. We lay in bed, holding hands and talking about our plans for the day. They didn't amount to much and weren't much different from other weekend days we spent in Dobbs Ferry: breakfast at the diner, the Rangers on television if they had a game, lunch, a nap, cocktails, and then some kind of dinner that didn't involve too much effort. We had turned into one of those couples who didn't go out much but who didn't need to; everything we wanted resided within whatever four walls we inhabited together.

We woke up around eight. Crawford rolled over and propped himself up on his hand, his elbow sinking into the pillow. "I've been thinking."

"Don't hurt yourself." I stretched, and threw the covers off. The sun was streaming through the window and warmed the skin on my arms.

"No, seriously, I was thinking."

"Oh, no, here we go again. Last time you said that to me, I ended up pantyless, trapped in your apartment."

He smiled. "Could you be serious for a minute?"

I pursed my lips, trying desperately not to laugh.

"Thank you." He rolled his eyes. "I realized that I haven't taken a real vacation in almost five years. Do you want to go away during the Christmas break?"

"What did you have in mind?" I asked, my interest piqued. Christmas break wasn't for several weeks but if he was thinking that far ahead, that was a good sign.

"A cruise? Aruba maybe? Napa?" he asked, and then looked away. "Vegas?"

"Anything but Vegas," I said, and made fake gagging noises.

He looked crestfallen.

"Do you want to go to Vegas?" I asked, thinking I may have hurt his feelings. The vision of a tacky wedding chapel floated into my mind and I quickly pushed it aside.

He recovered quickly. "No," he said. "I was just thinking of someplace warm."

I suspected he was lying about Vegas, but I let it go. "Let's go to Napa. It won't be really warm this time of year, but it could be very romantic," I said, and stroked his bare stomach.

"And I know how much you love romance," he said, smirking. He rolled on top of me and pinned my hands over my head, kissing me. "Let's think about it. Having you around all of that wine might make for an interesting trip."

"I only get uninhibited on painkillers. Wine I can handle."

We got tangled up in the covers and started peeling off our clothes, still in that stage of the relationship where making love twice a day was not out of the question. I wasn't sure how Crawford felt, but I couldn't get enough of him. I suspected he felt the same way and I was hoping we would continue to feel that way for a long time. I heard a knock at the back door at a crucial moment in our wrestling match and I groaned.

"Don't go anywhere," I warned Crawford as I got out of bed and reassembled my sleeping outfit—tank top and pajama pants, throwing on the sweatshirt that hung on the back of my bathroom door. My clogs were by the door and I shoved my feet into them, not looking forward to running across cold ceramic tile without them. I ran down the stairs and opened the back door.

It was Accordion Boy, brother of Brendan. "Hi, Mrs. Bergerson."

At first, I had asked him to call me Alison, but he said his mother didn't approve of him calling grown-ups by their first names. I didn't try to disabuse him of the notion that (a) I wasn't a grown-up, (b) I wasn't married (if she didn't want him calling me Alison then she surely didn't want me telling him that the guy in my bedroom wasn't my husband), and (c) that my name was Bergeron. No *s*. So, we left it at "Mrs. Bergerson" for me and "Mr. Bergerson" for Crawford. He and his brother had committed the incorrect name to memory and I let it go. When it came right down to it, I could never remember his name, either, so who was I to complain?

"Can I take Trixie out?" he asked. He was tall, like his brother, and had the smattering of freckles across his nose that seemed to be a trait in his family. He had strawberry blond hair that was cut short and beautiful blue eyes which supported what his brother told me about him: he had a real way with the ladies—wink, wink, nudge, nudge. His good looks would only improve over time, I was sure, and Jane would be beating girls off with a stick shortly. Besides the good looks, he also had a certain je ne sais quoi that I'm sure drove the teenage girls wild.

Trixie came into the kitchen, her nails tapping on the ceramic tile. I noticed that her leash wasn't on its usual hook by the back door and it occurred to me that I had left it in the car. "Come with me," I said to the boy. "I left her leash in the car."

Accordion Boy followed me out of the house, trailing Trixie behind him; we made our way across the backyard, chatting about the upcoming holidays and his midterm exams. I offered to help him study for his English test; I figured I had to do something for this kid and his brother. They walked my dog for free and would probably do just about anything else I asked.

Trixie, who is generally a very placid and rule-following animal, surprised me by darting off and plunging through the hedgerow into her former backyard, home of the absent Terri and Jackson. "Trixie!" I called after her. "Come back!"

She ran straight to the sliding doors that led to the kitchen and paced back and forth in front of them, barking. When it was clear that she wasn't coming back, I shimmied through the hedges and walked over to her, grabbing her by the collar. She didn't budge. "Fine. Stay there." I started to walk away, hoping she would follow me. "You're going to get hungry, eventually, and then you'll really want to come home."

It dawned on me that all she heard was "blah, blah, blah" but I was confident that she would come home eventually. She probably needed to have a moment at her former abode.

"So, when's your English test?" I asked the kid, who was poised next to my car, on the other side of the hedge.

The kid stared back at me, his mouth hanging open.

"Your test? When is it?" I asked, making my way across the Morrisons' backyard. First the dog, and now this. I apparently had lost any sense of authority that I once had if I couldn't get a dog and a fifteen-year-old to respond to me. I had almost reached the hedge when I noticed that the boy was frozen, staring at something behind me. I turned slowly and watched as Jackson came walking across the backyard, a huge knife poised above his left shoulder and aimed directly at me. I recognized it as the kind of knife you would get in the Wüsthof six-pack of carving knives, the one designated for deboning game birds. I had spent enough time watching my father debone waterfowl to know the damage that knife could do. It wasn't roadkill, but it was close enough.

"Go get Mr. Bergerson!" I yelled to the boy, watching as Jackson picked up speed. I watched the boy run off at the same time that Jackson let out an animalistic roar, and I put both hands up in front of me in an attempt to shield both my face and torso from the weapon.

The knife tore into my left hand and I gasped in agony and surprise. But with any sense I had left, I managed to push Jackson back onto the grass. I caught sight of Trixie out of the corner of my eye pacing nervously back and forth at the edge of Jackson's backyard. She was confused; who to save? Her former master or her new one? I started to run toward her, but Jackson had regained his footing and was upright again, running after me. He caught the back of my sweatshirt shirt and pulled me back. I began to fall backward, my arms pinwheeling in the air.

"Trixie!" I yelled, my throat constricted by my collar. The dog continued to pace, uttering a low-pitched moan. The backyard wasn't large but getting across it and away from Jackson proved too much for me. I fell with a thud onto my back, my head hitting the hard earth. The blue sky above swam before my eyes and I struggled to stay conscious.

I looked up at Jackson, who stood over me, the blood-ied knife hanging by his side. He wasn't the well-coiffed graphic designer who loved expensive hair gel anymore but the maniacal drug- and booze-addled murderer that Terri had painted him to be that time in my kitchen. I tried to sit up but I was too dizzy, so I stayed prone, looking up at the fluffy clouds, hoping that if there was a heaven, my parents were waiting for me when I got there.

But before I succumbed to this knife-wielding psycho, I needed to know one thing. "Why did you kill her, Jackson?" I gasped.

His answer was succinct and direct. "I was tired of the cheating."

"Me, too," I said. "But divorce seemed a lot less messy to me."

He wiped his hand across his brow and I saw the blood from my hand paint a dark streak on his skin. He was out of breath from his short run across the lawn and he strug-gled to catch his breath. I was in luck—I had been knifed by an out-of-shape assailant. "She wasn't going for that," he said. He knelt in front of me, his knees straddling my legs. He hung his head and tried to get his breathing back to normal.

I figured I should warn him. "There's a very large man in my house with an even bigger gun. And when he sees you filet me, he's going to shoot you in the head." I chuckled, slightly hysterical. "Just thought I should let you know." I picked up my hand and looked at the defensive knife wound. "Wow," I said, in wonder. "This hurts more than when I got shot. And that hurt a lot." My palm was in two pieces, clear down to the bone. My other hand was trapped under my leg and I couldn't get it loose, what with Jackson's weight pinning me down. "And even if you don't kill me, he's going to kill you for doing this," I said, showing him my injured hand.

"You talk too damn much," he said, and raised the knife above his head again.

"And your French stinks," I said, taking the heel of my palm and shoving it as hard as I could stand into his face.

The pain shot through me, white hot, but I managed to push Jackson onto his back. I got to my knees and staggered, half standing, pushing off the grass with my good hand. I curled my wounded palm into my chest and looked up, hoping to see Crawford come out the back door of my house. But my backyard was vacant, except for a very troubled Trixie, who continued to walk in circles, her head hanging low. When she saw me approach her, her instincts kicked in and she ran to my side, licking my good hand. Apparently, she had decided who she would defend.

Jackson got up and ran toward us but Trixie let out a sinister-sounding growl to warn him off. She separated the two of us, and in that instant, I saw in Jackson's eyes that he was deciding how quickly he could kill the dog before he got to me.

"If you hurt a hair on her head, Jackson, I will tear you limb from limb," I said, and knelt beside Trixie, holding her collar in my good hand. "This dog is the best thing to come out of your house. And this whole mess." I heard the back door open and the screen door slam shut as Crawford's calm and reassuring voice drifted across to me.

"Alison, get up and walk toward me with the dog. Jackson, don't move or I will shoot you," he said, the last part more of a promise than a threat.

I stood and pulled Trixie along. The front of my shirt was soaked with my blood and it clung to my chest, heavy and wet. I stumbled toward Crawford, who was shirtless and pointing the gun very steadily in Jackson's direction, despite being fifty feet from his target. His sweatpants hung on his slim hips and his feet were bare.

"Drop the knife, Jackson, and then put your hands where I can see them," he said, still calm. He took short steps toward Jackson, who stood on the other side of the hedgerow. "Go inside, Alison," he said. "The boy's already called 911."

Nothing doing. I wasn't leaving him outside with that guy, no matter what. Trixie and I stood behind him on the patio and watched the standoff.

Jackson held the knife over his head but he didn't drop it. He stared at Crawford, weighing his options. Crawford read his mind. "You don't have any options, Jackson. Let's do this the right way." He inched closer to the hedge. "She cheated on you, right?"

Jackson looked around, hearing, like I did, the sirens in the distance.

"Cheated on you a lot. With Ray even." Crawford continued his baby steps across the yard, his arms held out in front of him, the gun in a two-fisted hold.

Jackson nodded, his eyes filling with tears.

"You're in over your head here, man," Crawford said. "Drop the knife."

The sirens got closer. But Jackson stayed where he was, the knife at shoulder height.

"I have a gun, you have a knife. You know how this is going to end, right?" Crawford asked. "It's like rock, paper, scissors, except when you lunge at me, I shoot you.

That's how it ends every time. The one with the knife always dies. I've done it before, Jackson. It's not hard. And you'll never surprise me." He was close enough to touch the hedge now and I felt my heart pounding in my throat.

But surprise him he did, because just as every police car in Dobbs Ferry congregated at the end of my driveway, Jackson plunged the knife into his own chest, spraying blood farther than I ever would have imagined blood could travel. The look on his face was utter surprise at his own action, as if he hadn't had any idea that he was going to do it. He disappeared behind the hedge.

Crawford burst through the hedge and vanished, as well. I heard him yell to me to get the cops over the cacophony of sirens. I opened the back door and ushered Trixie in, catching sight of Brendan's younger brother in the hallway, his eyes wide and tear-filled. I grabbed a dishtowel from the counter and wrapped my hand as I made my way down the driveway, where I did exactly as I was told before collapsing into a heap on my front lawn.

Chapter 32

My left hand looked like a giant Q-tip, wrapped in more gauze than I had ever seen. The microsurgery to reattach some of the cut nerve endings was successful, but any career as a concert violinist had now been cut short by my coming into contact with a giant fowl-deboning implement.

Jackson had managed to severely wound himself but he didn't die. When he started to recover, he was questioned by the Dobbs Ferry detectives, cranky Joe Hardin and even crankier Catherine Madden. Turns out that Jackson thought he had hit on something good with the old dismemberment modus operandi; he could kill Terri, cut off her hands and feet, and cast more suspicion on the Miceli clan while he took off for parts unknown. Ray and Terri had truly been kindred spirits, because like Ray, Terri had amassed quite the little black book of conquests. She was a serial philanderer and Jackson had had enough. Everything she had told me about him had been true; he had spent a good deal of their marriage in rehab and, obviously, had the "anger management" issues that she had alluded to. I'll say.

The worst part of the story was that he had killed her in the house. They had left town the day that I had come to own Trixie; they had gone to Massachusetts to their summer house in the Berkshires in an attempt to rekindle their relationship and decide whether or not they would stay together and in Westchester. Terri, however, had left something in the Dobbs Ferry house and implored Jackson to return before they made any permanent moves. It wasn't Trixie she was after. And when Jackson found out what it was—a necklace that had been given to her by Ray—he had snapped. And just like I suspected and had told Crawford when I called him at work, someone had called 911 that rainy morning. It wasn't the wacky 911 system going haywire like the cop had told me; Terri had been bleeding to death in the house and managed to make one last call. A luma light and the appropriate chemicals revealed blood spatters in the family room and kitchen, consistent with someone being stabbed to death.

Jackson had stolen the red car from the Stop & Shop in the center of town and had dumped his own car there as well; he wanted to be anonymous when he took off. Poor Mrs. Dayer, the owner of the stolen car, had been visiting her sister and had gone out to get eggs. She was dismayed to find that even though she was visiting a swanky suburban town, crime happens, and her lovely little red Corolla was gone when she emerged from the store. Jackson was in that car when I was chasing him. He was on his way to dispose of Terri's hands and feet, which he revealed he had tossed into the East River, the repository of many a dead body or parts of dead bodies.

The hole that he had buried her in had been started by Trixie; that dog just loves to dig and had been working on that hole for a long time. Fortunately for Jackson, the developing hole, coupled with my absence during my stint in state trooper jail, afforded him the location and the time to bury Terri and get out of town before I even returned.

Jackson had forgotten one thing in his haste to leave: his passport. His goal was to start a new life in Canada, but bless their hearts, United States Customs had instituted a new rule that made everyone crossing our borders show a passport. In the old days, traveling to Canada consisted of a wink and a nod at the border. I don't know to what part of Canada Jackson was going to go, but the thought of him sullying my homeland with his stupid hair and murderous ways made me furious.

And just as Crawford suspected, the cop who didn't follow up on the 911 calls coming from their house had made a sudden and unexpected career change. Last I heard, Officer Bruno was a conductor on Metro North.

So, how did I end up with Trixie? I made Crawford pry that out of Hardin and Madden, who had pried it out of Jackson. Seems Terri hated that dog, which moved her up on my most-hated list. How could you hate Trixie? Jackson said that Terri knew how much I liked the dog and viewed their leaving as a good way to get rid of the dog, complicate my life, and make everyone happy in the long run.

As for Miss Blurry Tattoo Ass, Julie Anne Podowsky had made one more trip into the Fiftieth Precinct, but this time she didn't lie. She wasn't there to help but to admit something that had been eating at her since her first visit to the precinct: she had broken into Ray's apartment to find a sex tape that he had made of the two of them. Seems her father was a building superintendent in Queens and she knew her way around locks and had even picked a few in her day. She told Crawford that she had never found the tape and was wondering if the police had it. Crawford assured her that there was no sex tape and he said that when he told her that, she had turned the color of cement.

I must have done a pretty good job of wearing a poker face, because Crawford didn't seem to suspect that I knew anything about the tape. I was really proud of myself because, despite having the biggest mouth in the world, I had been able to keep the fact that I possessed the world's worst, most unsexy sex tape from Crawford.

Julie Anne Podowsky found an envelope in her mailbox the following week. I know, because I watched her open it from my position across the hall from the mail room, and smiled when I saw the relief etched on her face. It wasn't a letter telling her that she had gotten an A in Modern Literature, but it was something that I'm sure she wanted just as badly. Maybe even worse.

Mrs. Helpful strikes again.

Crawford came by my house early on a Wednesday morning, two weeks after everything had happened, and took me to school. Sister Mary had kindly given me a week off so that I could recover from my microsurgery. I had been prepared to take the rest of the semester off, but the doctor had assured me that my line of work wasn't terribly taxing and that I would still recover nicely, even while delivering the boring lectures that I was known for. I had discovered the joys of Percocet—even better than Vicodin—but weaned myself off lest my lectures stopped being boring only to become wacky and weirdly fascinating.

I got in the car with Crawford and leaned over to kiss him, whacking him lightly in the head with my Q-tip hand. "Hey," he said, rubbing the side of his head.

"Sorry," I said. "I'm still trying to judge distances with this thing."

"How are you feeling?" he asked.

I considered that question. "Pretty good, actually."

He looked at me closely before putting the car into gear and slowly starting down the street. "Are you still on Percocet?" He handed me a cup of coffee from the cup holder.

"Nope. Clean as a whistle." I took a sip of coffee. "Want a urine sample?"

"No," he said, obviously disgusted.

When we got to St. Thomas, he parked, as he always did, in the tow-away zone. He turned to me and rested his arm on the steering wheel. "So, what are you doing Friday night?"

I looked up at the ceiling, trying to figure out if I had plans. Of course I didn't, but I liked to tease him. "I'm not sure . . . what did you have in mind?"

"The Rangers are playing the Islanders."

I gasped. "You don't have tickets, do you?"

He rolled his eyes. "No. That's your other boyfriend."

"So what are we going to do? Stand outside an electronics store and watch it on television behind plate glass?"

"I was going to invite you over to watch the game but if you're going to be difficult about it . . ."

Crawford may not have the typical "guy" apartment but his television is bigger than mine. It's actually the biggest television I've ever seen. "Well, when you put it that way, I guess I can make myself free for the night. Can Trixie come?"

"Of course Trixie can come. I figure she's part of the deal now."

I waved my hand in front of his face. "And can I bring Q-tip Hand?"

He sighed. "Yes, you can bring Q-tip Hand."

"Then it's a date." I leaned in and drank in his clean laundry smell. "I can't wait," I murmured, giving him a long kiss, one that would last me a few days.

"Chinese or pizza?" he asked when we came up for air.

"It's too early to know what I'll want to eat. You'll have to wait until Friday." I opened my door and started to get out. He put his hand on my arm.

"I love you," he said.

"And I love you," I said and got out of the car. One last

look at him told me that he had the same look on his face that he always did when I told him I loved him: surprise. I was going to have to say it a lot for him to believe me, obviously. I watched as he drove off in the police-issue Crown Victoria before going into the building.

Dottie was clad in a spectacular all-green ensemble, her eye shadow iridescent and thickly applied to match her clothing. I knew I hadn't taken any Percocet that morning, but considered the fact that maybe *she* had. Only someone hopped up on opioids could have come up with that combination. She batted her eyes at me. "Getting better?" she asked.

I held up Q-tip Hand. "Guess so," I said, but without giving her any additional information, I sashayed down to my office. She was fascinated with all of the gory details of what had happened. I knew she read all of the local papers and was up to date on all of the cases because it was clear she wasn't doing any real work behind that desk, and the *New York Post,* rag of rags, was always tucked into her *Webster's New Abridged Dictionary*.

I went into my office and sat in the chair behind my desk. I wasn't in my office more than thirty seconds when there was a tentative knock at the door. "Come in."

Her head barely grazing the doorknob, Sister Calista darted in and threw something on my desk. I shielded myself from any expectorations but she just cackled wildly and pulled out as quickly as she had come in.

"Voilà!" she called as she click-clacked back to her office in her chunky orthopedic shoes.

The manila envelope skittered across the metal top of the desk and came to rest on the far left-hand corner. In it were the syllabi from Calista and all of her colleagues. And also in there, written in the beautiful calligraphy of an old nun, was a note:

Dear Alison: Here are your syllabi. My dear, you should have joined the convent when you had the chance. It's a much safer existence. With God's Blessings . . . Sister Mary Edward Calista.

Keep reading for a sneak peek at
Maggie Barbieri's next Murder 101 mystery

Quick Study

Available soon in hardcover from
St. Martin's Minotaur

"I don't know who you are, but I love you!"

The voice was deep, rough, and heavily inflected with the accent of one of the outer boroughs, and it belonged to the guy sitting in back of me at Madison Square Garden, home of the New York Rangers, my favorite professional hockey team. And the comment, which had been directed at me, was all the more interesting because I was sitting beside my best friend, Max, who had slipped her one-hundred-pound frame into a slinky size-two black cocktail dress, her cleavage prominently and proudly displayed for all to see. She's tiny but she's got a great rack. It's a veritable "rack of ages." Nobody, and I mean nobody, had ever noticed me when Max was around. And we had twenty years of friendship to draw on proving this point.

I was not in a cocktail dress, having opted instead to wear my new Mark Messier jersey (he was number eleven and the sole reason for the Rangers' Stanley Cup win in 1994, thank you very much), a pair of jeans that I had purchased in the last millennium, and sneakers that had seen their fair share of painting projects. My hair was pulled back into a ponytail, I had a smear of ketchup on my cheek and now, after jumping up to take umbrage at a call, a glassful of beer soaking my chest. I don't even like beer, but when in Rome . . . you know the rest. But apparently, when I yelled, "Shit, ref, you're killing us! That's a bullshit call!" after a bogus hooking penalty, I had forever pledged my troth to Bruno Spaghetti, as Max had dubbed him when we arrived, seat 4, row D, section 402.

He ran his hands through his spiky black hair and grabbed me in an embrace, his silver hoop earring brushing my cheek. Max, who had been standing for the better part of the last period and who thus had incurred the wrath of everyone behind her—many of whom had missed said bogus penalty because their only view was the back of her well-coiffed head—fell back into her seat, her cocktail dress riding up on her yoga-toned thighs. But Bruno didn't notice; he only had eyes for me. See, we were sitting way up high in Rangerland, a place that used to be called "the blue seats" in which only the hardest-core hockey fans sat. Now they're teal, which doesn't lend them the same menacing air. A gorgeous woman in a slinky black dress with spectacular boobs had nothing on a five-foot-ten college professor with a pot belly and beer breath who loved hockey and who could curse with the best of them.

It was my birthday and my boyfriend had given me the jersey and the tickets. Crawford—Bobby to the rest of the world—was a detective in the New York City Police Department and working overtime that night; hence, my birthday date was Max. Crawford had stopped by school on his lunch break to wish me a happy birthday, appearing in my office doorway at around one; I was preparing for my next class, a two o'clock literature seminar, and was delighted to be distracted from the critical essay on *Finnegan's Wake* that was putting me to sleep. I'm a Joyce scholar, but even I recognize that obscure is not the same thing as exciting, and that makes my relationship with the subject of my doctoral dissertation tenuous at best. I love a challenge, though, and had spent the better part of my academic career trying to figure out if Joyce was laughing *with* us or *at* us. I was slowly coming to the conclusion that it was the latter.

I could tell that Crawford was excited by the items in the gift bag he was holding behind his back. He leaned over and gave me a peck on the cheek; although he is a seasoned detective and an all-around good guy, he gets really nervous around the nuns I work with at St. Thomas University, my employer. Whenever he visits me at school, he looks like he's on his way to detention, even though I'm sure he never did anything more scandalous than pass a note in class. He took the bag from behind his back and set it on my desk, settling himself into one of the chairs across from me, a self-satisfied smile on his handsome, Irish face.

I love the guy but there's one thing that bugs me: every time he gives me an item of clothing, it's always extra-large. I'm extra-tall but not extra-fat, so this concerns me. Is this how he sees me? Or does he think women should wear tentlike clothing? I still haven't figured it out. I held his gift aloft and spread my arms wide to examine it, full width: a Messier jersey. Despite the size, I couldn't have asked for a better present. "Crawford, I love it!" I said and came from around the desk. I kicked my office door closed so I could give him a proper thank-you, sitting on his lap and putting my arms around his neck. "Now the best present you could give me would be your undivided attention tonight," I said hopefully, although I guessed this wouldn't be the case.

He shook his head sadly. "I can't. I pulled an extra shift so I could go to Meaghan's basketball playoff Monday night." Meaghan is one of his twin daughters; she was banking on a basketball scholarship to get her through college. I had come to realize that basketball was like a religion in that family; what teenage girl would count former New York Knick Bill Bradley among her crushes if it wasn't? He reached into his jacket pocket and pulled out an envelope. "Here. These are for you, too."

The tickets were the icing on the cake, but I was extremely disappointed that another Friday night would go by and I wouldn't see him. A little slap and tickle in my office just wasn't cutting it anymore. The relationship, and Crawford himself, were everything I wanted but not in the amount that I had hoped for. I tried to be the good and understanding girlfriend, but I felt like Crawford's wife was the NYPD and I was the jealous mistress. And in fact, for a very short while, I had been kind of a real mistress: unbeknownst to me, Crawford had been married when I first met him. But that's all in the past; she's almost married to husband number two and Crawford and I are still going strong, so things couldn't have worked out better for all concerned.

I had two choices for alterna-dates: my best friend Max, and my other best friend, Father Kevin McManus. I called McManus first, but he had a Lenten reconciliation service to perform and penance to dispense, so he was out. He reminded me that I had a couple of sins to confess myself—premarital sex being the worst and most oft-committed of the lot—but I hung up before he could recount all of them in detail. I went to Plan B and invited Max. She arrived at the Garden right before the puck dropped, breathless and a little tipsy from a cocktail party she had attended for a new show that her cable network was launching. She tottered toward me in four-inch heels and the aforementioned cocktail dress, and I immediately got a sinking feeling. Max is not what I called a responsible drinker. She holds her liquor less effectively than a dinghy with a hole in its bottom, which has resulted in more than one late-night, four-hour phone call to discuss the merits of kitten heels versus stilettos. I thought we might be in trouble. Once I got a whiff of her champagne-tinged breath, I was fairly confident.

Bruno Spaghetti noticed me the minute we arrived and commented on my Messier jersey. He was wearing a Steve

Larmer jersey, a testament to his hockey knowledge and devotion. No Johnny-come-lately Jaromír Jágr jersey for him; he was a Rangers aficionado and wore a jersey that harkened back to the good old days when the Rangers actually made the playoffs and even won a few games. "Lady, you can curse with the best of them!" he yelled, grabbing me in another embrace.

He hadn't heard anything yet. And I was fairly certain I wasn't a lady. Dating a cop had increased my cursing lexicon tenfold. Although Crawford was a gentleman and didn't curse at all in my presence, two trips to police precincts had expanded my horizons. I broke my embrace with Bruno Spaghetti and sat back down, signaling the beer vendor; he ignored me. I considered asking Max to flash some leg so I could get some service.

The Garden erupted as the Rangers scored their first goal, despite the fact that one of their players was in the penalty box. I was excited, but afraid of what kind of display of love this might elicit from Bruno, so I did the old excuse-me-pardon-me into the aisle.

"Bring me back a box of Sno-Caps," Max called after me, taking her cell phone from her very expensive purse. Max is a newlywed and calls her husband every twenty minutes or so. Her husband is also Crawford's partner, so I knew these periodic phone calls had become mildly annoying, at least to Crawford. He said that Fred Wyatt, Max's husband, still appeared to be completely smitten with her, even indulging in baby talk when she called. He's about eight feet tall and a thousand pounds and looks like a serial killer, so the visual eluded me, but Crawford assured me that it was chilling.

"They don't have Sno-Caps out there," I said. I had been to the Garden enough times to know what resided in the candy displays. Row D turned its collective hostile gaze toward me.

Max considered this. "How about Jujubees?"

"I don't think they even make Jujubees anymore." I strained to get a look at what was happening on the ice.

Max stood, thinking on her feet. "OK, how about Milk Duds?" At that moment, the Rangers scored another goal.

"Lady, if you don't sit down, I am gonna shove a pretzel up your ass!" Bruno Spaghetti had brought a pal—Max had named him Shamus McBeerbong—and he wasn't quite as enamored with us as Bruno was.

"Max, sit down," I cautioned her. "I'll surprise you."

She clapped her hands together. "I love surprises!"

Shamus McBeerbong sighed. "Bring her back something that keeps her in her seat," he said to me, and then to her, "Sit down, you stupid broad!" The rest of row D nodded in agreement, despite seeming a little aghast at his choice of language.

Max turned to Shamus and gave him the hairy eyeball. "*You* sit down!" she said, at a loss for a truly snappy retort. For effect, she adjusted her breasts defiantly.

"Max, sit down," I called again, waiting to see if the section would turn on her. She sat, just in time for everyone to see a melee erupt on the ice.

Once it was clear Max wouldn't be eaten alive by rabid Ranger fans, I went out to search for her Milk Duds and to get myself another beer. I'm not the biggest beer drinker in the world, but they don't serve chardonnay or vodka martinis at the Garden, and what's a Ranger game without a little booze? The Garden is a giant labyrinth comprised of long, tiled hallways that wrap around the seating area. I wended my way down one hallway toward the snack bar and was deep in a decision regarding Gummi bears versus Gummi snakes for Max when I felt a tap on my shoulder.

Jack McManus is the director of marketing for the Rangers and Kevin McManus's brother. He is also a man with whom I played tonsil hockey not too many months before. At the time, Crawford and I had been on a "break" and I had stuck my little toe briefly into the dating pool. Don't think I haven't been completely guilt-ridden about that ever since. But confessing about cheating on your then-married boyfriend with your priest's brother to your priest, who is also one of your best friends, is complicated. Jack is gorgeous and single; inexplicably, he was interested in me for a time. My face immediately went red when I saw him and I smoothed my hair back, pulling my ponytail tighter to my head, a gesture that wasn't going to improve my appearance any but it was worth a try.

"Jack!" I gave him a quick, loose embrace, memories of going to second base flooding my mind. "How are you?"

"I'm great," he said, flashing me a winning smile. "Kevin told me that you were here tonight and that you didn't have great seats, so I wanted to find you so that I could move you down."

Move me down. Three little words that, at the Garden, held so much import. Three little words that meant the difference between high-fiving Bruno Spaghetti and going out for an after-game cocktail with Ryan O'Stockbroker. I would have to tell Max, Bruno, and Shamus that we were leaving the upper tier. I had sat in Jack's seats before and they were practically on the ice. They were so close to the Rangers that once I had almost become part of a line change. I stammered a thank-you and told him to stay put while I gathered Max and the rest of our belongings. As I turned to go back to my seat, I spied Max walking gingerly toward me, trying desperately not to slip on the polished hallway floors.

"There she is now!" I said.

Jack took one look at Max and burst out laughing. "I thought Max would be a middle-aged bald guy."

"That happens a lot," I said. Max arrived at my side. "Jack, Max Rayfield. Max, meet Jack."

"You weren't kidding," Max said under her breath. "But he's way better than a poor man's George Clooney," my words coming back to haunt me. "He's the real deal. Real Clooney. *Ocean's 11* Clooney. Nephew of Rosemary Clooney. Clooney to the white courtesy phone . . ."

Fortunately, the roar of the crowd and the acoustics of the hallway masked her commentary; Jack was none the wiser.

Max shook Jack's hand. I noticed my coat hanging over her arm. "We're leaving," she said. "Shamus wants to make me Mrs. McBeerbong."

I explained to her that we weren't leaving and that Jack wanted to move us to fifth row, center ice.

"Can you get a decent martini down there?" Max asked, her maiden voyage to the Garden not fulfilling her original expectations. Maybe I had lied a bit and said that you could get a good martini, and maybe I had told her our seats were better than they were. And maybe I had fudged the truth a bit by telling her that more than one woman would be in a cocktail dress. Now that we were moving down to the expensive seats, that part might actually be true, since most of the people who sat there were either corporate types or models trying to marry Rangers.

Jack assured her that he would get her a martini as soon as we were seated. He took the coats from her arm and led us to the escalators where we made the journey to the hundred-dollar seats and the land of chilled vodka, never-ending vendor service, and hockey players so close you could touch them. Which I made a mental note not to do.

We settled into our seats just as the first period ended. Jack took our drink and food orders but stayed rooted in the aisle next to our seats, watching the Rangers skate off the ice. I noticed him give a little wave to someone and the lights went down in the rink.

The Rangers' announcer came on the public address

system just as a giant spotlight found me in my fifth-row seat. "Ladies and gentlemen! Please join the New York Rangers organization in wishing our number-one fan, Alison Bergeron, a happy birthday!"

Max turned to me, her eyes wide. The fans let out a giant roar, followed by thunderous applause.

I shielded my eyes, a motion I could see depicted on the Jumbotron that hung over center ice. I looked like a deer caught in the headlights—one with dried ketchup on her right cheek. I looked at Jack, stricken. He had a huge smile on his poor-man's-Clooney face as he leaned over to give me a hug.

The announcer continued over the deafening din. "And now, welcome our own John Amarante!"

John Amarante was the Rangers' long-time anthem singer. He appeared on the ice, as he usually does before games, but instead of singing the anthem, he broke out into a rousing rendition of "Happy Birthday."

Here's the thing: if the entire fan base at Madison Square Garden began singing to Max, she would have been thrilled. Not only that, she would have almost expected it, given her fabulousness. Me? I wanted to melt into the sticky, beer-stained floor. I had been in those seats once before, been viewed by every Ranger fan in the tristate area on my first date with Jack, and had borne the brunt of Crawford's ire for longer than I cared to recall. I prayed that the first period's highlights were being discussed and that my giant, petrified face wasn't being broadcast for all of New York to see. And that Crawford was out on the hunt for some kind of homicidal maniac whose antics would keep him busy for the next decade.

Max read my mind. "You better hope this isn't on TV," she said, fluffing her hair and exposing just enough of her spectacular breasts at the same time in case it was.

Jack bent down and pulled a bag out from under my

chair. A microphone appeared in his hand and when Amarante stopped singing and the fans quieted down, he prepared to make some kind of presentation. He put the mic in front of his mouth. His lips were moving, but I had conveniently gone deaf, just hearing the voice inside my head telling me, "You are so screwed." When he saw that I had gone into some kind of fugue state, he opened the package and unfurled its contents.

It was a Mark Messier jersey, identical to the one I was wearing.

Except it was autographed by Mark Messier. To me. With love.

Max looked at me disdainfully. "You are so screwed."